LOKI AND HIS MASTER

DEMON GODS

RHYS LAWLESS

Loki and his Master, Demon Gods

Copyright © 2023 by Rhys Lawless

Cover Design by Ethereal Designs

Editing and Proofreading by Sue Meadows at No Stone Unturned Editing

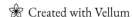 Created with Vellum

What does it mean?

CH

So you picked up the book and you're wondering what the CH logo on the cover means?

The answer is quite simple.

The CH logo stands for Cursed Hearts and what it represents is the fact that this book is part of the Cursed Hearts universe.

That means the books/series with this logo all take place in the same fantasy world, share the same mythology and rules and some characters may have appeared before or will appear somewhere in the future.

For more information on the Cursed Hearts universe and a suggested reading order (although not always necessary/make sure to check the blurb on whether a book can be read as a standalone), you can visit my website at rhyswritesromance.com/cursed-hearts-universe

Tomasz

"Are you sure you want to do this?" the old woman asked.

She didn't appear old, per se, but looking at her, the only thing that came to mind was Matka Ziemia, the powerful Slavic deity I'd grown up to equally love and fear.

"I'm sorry to disappoint, young man, but I'm not her," she said as if she could read my mind.

Right. I had been warned about her.

Be careful what you think of, my boss had said.

It seemed he was right.

"It-it's okay," I managed to mumble.

I was terrified of her, yet drawn to her bright green eyes, which seemed to have an inhuman glow in the darkness of the underground chamber.

The same eyes that seemed intent on burning me

with their intensity. Instead of returning her gaze, I focused on the fire in the pit between us.

It seemed a little cliché for this sage old witch to be hiding in a dark cave lit by torches and balefire, surrounded by old hardbound books and cobwebs, but I guessed some witches took themselves a lot more seriously than others.

"So?" she said under the hood of her black cloak, her curly hair spilling out from beneath it, creating a frame around her face. "What is your answer, young whisperer?"

The fire pulsed. It thrummed in my ears. I didn't know how it could do such a thing, but that was the only way I could explain it.

Or maybe I was losing it.

I was sitting in an underground cave in the middle of Camden, after all.

But its beat, its song, brought up all the images, all the horror, all the loss.

The memories I wanted to erase with every fiber of my being, but doing so would mean I'd live under the illusion that they were still alive and they weren't.

And those who murdered them needed to pay.

"So much anger. So much hatred," she whispered.

"Let me guess. You're going to tell me I need to let go, to clear my mind, that revenge is never the answer?" I told her, looking at her with defiance I hadn't been feeling before.

She cocked her head, and without missing a beat opened her red lips. "No. Use it," she said.

The memories assaulted my mind again. The chaos. The mess. The blood.

And for what? For a stupid, *fucking* egg!

The flames of the fire seemed to burn brighter, licking my skin and lending me their heat. Within seconds my insides were just as hot. I caught my breath, felt my heartbeat pounding in my ears, tasted the bile on my tongue.

"Do it!" I told her.

I stretched my hand over the fire and she held out a dagger.

No. Not a dagger. A sword.

The silver blade glinted, reflecting the light and I caught the markings on the surface. Knots. Decorative knots that seemed to never end.

With the tip of the sword she pricked my finger and let my blood trickle down the blade and paint it red.

Then she got up and walked into one of the many doorways, tunnels branching out from the center of the room, dragging the sword, a red line coloring the floor behind her.

Even though she'd only taken a drop or two, the blood gushed from the blade.

What have I just done?

"Are you coming?" she asked before disappearing completely.

I rushed to my feet. It was dark in the tunnel but somehow I knew where I needed to go and when I needed to stop. When there was light again I found myself in a long, cold room with a stainless steel wall.

Along the wall were small doors. Rows and rows of them.

Wait a minute. Is...

"Is this a morgue?" I asked her as she opened one door and confirmed the answer to my question. "I thought we were summoning a demon."

She leaned over the large man in the drawer. He was covered in a thin gold membrane but was otherwise butt-naked.

The witch looked up at me and smirked.

"A demon, young whisperer, needs a body," she answered and before I even had a chance to digest her words, she lifted the sword and impaled the man with the bloody sword.

Shit.

Maybe this was a bad idea.

"Too late now, little whisperer. Your demon is about to awaken."

Tomasz

A few weeks earlier

Blood.
       Stillness.
       Cold.
Death.
Blood.
Stillness.
Cold.
Death.
Blood.
Stillness.
Cold.
Death.

"Tomasz? Tomasz are you okay?" my boss shouted.

I barely heard him.

I barely saw him.

I just kept going until I collapsed onto the mustard-yellow sofa and attempted to breathe although it felt as if I'd swallowed glass.

Saskia climbed onto my lap and curled up there. She didn't have much to say. She could feel my pain. I could feel hers. We'd both lost...

Lost them.

No. It couldn't be true. It couldn't be real.

"Tomasz? What's going on? Why are you covered in blood? Are you hurt?" Caleb asked, dropping to his knees in front of me and ignoring the customers waiting in line to get their coffee.

I tried to focus on his gray eyes but mine were blurry and burning.

"Blood," I whispered. "Blood, Caleb. Blood."

Caleb stroked my hand with his gloved fingers and leaned closer, trying to get me to look at him.

I tried to. I really did, but all I could see in front of me was the color red.

And their empty faces.

"M-may I?" he asked, lifting the glove from one of his hands.

I must have nodded, but I didn't feel the motion. Seconds later my boss's bare fingers encompassed my hand and I watched as his breathing hardened under the weight of my emotions.

"Oh my Gods, Tomasz. Oh my Gods! You're in shock. I...I'm going to try and help. Don't resist, okay?"

A wave rushed through me like salt over a wound and tears ran down my face.

Another wave and it all washed away. The blood, the faces, the pain. I was able to breathe again.

But Caleb didn't stop. He kept sending waves of comfort to me, channeling peace over the war inside me with his empathic power.

"Lorelai, get the whiskey from my office," he said.

He reached for his bejeweled bracelet and pulled a gem from it. A yellow crystal that glimmered in the daylight.

"Erase," he whispered.

The crystal burst into dust in his hand and he turned to blow it at the customers watching us. The dust of the magic spell surrounded them all and faded away.

When it cleared, everyone shook their heads as if they'd been distracted by something, and turned to the bar, completely ignoring Caleb and me.

"Come on. Let's move to the back. That was my last memory spell and I can't be dealing with the police again," he told me, helping me off the couch and moving to the very back of the café. It was a little more private since there were no windows and a divider blocked the view from the other tables and the bar.

Saskia tiptoed beside me, staying close to my feet

and even though I didn't need to look at her, I knew she kept watching me, making sure I was okay.

On our way to the back, Caleb snatched a bottle of whiskey from Lorelai who watched me with curiosity and concern before she went back to serving the customers.

Soon we were sitting across from each other with a glass full of amber liquid each. No ice.

"Are you feeling better? Do you need more?" Caleb asked, reaching for my hand.

I shook my head and he nodded. "I'm better. Th-thank you."

"Of course."

Saskia climbed onto the table next to me and put her face in my glass, trying to lick the whiskey.

"Hey!" Caleb flicked her face gently. "That's not for cats," he told her.

Saskia turned to me and gave me a stern look that almost made me laugh. And I probably would have if I didn't feel so rotten inside.

"Is he for real? Can you tell him to fuck off?" my cat told me.

Caleb just heard a meow. Only I could hear Saskia speak. And sometimes I wished I couldn't.

"He's trying to help," I told her.

She rolled her eyes.

"Whatever. You're getting me drunk later and I don't give a rat's ass what humans think," she said.

"Deal," I told her.

For the hundredth time Caleb watched me talk to my cat as if I was a madman.

Even though Caleb was also a witch and I'd been working for him and Lorelai for a year and a half, I still hadn't told him about Saskia or my family's complicated history.

Our history was meant to be a secret. Even within our own community.

"You and your cat have a weird relationship," he said after a deep breath. He took a swig and I mimicked him. "What happened? Do you know?"

The memories from before threatened to assault my senses again but Caleb's empathy kept them at bay a while longer.

The faces of my mother, my father and Oliwia, barely recognizable, covered in blood and agony, staring glassy-eyed back at me, unblinking.

"I don't know," I said. "I just...I went home for our usual, weekly get-together and...and they were all there...*just*...dead. Just dead."

Caleb took my hand in his again, but he didn't send any peace or calm to me. He always asked for permission before he used his powers.

"I'm so sorry, Tomasz. That's awful. What's the address? I can send the Council over to start the investigation straight away," he said.

"Pfft," was my response.

The High Council of London witches was a mess. Always had been. I remembered all the times my mother would tell me to keep out of their business and out of their way because they had made a mess of everything. The Polish expat coven my family were part of was much better suited to help us and our needs.

And it had been even worse when two years ago all the corruption in the High Council came out in the open, thanks to Caleb and his boyfriend.

Not that he'd ever said anything. He liked to keep a low profile but his reputation preceded him.

Mom and Dad hadn't liked me working for Caleb. He was a High Council witch (ex, if you asked him) and they didn't trust him. But I wanted to learn, expand my horizons beyond my limited powers and Caleb was the kind of man I aspired to be. Strong, powerful, independent, rule-breaker.

"I've got very good friends within the Council and they can help if I ask them to," he said.

I doubted that. I very much doubted that, but I gave him the address anyway as the horror took me over again, completely crippling me.

Caleb made an attempt to help, but I stopped him before he touched me. As good as it was not feeling the brunt of the tragedy that had taken my family, I couldn't rely on it. If I relied on it I could fool myself they were still alive and they weren't.

They weren't.

They'd been murdered and I needed to find who'd

done it.

"I'll call them now. I...are you sure you're okay?"

I nodded.

"I've got this, don't I?" I told him and raised my glass pointedly.

He retreated to his office and left me alone with Saskia. She wasted no opportunity to lick the contents of Caleb's glass.

"Hm, this is the cheap shit. If we don't deserve the good shit right now, when do we?" she asked.

"Shut up, Sass," I said and touched the rim of the glass to my lips.

"Złagodzić mój ból," I whispered three times.

Ease my pain.

Not that it would. My power wasn't strong, especially when it came to healing or using it on myself.

But it would do.

Little shots. Whispering by whispering until I hopefully, one day didn't feel as if my entire world had been destroyed.

Shot by shot. Whispering by whispering.

I drank the whiskey and let my whispering do the trick.

It didn't last.

It didn't last neither the minutes, nor the hours, nor the days, nor the weeks that passed. The only thing it did was make me angrier.

Angrier because I didn't know who'd killed them and I didn't know how to find them. Angrier because I hadn't been there to protect them. Angrier that I was alive and they weren't. Angrier that no one else's world seemed to have collapsed. Just mine.

———

"It's not here," Saskia said, coming up from the basement.

I had to whisper me some warmth because the house was so cold. Even after two weeks it was freezing. It made my hairs stand on end.

"I know. I've already looked," I told her.

"Fuckers!" she cursed and her true form threatened to come out, but she controlled herself.

I avoided looking at the kitchen, where I'd found them. I avoided the room when I could.

My phone buzzed and I glanced at my screen.

CIOCIA:

We need to talk about funeral arrangements. Pick up.

My aunt wouldn't shut up about it.

How could I bury them when I didn't know who'd killed them? Burying someone was all about peace and they couldn't find theirs until their killer was caught and paid for what he'd done. Why couldn't she see it?

"You think that's what they wanted?" Saskia asked.

"Of course that's what they wanted. The question is how did they know about it?"

Saskia climbed the hallway table and tipped her head to the side. If I didn't know any better I'd say she was cute with her little button nose and her bright yellow eyes.

"Secrets have a tendency of spilling. Especially in our coven. There have been rumors about our family for years," she said.

"So it's another Polish witch," I said.

"Could be. Or it could be anyone. There's no way of knowing."

"And unlike Oliwia I don't have the connections to find out through the rumor mill," I said.

My sister had been so much better keeping in touch with the community and our roots.

She also didn't work for a High Council business unlike me, which helped.

"So all this for a fucking egg? I would have given it to them if that was all they wanted," I said.

My insides bubbled over. My blood boiled. My family had died, been butchered, over a fucking egg!

"Whoever it is, needs to pay!" I said.

"Damn right they do. But first we have to find them," Saskia replied.

"You head home, I've got to go to work. I'll check with Caleb to see if he can get us an update. They've been at it for weeks now. They should have something," I said.

"Don't count on it. This is the High Council we're talking about," she said.

"I'm not," I reassured her and left the family house.

My parents had proudly bought it all those years ago with their hard work, sweat and tears, looking forward to passing it down to the family, carving a continued history in England and now I didn't think I could ever live there ever again.

"You know you can take more time off, right?" Caleb told me as soon as I walked into Java Jinx.

"Yeah, you keep saying, but I don't want it. I need the money, and the distraction."

I put my jacket and my bag away in the staff room and walked back out in my purple branded T-shirt and got to work.

My heart pumped so fast and so hard it felt like I was going to explode. My temples thrummed and my breathing was erratic.

Same as it had all been since their death. There was no peace or quiet inside me anymore. Every waking moment was dedicated to finding them—the monsters who'd killed my parents.

But I suppressed it all and pretended as if it was all okay. According to Saskia I was doing a piss-poor job of that, but it was all I could do.

It felt like forever when the morning rush quietened and I finally got the place to myself with Caleb.

"Spit it out," he said before I even got the chance to open my mouth.

"Is it that obvious?"

"I don't need to touch you to know. And no, I've got no news from the Council, and I've pushed," he said.

"This is bullshit. We're witches. How can they not find who did it," I spat and almost broke a glass I'd been holding.

Caleb glanced at the latte glass and took it off me before he leaned on the bar and stared at me. "I know," he said. "I know better than anyone."

I shook my head.

"You don't though. You don't understand the pain —" I started and felt the sting of tears, but I kept them back.

"I do, Tomasz. If there's anyone who knows what it's like finding your loved one butchered, it's me," he said in a deep, serious tone.

He never spoke about his life or his past so I had no idea what or who he was referring to, but I didn't argue with him.

"What did you do?" I asked.

Caleb bit his lip and looked to the side, toward the front door with an empty, distant gaze.

"I found and killed every last one of them," he said.

His words sent chills to my bones because I believed him.

And I envied him.

"I wish I could...I wish I could do the same. But even if I find them, what harm can a shitty little Szeptun do? What good are my powers if and when I come face-to-face with them?"

I meant to spit that out, to hiss, to show my anger but all I managed to do was cry and sound just as pathetic as I felt.

"You're not shitty anything, okay?" Caleb reassured me. "I wish I could help. I'd get revenge myself, but...I gave up that life for good when West was born," he said.

That was his baby son. He also had a daughter, Nora, a manic little three-year-old.

"It's okay. It's not your battle. I just...I wish I could do more. I wish I was more. It's starting to feel like I'll never find who did it and I'll never get my revenge, and my family will never get their peace. And I'll never find mine."

More tears rolled down my cheeks. A couple landed on my lips, salty and wretched. How many more tears would I spill? How much pain would I endure? Was this my life now? Was I doomed to live in grief and pain?

"There's someone who can help," he said and his voice seemed to boom inside of me. Was this...was this hope?

"Who?"

"A witch who helped me a while ago. She keeps out of witch business and usually doesn't help us, but she might be able to...do something for you," he said.

"I don't understand," I said. "Is she a detective?"

Caleb shook his head. "No. She's old though. And knows more than everyone I know combined. Spells, potions as old as her. She might have something you could use."

I arched my back and wiped the tears off my face.

Maybe all hope wasn't lost after all.

Maybe there was still a chance to get my vengeance.

"Who is she? Where is she?"

"Her name is Mother Red Cap," he said, giving me clear instructions on how to find her lair and gain access to it.

"Can-can I finish early today?" I asked him.

I didn't know if I could wait until four to go find her. I wanted to go now. I needed to ask if she could help me. If she had a way.

"Of course," he said.

Within moments I was wearing my jacket and holding my backpack. "Thank you, Caleb. You have no idea how much this means to me."

He nodded with a sad smile and patted my arm.

"Just be careful, okay? Revenge can lead you down a dangerous path that could kill you. And trust me, dying isn't fun," he said.

I didn't linger on his words, but I knew they'd haunt me for the rest of the day, trying to figure out what he meant by that and whether he had died and come back to life before. I didn't know how that was possible.

"Oh, and Tomasz," he called out just as I opened the front door and the traffic of St. Paul's Square blasted my eardrums. "When you find her, be careful what you think of."

LOKI

M y guts turned. My eyes rolled so far back they made my temples thrum with a headache. My heart raced.

No matter how many times I did this, there was no getting used to it.

Having your soul yanked right out of the Helheim and shoved into a body was as excruciating as it sounded.

So was it any surprise when I jolted up screaming and shouting?

It took seconds that could have been centuries for my soul to adjust to the brand-new body and take control of motor functions, but when it did I could finally see.

A wall made of steel and a wall made of stone. A flame. And a woman.

"It's okay. You're okay," she kept whispering as if

she was trying to soothe me, but if she was she had no idea what chaos the experience was. "You're going to be okay. Just give it time, master. Give it time. Deep breaths."

What in Hel?

Had that woman read my mind or was I still shaken from what had just happened?

"Breathe, master. Breathe!" she said.

I did as instructed.

Master.

Was she a follower?

She must be or why else would she call me master?

A witch, most likely. And if she could read minds I had to be careful of my thoughts.

"Here. Have some water. Easy. Easy."

I sat up, her hand warm on my bare back, and took hold of the glass she held to my lips.

The liquid was refreshing. More refreshing than I remembered water being during my time in this realm. But that was what happened when your soul was stuck in Helheim without need for sustenance.

Oh, how I'd missed Midgard.

If water was fun, I couldn't wait to get back to old habits.

I stretched my limbs, curled my toes, took in the build of this foreign body I'd been thrust into, curled my fingers into fists.

Strong. This body was strong.

"Only the best for you, master," the woman said

and if I wasn't sure before, I was convinced she was a mind reader now.

It was time I acted like the master I was.

"Thank you, kind witchling. What should I call you?" I put the glass down and put my feet on the ground.

The witch held out a pile of clothes for me and I took them from her.

"Everyone calls me Mother Red Cap."

My lips tilted into a smirk.

"I've heard of you. You're older than you look."

It was her turn to smirk. "I'm honored my name has passed your ears. When was your last trip to Midgard?"

I shrugged. "Some time in the early nineteen hundreds. What year is it now?"

"It's 2023, master."

So I'd been gone for a century. A lot must have changed since.

"You wouldn't believe how much," she answered.

I took the first article of clothing from the pile, a white shirt made of cotton. Then a black item made of a fabric I was unfamiliar with.

"Undergarments," she told me.

I nodded and put those on and next was the pair of trousers made of some rough blue material.

"That can't be comfortable."

"You'd be surprised."

I dismissed any concerns and put the trousers on.

The fabric hugged my legs but to my surprise it wasn't as constricting as it appeared. After that I put on the socks and a pair of white shoes that looked all wrong quickly. I couldn't spend the rest of my day worried about fashion when there were more pressing issues.

"So...now that I'm decent what can I do for you, witchling? I assume you invoked me for a reason," I told her.

"Most certainly. Follow me, there's someone you should meet."

She sauntered out of the room and I followed closely, taking in my surroundings.

Judging from her accent and reputation I must be in England. London to be exact. I'd recognize that stench anywhere, any time.

"Correct. We are in Camden," she answered without looking back at me.

She walked down one end of a tunnel until she came to a round wooden door, which she pushed and held open for me. I came out into a central chamber with a fire pit in the middle. A hunched figure sat in front of it with their back to me.

Bookcases lined the walls, containing books and precious artifacts I was certain belonged to museums.

There were multiple exits but only one door had a well-scraped threshold. It was time for this charade to end.

I grabbed the witch's neck and pushed her against the door.

"Tell me, witch, who are you really?"

The woman struggled, using both hands to try to loosen my grip but she was just a witch and I was a god, infinitely stronger and smarter than her.

She croaked in an attempt to speak and since I was no mind reader I loosened my hand.

"Stop him, whisperer!"

I tightened my grip again before she could say anything else and glanced at the figure in front of the fire.

He was now standing, looking at me with terror in his eyes.

Mmm, I've missed the taste of fear in humans.

It was such a gratifying sensation. It filled me with so much satisfaction, so much pleasure.

"Wrong move, witch," I told the woman and winked at her.

I watched as her pupils dilated and her nostrils flared.

I let go of her, leaving her trapped in my illusion of ravens feasting on her eyes. She screeched and dropped to her knees. I turned my attention to the other witch. She'd called him a whisperer. I didn't know what that meant but I wasn't going to risk it. I'd kill him before I ended up on the other end of his power.

I left Mother Red Cap writhing behind me and leapt across the room toward him.

He was so slight I was pretty sure I could break him with a word.

As I was mere feet from him I raised my fist and punched him.

He put his hands in the air and shouted. "Stop!"

I just about registered his voice but his word reverberated through my entire body, pulsing through me, twisting every single one of my muscles that dared flex.

What the Hel?

The man—boy really—looked at me through the gaps between his fingers and blinked with a grimace.

He was a pretty little thing with an intense, cool, gray gaze with golden flecks dancing in his irises and freckles the same dark ginger of his hair dusting his face.

I bet he'd be fun to play with. If only I didn't need to escape whatever nightmare this is.

The boy moved delicately through the space, staring at me the whole time. He waved his hand in front of my face but while I could follow him with my gaze there was nothing I could do about it.

What happened to me? What had he done? Was that his power? If it was he wouldn't look so shocked. I was sure of that.

"Wh-what the hell?" he whispered with a slight accent that told me he wasn't English.

Admittedly, he was quite the sight to behold. If only I had control of this new body so that I could explore his—

"Mother Red Cap! Are you okay?" He glanced

behind me as the figure of the older witch shadowed his path.

"I'm fine, young whisperer. Mind tricks don't work on a mind witch. Not for long anyway," she told him and turned to me with a smug expression.

"What happened? Why is he...frozen like that?" the boy asked.

"Because..." the witch retrieved something from the boy's back pocket and showed it to him.

A dagger. A dagger he wrapped his hand around.

"I swear this was bigger a few minutes ago," he said.

"Yeah, it has a way of adjusting to its user."

"What is it?"

I glanced at the blade and my insides turned.

The Hofund.

Of course. No trip to Midgard would be complete without that darned thing.

"It's his worst fear," Mother Red Cap said. "It gives you control over him. You're his master now." She looked so pleased with herself telling the boy that.

So much for her calling me master. She wasn't a follower. She was a fraud.

"Now, now, Loki. Just because I used the Hofund on you, doesn't mean I don't respect you. It's not like I had an option anyway," she told me.

She had me there.

Thanks to fucking Heimdall the only way I could

be invoked was by being a prisoner to the wielder of the Hofund.

The boy turned and took me in as if for the first time. His lips parted as he took a deep breath.

"So, that's him, is it? Loki? The god of mischief?" The terror was present in his tone but whereas I'd savored it before, this time it made me...sad.

I didn't want the pretty little thing to be scared of me.

"And I control him with this?"

The blade reflected the fire. I snarled.

What the hell was I feeling sad for? That was what had gotten me into trouble in the first place. He was the enemy. And so was she.

"We...we're not the enemy. This young witch needs you," she said. "He thinks we're evil."

The boy turned to me and shook his head.

"No. I...I don't want to hurt you. I need you, Loki-mister-sir."

The pulsing inside me ceased and I had control over my body again.

"Will you help me pl—" the boy started but before he could finish his sentence, I snatched him by the wrist, pulled him onto me and grabbed the Hofund from his weak hand.

"Don't—" Mother Red Cap said, but it was too late.

I ran the blade across the boy's neck and he yelped.

The searing pain of the Hofund burned my own

skin and I choked as the blood from my sliced neck colored my white shirt collar red.

"You know the Hofund can't harm its master, Loki. Why even try?" Mother Red Cap said as I let go of the boy and fell back to the ground, clutching at my neck.

"Shit. Is...is he going to be okay?"

The older witch walked casually around the room as the boy dropped to his knees and grabbed my shoulder.

"I'm so sorry. I didn't know that would happen. I..." He looked around him as if battling with himself and then stooped lower, his lips ghosting over my ear and whispered something three times. "Uleczyć ranę, uleczyć ból."

A szeptun.

Now it made sense. Now I understood why the other witch called him a whisperer. Whisperer was an understatement compared to his true nature.

He was a shaman. A healer. An enchanter.

"Damn it. It didn't work. Of course it didn't. I'm useless," he cried out.

All Father, the way he's acting you'd think I was his lover.

If only.

"He's going to die."

"He's going to be fine." The witch stood over me with a green gemstone in her hands. "*Cura.*"

An emerald dust encapsulated me, my skin

absorbing the magic of the spell. The next breath I took was full and clear.

"Oh thank God. Are you okay? I'm so sorry," the szeptun said and helped me sit up.

"Don't apologize. It's his fault. He knows the sword can't harm you," Mother Red Cap told him, taking a seat opposite me.

"You know it's in my nature to try," I told her.

The boy picked up the dagger-sized sword from the floor and held it out to me.

"You can keep this if you want," he said.

"It's no use. I can't do anything with it. *You* are its wielder," I told him and I felt the familiar knot in my throat.

I would never be free. Never truly be free. As long as I was bound to the sword my life belonged to whoever wielded it.

"Oh."

The szeptun sat down too, a few feet away from me. Even though Mother Red Cap just told him he could control me, he was still scared of me.

Great. That's gonna go well for me.

"Now that you followed your natural instincts and almost died are you ready to hear us out?" Mother Red Cap asked.

"What do you want from me?"

I was doomed to be in servitude for the rest of my long existence. That was what happened every time I was invoked. My masters always had a dirty job for me to do and when that was done they sent me right back to Helheim as though I was nothing.

So what if I seduced them, what if I tricked them, what if I fell for them? The end result was always the same.

"I need you to kill the people that murdered my family," the szeptun said.

Only this time was different.

This time *I* had a job in Midgard too.

Tomasz

"Okay. I'll do your bidding," the man in front of me said.

It was hard to believe he was the one and only Loki from Norse mythology.

I didn't understand how that worked. Mother Red Cap had called him a demon, I knew him as a god. Which exactly was he? And did I really want to know?

The dagger in my hands felt like the biggest weight in the world and also my very own shield against all the madness that seemed to encompass the man in front of me.

He had a big build. His muscles stretched the fabric of his shirt so much it looked like it was gonna burst at the seams. He had a messy, curly pomp and a long beard that made him sexier than he had any right to be. His appearance certainly qualified him as a daddy.

At least that was what daddies looked like in online porn. I wouldn't know from personal experience.

What I did know was that watching him too long made the straining in my pants harder just like the daddies online did. Or being glued to him like I had moments ago when he'd threatened to slice my throat.

You'd think my number one thought would be "oh shit, I'm about to die" but instead it was "oh gods, I'm about to come."

I only hoped he couldn't sense my erection like an incubus because then I was screwed.

Although, to be honest with myself, as hot as I found the god of mischief—how was it possible he was standing in front of me—one glance at his eyes and my arousal was replaced by something else.

Unease.

I didn't know if it had anything to do with the fact one eye was green and the other golden, but whatever it was made me feel...

Unsettled. That's the word.

"I think I speak for the young man here when I say he's very grateful," Mother Red Cap said.

I shook my head to look at her.

Her lips twitched to the side and her eyes glimmered and I remembered what Caleb had told me.

Shit.

She heard me think all that.

Heat tickled my cheeks and I had to take a few

deep breaths to calm myself or bring attention to my embarrassment.

"Great. It's all sorted then. Thank you for your cooperation, master Loki. You two are free to go," she said.

Wait. Did she just say...

"Free to go? Wh-what do you mean?"

Mother Red Cap chuckled and looked from me to Loki and back to me.

"Well, exactly what you heard, young man. What? Did you think I was going to join you? My job here is done."

"But..."

What if he tries to kill me again?

"Don't worry, young whisperer. I believe Loki has learnt his lesson, hasn't he? Hurting you only means hurting himself and I'm sure he's not stupid enough to try that again. Isn't that right, master Loki?"

Loki stared at Mother Red Cap with contempt.

What if he looked at me with such contempt? What I was going to do then? I'd probably pee my pants.

I wasn't strong, or powerful, or even confident like my boss. I didn't know how to deal with higher beings like Loki.

"Your continued use of the word master is insulting when you refuse to follow it up with your actions," he told her.

"I may have bound you to the young whisperer,

but I still respect you, master Loki. I hope you understand the precautions. They weren't set by me. They
were set because of your...*behavior*."

I was certain I should be paying attention right
now and ask for an explanation of what the fuck they
were talking about, but I was far too concerned with
having to be alone with the god of mischief.

My hairs on the back of my neck stood and I didn't
even know if it was from fear or desire.

"Whichever it is, just remember you're his master
and he does your bidding. The sword is bound to you
and nothing he does can change that," Mother Red
Cap said.

I bit my lip. I didn't know what she was implying,
but if she thought I was going to use Loki as my
personal sex slave she was sorely mistaken.

"Hey, whatever floats your boat."

Shit, Tomasz. Control your thoughts.

I focused on the dagger in my hands, the knots on
the blade. The blood had dried up and it seemed more
like burn marks.

"So this thing will keep him from hurting me?" I
asked her.

I knew she'd said it, like, a hundred times already,
but I needed to be sure.

"Yes. And it doesn't matter if you're holding it or
not, you're still its master and he is bound to it and, by
extension, you."

I turned to the man of the hour with a grimace and bit the inside of my cheek.

"I'm sorry. I...I didn't ask for this, but considering the fact you tried to kill me, I have to make sure—"

Loki shrugged. "Don't worry. I'm used to it. You can't blame a man for trying to be free. But like *she* said you're in control. You want me to kill your family's killers, I'll do it. You want me to burn this whole place down?" He turned to look at the older witch and smirked. "I can do that too."

I watched the tension between the two of them and I wondered if there was a history there or if Loki just loathed authority.

"He's right. Do you want to burn this whole place down?" she asked without turning away from his stare.

"O-of course not."

"What do you want?"

"I want revenge."

Mother Red Cap raised an eyebrow and grinned. "You hear that? He wants revenge. You're good at that. So get over yourself and do what your master wants you to."

Loki huffed and looked at me. Mother Red Cap's face glowed as if she was proud she'd won the staring contest.

I couldn't blame her.

If only I had the guts to do the same, but those eyes put me on edge.

"What do you want me to do...*master*?"

That last word came out with so much disdain it made me even more uncomfortable.

How was I supposed to be in his company?

I should have listened to Mother Red Cap's warnings but how was I to know invoking a demon meant having to socialize with him. Or even worse, command him.

"Remember who you're doing this for," Mother Red Cap whispered.

I straightened my back as if on reflex.

She was right.

Get over yourself, Tomasz. You wanted your revenge, you've got a chance at it.

"I...I want to go." I stood and watched as Loki accepted I didn't want Mother Red Cap harmed and stood too.

"Good luck," she sang as we proceeded toward the exit.

We walked the long tunnel lit by torches until we came out at the underpass under Camden High Street and the hustle and bustle of London infiltrated my ears.

Loki grimaced in disgust.

"Everything okay?"

"Just as loud and gross as I remember it," he said.

"Welcome to London. Again." I stretched my hands out and as I did I knocked a guy passing by off his bike. His helmet ended up in Regent's Canal. "Shit. I'm so sorry."

The guy looked genuinely pissed until he glanced at Loki and he went milky white.

"It's-it's okay," he mumbled, running off.

I glanced at Loki but he offered me a smile and not much of a clue of what he'd said or done to the innocent human.

"What next?" he asked.

I nodded behind him then walked out into Camden Lock and took the steps up to High Street.

"We need to regroup. Well, I need to regroup and process what Mother Red Cap did. It's been a long bloody day and I've been working since 7 a.m. I'm sure you're tired too. Waking up in a new body must be... exhausting. And by the way, I want you to know that whatever happened in there was not my doing. I know she said I'm in control but...you know this is a team effort. I don't see this as—"

I glanced behind me and I found no one.

I searched for Loki but I couldn't spot him in the crowded street.

And then a car screeched to a halt and I located him just fine.

He was standing in front of a black cab, the bonnet folded around him as if it was a blanket and not metal.

The cabbie came out of his car and started shouting at Loki as everyone watched the events unfold. Loki wasted no time. He grabbed the driver by the lapel and lifted him against his car.

The driver kicked out trying to break free. Loki snarled at him and formed a fist.

"Stop!" I said, squeezing the hilt of the dagger in my back pocket.

I'm a fool. I'm a complete and utter fool.

What had I expected? That a little chat around the campfire would turn this blood-thirsty god—demon—would be enough and he'd turn into a shy wallflower?

Of course he'd tried to escape. Of course he'd tried to run away. And I was stupid to think he wouldn't. To think he'd actually want to help me. To be with me.

Loki stopped moving and I could see the panic in his eyes as he searched for me.

"Come back to me," I snarled under my breath and he put the cabbie down.

I had to watch my back with this one. Yeah, maybe he couldn't hurt me, but I was sure he'd do his damn best.

"That's a nice knife you got there. I bet you'd make a mint out of it," someone said beside me.

I turned to find a guy in a hoodie and a beanie, a kid really, staring at my dagger with a smirk.

"Ah yeah, I guess," I said.

"Wanna swap?"

At that he took his hand out of his hoodie pocket and flashed me his switchblade.

"I'm okay, thanks."

"I wasn't actually asking." He pressed the knife to

my ribs and with his other hand beckoned for my dagger.

For crying out loud. Why did these things always happen to me? And why couldn't my szept hurt people? How was I supposed to protect myself when the only thing I could whisper was luck, happiness and laughter?

"Uhm..." I said.

"Come on, dude. I don't wanna have to knife you in front of all these people."

"I'd love to see you try," a harsh voice said behind me.

The guy in the hoodie turned around to face the trickster god himself.

Not that he'd know it. All he saw in front of him was the imposing physique and terrifying look of a man twice his size.

"Beat it, grandpa."

Loki smirked and in flash snatched the guy's hand.

Crack.

The thief screeched and Loki let go of his hand. It appeared awfully crooked. He pushed him out of our way and looked at me.

"Which way, *master*?" he asked.

His eyes pierced through mine and I felt them boring down into my very soul but for some reason, I wasn't unsettled by them anymore.

No. Nothing unsettling at all. But I held him in the palm of my hand. Literally.

And what was more, I hadn't even needed to tell him to save me. He'd done it all by himself.

I walked away from the scene we'd caused.

"Thanks."

He kept in step with me and when we crossed the street I turned to look at the commotion up the road. The cabbie still shouting at us. The thief still crying out, crouched on the ground. People going about their business as if nothing had happened.

"Don't flatter yourself. He was going to steal the Hofund. We can't risk it falling in the wrong hands," he replied.

I didn't care. I didn't care whether he could be trusted. Or if I'd have to sleep with one eye open. Or if I'd have to watch my back around him.

For the first time since my family was butchered—hell, for the first time in my life—I felt powerful.

And hopeful.

Loki would find the bastards who'd killed my family and he had the power to end them.

And all just because I told him to.

Was this what it was like being powerful? Was that how Caleb felt?

Maybe having a god bound to you wasn't that bad after all.

LOKI

Midgard had changed since I'd been here the last time.

The people had changed.

They appeared far less reserved than they had in the 1920s.

Large vehicles filled the roads, tall metallic buildings rose all the way to the skies and tiny devices seemed to be the center of everyone's attention.

It was all too much to take in especially when we were brushing through the streets as if our undergarments were on fire.

There's something that hasn't changed.

Londoners loved looking busy even when they weren't. Only now they also looked...stressed.

What do they have to be stressed about? They don't have masters controlling their every move like I do.

Soon we were inside an underground train.

However, it didn't even go under the ground, which made no sense.

"That reminds me. You never told me your name. Unless you'd like me to call you master."

The young szeptun's eyes opened wide and his cheeks turned a nice shade of pink. "Oh my...of course not. I'm not...I know technically I am, but I didn't know that part. She didn't tell me I would have that kind of power over you..."

He sounded so endearing when he opened his mouth with all that insecurity about him. But I shouldn't let that fool me. He might be insecure, but for all I knew it could be an act. And even if it wasn't he was still my master and I was nothing but his slave.

"What I'm trying to say. Tomasz. My name is Tomasz Nowak."

He offered me his hand as if we were perfect strangers who had just met. I shook hands with him and smiled, continuing the ruse he'd started. I was nothing if not a great actor.

"You can call me Tomasz. And you-you're Loki. Duh." He slapped his forehead with a clumsy air to him that almost made me chuckle for real.

It was almost impossible to believe a beautiful creature like him would be so...

Goofy.

I had no idea what the word meant but it seemed to fit him perfectly.

The word rose to the surface of my consciousness

naturally and I recognized it for what it was. A remnant of my host body's soul.

In a few hours or days I'd have more of those remnants to fill in the gaps and catch me up with life in the twenty-first century but until then I was...a man out of time.

"I mean, what do you want me to call you?" he asked.

Free would be ideal...

"Loki is fine," I told him.

Tomasz nodded, smiling before looking around. The train was empty. There was a woman sitting a few seats behind us but she was fast asleep against the window.

"So...as you may have guessed, Mother Red Cap didn't give me all the information before she invoked you. That's why I want you to know I'm not going to take advantage of my power over you."

Pfft, where have I heard that before?

"What exactly *did* she tell you?"

He shrugged. "That she could call forth a demon that could help me get my revenge. And that his—your name would be Loki."

"Witches like her get a kick out of being vague."

He nodded. "The thing is I don't know what you are. Are you really the god Loki? Or are you a demon? Which is it?"

"You mean to tell me you don't know? Aren't you a witch?"

I readjusted in my seat and turned my upper body toward him. He was so close I could count the freckles on his face. So close I could smell his perfume.

Fruity. With hints of apple and citrus.

A wave of desire came over me and I remembered my last master.

He, too, had been an attractive gentleman with a score to settle with the High Council.

But like all my masters before him, he too had gotten rid of me as soon as I'd done his bidding and warmed his bed.

Tomasz would be no different.

So get a hold of yourself, Loki.

"I...we were never...no one thinks demons and gods are real. So all I know is from fiction and it's, like, way off the mark," he replied with a tremble on his lower lip as he stared right back at me.

No, not at me. At my mouth.

Was it possible my new master was attracted to me?

I can use that.

"So what are you?" he asked.

I gave him the once-over before looking him back in the eyes as a plan formed in my head. "I'm both."

He seemed shocked by that.

"We came first. We're the first witches. We've had many different names over the millennia. The ones that seemed to have stuck are demons and gods. We're both, depending on who you ask."

Tomasz pursed his lips, processing the information. Then with a tilt of his head, he asked another question. "Then why do we not know anything about you? Why have I never met a demon-god before?"

"Because...thousands of years ago, a little bitch god got so upset with her parents that she decided to trap them and the rest of us in different dimensions—mine was Helheim—destroying our bodies in this realm and imprisoning our souls. So we've been trapped ever since. The only way to cross over to Midgard was to possess a human body since our original bodies were destroyed a long time ago. And each of us has a different ritual to be invoked."

That's right. Keep it friendly. Give him all the information he needs. Gain his trust.

"But you've been to Midgard before. You said you were here a century ago," he said.

"I have. I've been here many times over the centuries."

"I thought you said you were trapped."

I smirked. "There's more than one ways to leave Helheim. I happen to have...uhm what do you call it? Inside information."

Tomasz seemed impressed by that and equally perplexed, if his wandering eyes were any indication.

"Shit, that's our stop." He jumped off his seat and ran to the door, the hilt of the dagger glowing at me.

I got up and followed after him. My new master.

A master.

How insulting.

I'm the god of mischief and chaos. I should be free.

"My home is just around the corner," he said as we passed an orange underground sign that read *Hackney*.

As he explained, he was literally around the corner. His home was a rectangular little room. A small kitchen area to the right, a sofa and table at the end and a staircase leading upstairs to a little mezzanine.

Was this what they called home these days?

How did four people fit in this place?

Regardless of my thoughts about the space, I walked around looking for any clues.

The walls held no secrets. The space under the limited furniture hid no traces. I took the stairs up to the mezzanine only to find a bed and two bedside tables. Despite my surprise that also gave me no indication.

"Wh-what are you doing?" Tomasz stared at me as I came down the stairs.

"Searching."

Wasn't it obvious?

"For what?"

"Your family's murderers."

"They weren't killed here. That's my home. Not my parents'. They weren't killed here."

I gave the place another glance and turned to my master.

"Then what the Hel are we doing here?"

Tomasz hung up his coat and grimaced.

"I told you it was best to have a rest and regroup. It's been a long, eventful day."

"Not for me."

"But it has for me. I have been up all day working, then almost got killed by a demon so excuse me if I want to rest. Gather my thoughts. Process everything that's happened."

I stared at the kid and thought about what he'd said.

I couldn't blame him for wanting to relax, but what the Hel did he have to worry about? I was the one who was trapped. He was free to do as he pleased.

And I had to find a way to free myself.

Surely there must be a way.

If I could sneak out while he was asleep I couldn't be controlled by him.

Yeah. Maybe that was what I needed to do.

"And what were you even looking for?" he asked.

"Clues they may have left behind."

The szeptun shook his head and walked over to the kitchen.

"Do you really think it'd be this easy? If it was they'd have found them already. Do you think I went to all this bloody trouble—and I mean that literally—of invoking a demon to play CSI?"

"I don't know what that is."

I approached him and leaned against the wall with my hands crossed.

"Would you like some coffee? Tea? Water?" He put

the dagger on the counter and turned to me.

"Have you got nothing stronger?"

"Beer?"

"Now you're talking."

Tomasz walked toward me with determination and a pleased expression on his face.

He looked as if he wanted to devour me, but instead he pushed me and opened the wall I'd been leaning on.

A secret compartment?

I searched behind the wall and there appeared to be a box with a light on. And it was cold.

What kind of magic was this?

Fridge.

The word came in my head and all of a sudden I knew what the contraption was.

Tomasz gave me a can and I held the frozen thing in my hand. I didn't know what to do with it at first, but then I cracked it open as if I'd done it many times before. I assumed the previous owner of my body was also a beer drinker.

It was after I'd taken a sip—and then a big gulp— that I noticed the szeptun was staring at me. "What?"

"Nothing." He shrugged. "You're just...you're a weird creature."

He didn't elaborate.

Instead, he approached a small machine on the countertop and put a mug next to it—an espresso machine, said the little voice in my head.

Whatever he did next I didn't pay attention, because the dagger was right there, on the kitchen counter, free to grab. If only there was a way to break the binding spell on it, but Hel, I'd spent centuries looking for it and had never found it.

Damn you, Heimdall. Damn you.

Tomasz stood in front of me with a mug and stared at me. The coffee smelled divine so close to my nose. I'd never been one to enjoy the beverage but maybe there was something to it?

"Are you okay?" he asked.

I looked away from the dagger and right into his eyes. "Yeah. All good. Like you said. Rest tonight and regroup tomorrow. Any idea where we start?"

"I was hoping you'd know." He narrowed his eyes and bit his lip. He did that a lot. "But then again you thought you could find evidence in my flat just by looking around so what do I know?"

He'd just insulted me, but all I could focus on was his lips. They were so plump and shiny. And so inviting. I wanted to run my tongue across them and get a taste of the young szeptun.

His cheeks turned red.

Could he read my mind?

Nah, that was impossible. If he could he would have put his guard up, but he hadn't.

Maybe because he knew I couldn't hurt him even if I wanted to.

No, he couldn't read my mind. But he was staring

at me as if he could.

He licked his lips again almost in response and I forgot to breathe for a moment.

He was breathtaking.

Deny it as I may, he was. Just because he was my master didn't mean he wasn't. He was so perfectly sculpted I could have mistaken him for a god, and yet he was nothing but a little whisperer.

"So...you don't?" he croaked.

It took me a moment to realize he'd spoken and I had to shake my thoughts free of him for a moment so I could concentrate on his words. "I don't, what?"

"You don't know where to start finding the killers?" he said with a little bit more confidence in his voice.

What are you doing, Loki?

I stepped back and put some distance between him and me. "I didn't say that," I replied.

We've been down this road before. We can't go down it again.

He's your master. He only wants one thing from you. To get him the revenge he craves. And then he'll betray you just like the rest of them.

That's why I need to betray him first. But how when he holds my leash?

"Oh. So you do have a plan?"

I nodded.

Yeah. My plan is to free myself from you.

Before I make the same mistake I always have.

LOKI

"Here you go." Tomasz handed me a towel and I closed the bathroom door behind me. *Finally some alone time.*

Spending so much time with the person who was meant to be your master was exhausting. And that was partly because half the time I didn't know whether I wanted to kill him or fuck him.

Well, I'd tried the latter and it had never worked before.

What was it with me falling for my masters? What was wrong with my head that I couldn't resist them?

Well, it wasn't entirely my fault. Most of them had been beautiful people. It was hard to deny my desires.

But I would this time.

This time it'd be different.

I'd be different.

No falling for the young szeptun.

No matter what he did, no matter what he said, I'd stick to my guns and my plan.

I looked around the small box room that passed for a bathroom and sighed. It was so small, so restrictive. I could barely breathe in here. It was like a cage.

But at least I was alone.

I didn't know whether that was for better or for worse.

I followed my body's instincts and slid the shower door open, turning the tap on. It showered hot water everywhere. What a marvel to behold. How astonishing for hot water to be available on command and in such infinite supply. Civilization had progressed dramatically in my absence.

The gaps were slowly filling in my head, courtesy of my old host. As grateful as I was, I needed to get rid of his stench of death. That and the blood ritual the old crow had performed to invoke me.

I didn't know how long it had been since the old host had died, but I could tell the body had been preserved for quite some time. The salves, potions and spells used to preserve the body reeked, but I could still smell the death underneath it all. I didn't know how or why the witch kept cadavers in her cave but it felt ominous to me.

I guess there's a lot of things I don't know.

I stepped into the shower and embraced the wet

heat encompassing my body and the low groan that escaped my lips was inevitable.

Damn, this feels good.

I ran my hands over my hair, untangling knots and releasing dirt caught in it.

The arms on this body. The pectorals. The muscles.

It was most certainly a glorious body to be in, but I wished I could talk to the host. Find out more about it, about him, about his world. It was always such an intimate time being awakened in a new body.

Usually, demons were invoked in live bodies and the act would slowly kill the old host, but it was a sacred process. A lot of our followers used to crave the sweet, slow release of death under our rule. But Mother Red Cap had taken that away from me.

Never mind, however. I could still enjoy the power and authority my new body exuded.

As I got lost in my thoughts of possessions and running through all the ways I could escape my new master, I spotted a big bottle on a shelf that said *cedarwood and rosemary body wash*. I picked it up. Whatever I could use to get rid of all the smells in my body were most welcome. I poured a generous amount of the lotion in my hand and as I put the bottle back I noticed something pink behind it, but before I examined it closer I worked up a lather on my body.

It was small, curved and had a rather peculiar long hook.

I'd never seen such a thing, but my old host must have because as soon as I picked it up the words butt plug came into my head. I held it mere inches from my face, inspecting it, trying to embrace the fact that young Tomasz had used this on himself.

That it had been inside him.

I bit my lip as a trickle of pleasure shot through me. The meat on this body was astounding, which meant I couldn't resist touching it. I didn't think I'd ever had control of such a huge cock, not even in my original body—good thing I could shapeshift. But it wasn't the same.

I brought the toy closer to me and smelled nothing but the same body wash I'd smeared all over me. But even though it had been cleaned there was still a scent that hadn't—couldn't—be cleaned off.

A scent that was pure sex.

It made me catch my breath and my cock to throb, begging for the person it had originated from.

Stop it. That's what's got you into trouble before.

I glanced down at my dick and at the toy in my hands.

It'd be a shame to let this erection go to waste.

Besides, I don't think thinking about fucking the little witch and doing it is the same thing.

Thoughts can't hurt.

I took a deep breath with determination and pressed my back on one of the tiled walls.

The cold surface made me tremble, only adding to the need coursing through my body.

I wrapped my hand around my length and focused on Tomasz's scent.

Did he play with this little thing often?

Is his hole tight?

Does it hurt when he inserts it in himself?

Every unanswered question was matched with the vigor of my strokes. Every image in my head, bringing me closer to release.

I could picture him beside me, taking a shower, unaware of my presence. Massaging his body. Playing with his limp dick. Watching it as it grew bigger and filled his hand. Reaching for the pink toy and slipping it inside him. Watching him wince.

Every image made me want it to be realer and realer. But I'd made a promise to myself. No messing around with the master again.

No one said I can't mess around with his stuff though?

The more I rubbed my length, the wilder my imagination got, the hoarser my throat got, a growl that threatened to spill like my release.

Before I came to my senses, I pressed the pink toy against my own hole and pushed it inside.

The dry friction made my muscle clench and I winced.

And then the vibration started and I all but unraveled before I even realized what was going on.

It took me several moments before I found the button at the bottom of the butt plug I had pressed in my attempt to fuck myself and the more I pressed it the more intense the vibrations got.

I could just about explode.

Instead, I could fantasize about jumping into yet another new body—Tomasz's.

Is this how he feels when he does it to himself?

Does he feel as horny as I do?

Does he bite down a growl like I am or does he let it out?

The familiar claw of an orgasm gripped my stomach and I covered my mouth to stop myself from letting out a scream that would give away what I was doing.

My cock pulsed, painting the shower glass white for a moment before it was washed off by the water.

My chest filled with air and satisfaction and my knees buckled under my weight.

Oh that felt good. It's been so long.

———

"I made some dinner if you're h—," the boy said as soon as I came out with the towel wrapped around my hips.

He paused, staring at my semi-naked body with parted lips and red cheeks.

"I'm famished. Let me get back into my clothes."

I turned and marched back in the bathroom before I went for round two with the real man this time.

"Oh, uhm, no, don't put the shirt back on. It belongs in the bin. Let me see if I've got anything," he shouted and moments later he handed me a jacket. "It'll probably be super tight, but it's better than trying to fit in my clothes, believe me."

But I would love to try and fit my cock inside you.

Oh Hel. Clear your head, Loki. You're not doing this again.

"Thanks." I took the jacket from him and like he said it was rather tight. As soon as I zipped it up some of the stitches burst, but it was better than being topless in front of the kid. He wouldn't stop looking at me as it was.

Then again, I could use that to my advantage.

"What have you made?" I walked over to the kitchen to find a plate of dumplings.

"Well..." Tomasz approached and batted his lashes. "When I say made I meant I put the pierogi in boiling water for two minutes. But if you don't like it I can order pizza."

A part of my brain ignited at the mention of pizza, but the pierogi would do fine.

"I'm good. And if I can wash it down with beer, I'll be even better."

The boy seemed pleased with my response as he opened the fridge and handed me another can of beer.

I took a seat at a flimsy table and Tomasz joined me with a beverage of his own.

"Did you enjoy your shower?"

I smirked at him before I took a bite of a pierogi. "Oh, I enjoyed it very much indeed."

He smiled, pleased with my response, chewing his food as I stared at him. And then his eyes went wide and his cheeks turned a very familiar color.

All Father, does that boy blush easily!

Would he blush as much if I fucked him?

He pushed his chair back and ran to the bathroom.

Just as I raised my beer to my lips, something pressed on my lap and made me jolt.

A black creature—a cat by all accounts—was sitting on me, inspecting me with big yellow eyes, tilting its head from side to side.

"Oh Sass, no! Don't—" Tomasz shouted as soon as he returned to the room.

The cat didn't pay him any mind when it laid down on my lap and curled into a purring ball.

Tomasz put his hands to his hips and his jaw dropped.

"What are you doing?" he asked.

"Nothing," I said.

He waved me off.

"No, not you. You. I...I thought you were about to rip him a new one."

I frowned and looked down at the cat who raised its head and let out a nonchalant meow.

"What do you mean you'd never. Need I remind you the number of people you've scared to death?"

Why was he talking to the cat as if it was a person?

Was it a familiar maybe?

Or was the young szeptun a bit crazy?

Whichever the case, my plan stayed the same.

Free myself of my new master, no matter what it takes.

Tomasz

As if it wasn't enough I'd just let a god into my shower while my sex toy was on full display, now I had to deal with Saskia being weird and the god himself staring at me as if I was crazy for talking to her.

"No more rats to hunt?" I asked Saskia, gritting my teeth.

"No. None," she answered, not seeming to give a shit about me.

"Ah yes, of course. London is known for being short on rodents."

She rolled her eyes.

I glanced at Loki and swallowed a knot.

With a huff, I bent down and grabbed the insolent domowik from Loki's lap. I grazed something hard in my attempt to get her off him and paused for a moment before I realized what it was.

Shit.

Would I ever stop making such a fool of myself?

"What are you doing, Sass? You're embarrassing me," I whisper-shouted at the cat as I walked away from him.

Sass smirked. "Oh come on. Don't tell me you wouldn't sit on his lap if you could. Especially when he's hard as—"

"Shut up. Don't be gross."

"Don't lie to me, Tomasz. The man is gifted. And he feels huge—"

"Sass!"

"Fine. Fine. Pretend I'm lying."

I held her up to my face and she slitted her eyes as if trying to read my mind.

"Maybe you're not, but I'd expect you to be more respectful of our guest."

"Ha! I knew it. And he's not just a guest. He's a god! Is that what you've been up to all evening?"

I shrugged. "What if I was?"

"Mmm, I like it. I don't know where you found him but me-uh-ow."

I sighed. "I thought you hated people."

"Yeah, people. Not gods!"

"How do you know what *he* is?"

"Oh honey, it's written all over him. Besides, you can't fool this snout. He looks like a god, he smells like a god, I bet he—"

"Sass!" I warned.

"What? I was only going to say I bet he walks like a god too."

I raised an eyebrow but she seemed undeterred by my judgment.

"Everything okay?" Loki asked.

I turned my head to smile reassuringly for a moment at the man across the room.

I didn't mind my studio flat. I was the only one using it, after all. And Saskia when she wasn't out hunting mice or scaring people to death. But if there was ever a need for a bigger house it was when I had to reprimand my domowik without sounding insane.

"If I put you down do you promise to behave?" I muttered under my breath.

"Of course. What do you take me for?" she answered.

"Honestly? I don't know anymore."

I'd never seen Saskia so drawn to a person like she was drawn to Loki. It was fucking weird.

Maybe there was something about gods that was compelling for us lowly beings, because I couldn't blame her.

Hell, I'd probably sit on his lap if I was a cat too. Or even if I wasn't. I wanted to feel that *"huge—"* Sass had felt.

"I'll behave. I swear," she added and I put her down.

The night had settled over London outside my window. I was about to let a god—a demon—sleep in my flat. A god who had tried to kill me the first chance he'd gotten.. A god I couldn't stop staring at or making a fool of myself in front of.

"You're in control."

That was what Mother Red Cap had said, but could I trust her? I knew her as well as I knew the trickster in my house.

I took a deep breath and turned to face him.

"Sorry about that." I approached the table and sat on the chair I'd occupied only minutes ago.

Loki popped an entire pierogi into his mouth and glanced at Saskia sitting on the floor in front of us.

"Is she your girlfriend?" he asked.

"What? You think I have a cat for a girlfriend? I'm not that desperate yet." I almost choked on my lemonade.

"I thought she was a familiar, but hey, what you do behind closed doors is your business alone."

He did have a point. I guessed if someone didn't know what Saskia was, they would presume she was a familiar considering her human-like behavior and attitude. Although the latter I was the only privy to.

Familiars were the fated mates of witches. Animal shifters destined to protect us. However, the chances of finding your familiar mate in this world was just as favorable as humans finding their soulmates. One in a million.

"No. She's not a familiar. And *definitely* not my girlfriend."

As if to stress the point, Saskia coughed—more like choked—out a hairball.

"Okay," he said.

"That's right, daddy. I'm free as a bird," she meowed seductively at him.

Good thing he couldn't understand her.

"Sass!"

"Fine. Fine. Behaving," she mumbled and started grooming herself.

"So, she's just a cat?" he asked and I nodded before I realized Saskia's grooming session had turned into a sex show.

She sat with her legs wide open licking between them and staring at Loki like the thirsty bitch she was.

"Saskia!" I growled. "You're being disgusting."

"I'm being racy. There's a difference."

"He's human and you're a cat." I tried to mutter under my breath but I was annoyed with her.

"He's a god. He doesn't care about such trivialities. You know he gave birth to a horse, right?"

"You're exhausting."

"And you're a prude."

Loki watched us with a discreet smirk and furrowed brows.

"I'm sorry," I apologized.

He crossed his arms and leaned back on his chair. "Oh do go on. This is highly entertaining. But when you're done, don't pretend she's a cat. It'll insult both our intelligence."

I rubbed my face, glared at Saskia and downed the rest of the lemonade as if it was whiskey. "She's not a cat. She's a domowik." I sighed.

No one was supposed to know about her. No one was supposed to know a lot of things about my family, but well...they were dead so what did it matter anyway?

"A domowik? Huh. It's been a few hundred years since I've heard that word," he said.

I set my glass down and leaned forward. "You mean, you know what they are?"

"I've heard rumors, but they're so rare and so out of my time that I don't know if those rumors are true. Care to enlighten me?"

How peculiar. Only hours ago he was the one doing the enlightening and now the tables had turned. How did a demon, god, whatever, not know what everything in this world was? Hadn't he said demons had come first?

Maybe Mother Red Cap was right. Maybe I *did* have control. And not just because he was bound to me. If he didn't know about domowiks then maybe he didn't know their history with szeptuns either.

"Domowiks are—"

Saskia coughed. "I'm right here, you know."

"Saskia is a...was a human. Until she was trapped in animal form and blessed with immortality..."

"'Blessed'? More like a curse, but don't get me started," she mumbled and walked away from the table.

I couldn't blame her. Her story was not nice. The only reason why she was able to go about life as if it wasn't painful was because of how many centuries had passed since it had happened.

"They—she is supposed to guard my family. She belonged to my father before me, and his mother before him. She was supposed to be my sister's, but—"

"The murder," he replied quietly, almost respectfully, and even though I hated thinking about it, that word, it didn't hurt as much when he spoke it with such humility.

"She split her time between us all. She was staying with me when it happened."

Loki reached across the table and covered my hand with his with a warm, firm touch that made my hairs stand on end. "I'm sorry."

I froze for a second. Which turned into two. I was afraid if I moved it would break whatever sanctity this moment had and it was the first time I'd felt that since being introduced to him. The first time I felt as if he was genuine and not trying to find a way to ditch me or kill me.

"Anyway." I broke the moment when it became too much to bear. Being touched delicately by a demon...god was no joke. It was intense. "Saskia. She's trapped in her animal for the rest of eternity. Or as long as my family exists, I guess. There's no way to break the spell and the secret of her curse died with the witches that created her and others like her."

"And are you the last of your family?"

I nodded.

"And that's why I'm here."

"Yeah," I whispered. "I want to find the people that took my family from me and make them pay."

His hand still held mine. "And I'll help you with that."

"Th-thank you," I answered him, looking at his calloused fingers.

The fridge hummed, filling the room with its monotone whirring for a second or two before he spoke again. "What happens after you're done with your revenge?"

I glanced at him. "What do you mean?"

"What will you do after I find those responsible and make them pay?"

I bit down on my lip and shrugged. "I haven't thought that far ahead."

What would I do after?

Before their death I'd been working up the courage to ask Caleb to be my mentor. To teach me his witch ways. To keep working with my sister on mastering our szept so I could one day become a healer like her and my dad.

But now?

There was nothing there. I couldn't see past avenging their death.

"And me?" he asked.

"What do you mean?"

"What happens to me when we're done?"

I dared to look at his green and golden eyes and sighed. "I-I don't know."

He pursed his lips and his nostrils flared. "So you're planning on keeping me under your servitude."

"What? No. I...I didn't say that. I know it sucks that you're bound to me, but I don't want you to feel like I'm taking advantage of you. I didn't ask for that. I asked for help. You're as much in control as I am. If there's a way to set you free, I promise I'll do it."

He raised the beer can and drank from it with a tension that hadn't been there seconds ago.

"I swear. I'm not out to use you. This is a partnership. I just need your help. Once we're done, I'll ask Mother Red Cap, find a way to set you free. Or return you to Helheim if that's what you want."

He shook his head. "That's what they all say before they...*stab me* in the back."

"But I mean it."

"How do I know that?"

I readjusted in my seat put both my elbows on the table. "How can I prove it to you?"

He scratched his chin, humming. I took the time to admire how glorious his beard was and how sexy his face.

"Why don't you set me free now?"

I narrowed my eyes. "Because you tried to kill me and escape. So while I don't want you to feel enslaved to me, I also don't trust that you'll stick around to help me. Maybe if you show me I can trust you—"

He raised his hand. "Fine. I had to try. You understand. It's in my nature. You can't let me free just yet. You said this was a partnership though."

"It is."

"If you mean it, then surely you won't mind helping me."

Just when I was starting to go soft on the man, he went and did or said things like that and my guard went all the way back up again.

"Help you how?"

"I need to find someone."

"Who?"

"That's none of your business."

"If you don't tell me, how am I supposed to trust you and help you?"

He seemed to ponder my question with another gulp of beer and when he set it down he leaned closer, so close that our faces were mere inches from one another and stared me right down.

"Fine. Someone has taken my children. I need your help to find them."

LOKI

"Your children?"

I nodded.

"And your children are..."

"Also demons, yes."

It was probably a big mistake sharing the information with him, but if I knew one thing in life, it was how to keep my options open. And one of those was gaining his trust in case I needed to use it.

Hopefully, it wouldn't come to that.

But I knew better.

"Wh-what happened?"

"Someone invoked them."

I made an attempt at drinking more beer but the can turned out to be empty. Tomasz noticed and got me another without hesitation.

"Are they also bound?" he asked under his breath before he returned to his seat.

"They're not."

I was the only demon I knew of that had been bound to humans since time immemorial. It was the most humiliating thing. A demon tied to a human? It had been unspoken of. Until Heimdall.

Fucking Heimdall.

"So why do you think they've been taken?"

Tomasz leaned his head into his hands and looked even more innocent than he had any right to. Not when he was my master and could order me to do whatever he wanted.

I stared into his eyes, pushing down any feelings and thoughts that kept rising to the top.

Maybe he's not like the others.

Maybe this time it'll be different.

Maybe he's someone who can love me.

It was thoughts like these that didn't have any place in my mind. That didn't belong to god or demon.

And yet they kept ringing round and round my head as if they were teasing me. As if the All Father was playing tricks on me, which wasn't fair because I was the master of them.

Maybe he can love me for me.

I almost lost my composure and laughed at myself.

Who in their right mind would ever fall in love with the god of mischief and mayhem?

Who would trust someone like me with their heart?

Pathetic. I'm a god bound to a mortal and my biggest concern is being loved?

By the person holding my strings no less.

"I know they've been taken. They were both pulled away from Helheim at the same time. And neither of them have been back since," I said, shaking my head along with my stupidity away.

"Is that unusual?" The young man grabbed his glass with both hands and barely took a sip as he stared at me with a mix of concern and confusion.

"Maybe not for Fenrir, but it most certainly is for Hela. She runs the place," I told him.

"Your-your daughter is Hela? As in the goddess of death Hela?"

I nodded.

"Is that how you were able to escape Helheim all these centuries?"

"That's right. And since she's the queen of her realm even if she was summoned into to a human body, she should still be able to communicate with me, or return if not only momentarily. And she hasn't. She hasn't been back at all."

Tomasz reached across the table and brushed my forearm with his fingers. His touch was just like the rest of him—unobtrusive, delicate, and reluctant. And yet it ignited my insides, assaulting me with the memories of what I'd done in the shower. Of the things I'd imagined him doing. Of the things I imagined doing to him.

"Do you have any...suspicions?" he asked and his voice sounded like a whisper that charred whatever part of me had been left unaffected by his presence.

I had to clear my throat before I spoke again, lest I give away how much of an influence he had on me.

"I do. I-I know who-who's got them. Heimdall."

He pulled back and even though the fire continued blazing inside me I could breathe a little easier again. "The watcher of Asgard?"

"And guard of the Bifröst. A major dick!"

Tomasz's eyes went wide. "Well, if the man really took your kids, then I'm not surprised you're not a fan."

My response was drinking with a huff.

"Problem is finding him," I said after a few gulps.

"So basically we both need to find people and we both have no clue where to start."

"He wouldn't hide. He wants me to find him. So I wouldn't be surprised if he made a show of it," I said.

Tomasz scratched his chin and pushed his lips from side to side. "I think I've got an idea where we can start," he said but before I could ask him to elaborate, he pushed his chair back. "But I'm knackered and I desperately need my bed."

Images of Tomasz naked in bed flashed before my very eyes, tempting that fire inside.

Did he have toys up there too?

"Yeah, sleep doesn't sound so bad," I told him even though demons didn't need it.

I got up as well and Tomasz's cheeks turned peachy as he fumbled around the house trying to set my bed for the night.

A few minutes later the sofa had been turned into a bed with a sheet barely covering the surface, a soft pillow and thin blanket for cover.

"I'm so sorry. I know you're probably used to much more luxurious settings."

It was true. Every time I'd been in Midgard I'd been part of the cream of society, being admired, worshiped and spoiled rotten. But after several eternities in Helheim I didn't care. Anything was better than the dark abyss.

"Don't worry. I'm nothing if not adaptable."

I tried to yank my way out of the T-shirt he'd given me and there was a ripping sound.

"If you want, we can go get you some clothes your size tomorrow before we go into work," he said, staring really hard at the T-shirt I'd thrown to the floor.

"Sounds good."

Tomasz smiled and pivoted to take the stairs up to the bed without another glance at me as if I'd insulted him somehow or said something wrong.

Or maybe he's avoiding looking at my body.

The memories of my private time in the shower rose to the surface and I had half a mind to follow him upstairs and show him what a demon could do. Thankfully, the other half of my mind was being logical and reasonable so instead I laid down on the sofa and watched the ceiling.

Tomasz kept mumbling indiscernible things and his domowik would meow in response. And then once he and the cat had settled I could hear him shuffling, or turning. I could detect when he pulled the cover of himself and when he folded his pillow.

It should have felt like forever before he was asleep, but I'd lived forever so the time it took him barely registered.

I got up, grabbed the T-shirt from the floor and made my way toward the door.

I didn't want to, I felt guilty doing it, but I didn't know if I could trust him. I didn't know if I could ever trust any of my masters.

Not even the cute ones like the szeptun sleeping right above.

"Sorry, kid," I whispered into the silent flat and pushed the door handle down.

It slid down with ease but when I tried to open the front door I couldn't.

Did he lock me in here?

The little shit.

I bent down to check the door but the latch didn't seem to be engaged.

For all intents and purposes the door was unlocked. I just couldn't open it.

Did he...

He couldn't have.

But the more I tried to pry the blasted thing open the more convinced I was he had.

He'd commanded me to stay in this flat.

That was the only explanation for why I couldn't open the door and run out into the night.

My chest tingled with a familiar warmth.

Little shit! I didn't think he had it in him.

Who would have known the innocent, shy guy who didn't want me to feel like a servant to him would be wise enough to command me.

However cute and surprising his action was though, it proved my point.

He can't be trusted.

But then again, neither can I.

TOMASZ

I opened my eyes as the noise suffocated me and the light licked my lashes but offered no warmth.

Another day had begun.

And yet no matter how many I lived through I still woke up every day resentful my family wasn't there to see the sun rise again.

Or to tell me how skinny I was, bicker over food and chores, and tell me for the millionth time that I was wasting my talents away working for a High Council operation.

Every day I didn't get the chance to speak to them, every day I hovered my thumb over their number knowing there would be no answer, was as painful as the last.

Is it ever not gonna hurt like this?

Am I ever gonna feel normal again?

Something moved beside me and I looked down at Saskia stretching with a big yawn.

It was times like this that she appeared just like any other cat.

Cute. Adorable. So perfectly fluffy.

"Fuck me, that was a good wet dream. Do you think a god can fuck you in your sleep?"

And then she'd open her mouth and I'd remind myself I was friends with a truck driver. Or in this case, a phone sex operator.

Well, friends was an understatement.

She was stuck with me and I with her. Not that I could complain. If anything she was my only company.

"Can you not be so uncouth?" I muttered, mimicking her yawn.

"How many times have I told you you can't pull off that word? You just sound like you're all fuzzy from sucking off a polar bear."

"I hate you, you know that?"

She sauntered to the end of the bed and only turned to me briefly before jumping off.

"I'll go cry in my demon daddy's lap. Now come on. I need a huge fucking cup of coffee."

Demon—

Shit. I'd forgotten about him.

Just like the rest of my life lately he'd felt like a dream.

And what a dream.

Shit. I'm starting to sound like Saskia.

I sat up in bed and the sunlight reflected off the dagger on my bedside.

"You can't leave this flat."

That was what I'd whispered to it last night. Despite everything we'd talked about and agreed I didn't fully trust him yet. For all I knew, he'd even lied about his kids just to get me to soften up. He'd been so obvious when I'd told him I didn't want to take advantage of him. I didn't know if he thought he was being inconspicuous, asking me all those questions, but his eyes had flared when he asked me why I couldn't find a way to release him before he helped me.

It pained me that I couldn't, but I knew—I fucking knew—if I did, he'd be gone before I managed to utter a word.

Or even worse, he'd slice my neck open like he'd tried to do when he'd first seen me.

Had he tried to leave last night? Would he tell me if he had?

"Oh hello daddy!" I heard Saskia downstairs and I had to shove my pondering to the backburner before my domowik sexually assaulted my demon.

He's not my *demon.*

Just as I thought, I found Saskia sprawled all over the coffee table with wide eyes ogling the topless Loki sleeping on the sofa.

Shit. I forgot about that.

He'd taken his top off so effortlessly, so recklessly

last night, as if I wasn't even there. Or as if he didn't care.

I wasn't used to men stripping in front of me. And I'm sure even if I was, I'd still not be used to men like *him* doing so.

So big, so imposing. With muscles and fuzz for days.

It had taken everything in me to not leer at him. And all my resolve to get him out of my mind as I lay in bed last night. Or think back to the fact he'd seen my butt plug in the shower. Or how hot it'd be if he were suddenly in my bed testing what a good job my sex toys had done stretching me.

Getting boners when your bitch of a talking cat sleeps in your bed was not the best mood-setter.

"Sass, stop being a perv and leave the man alone!" I whisper-shouted.

"Darling, please. This is no man. He's what orgasms are made of."

I marched to the coffee table, averting my gaze from the topless demon god on my sofa before I ended up copying Saskia, and grabbed the bloody cat, carrying her to the kitchen.

It didn't make much of a difference, granted, considering he was, like, five feet away from us, but it was better than waking up with a creepy domowik mind-fucking you.

I filled the coffee machine and turned it on as my

phone flashed *Ciocia* across the screen, but I rejected my aunt's call without a second thought.

I turned to Saskia and to her credit she'd stayed perched on the kitchen counter, but she was still staring at Loki.

"You do know his body is human right? There's nothing special about it," I told her.

Oh, the eyeroll she gave me. "I bet you wouldn't think that if he was taking you up the ass."

"Bitch."

"Besides, it's not just his body. It's his...energy. I can feel it on my lips."

I crossed my arms and stared at the coffee pouring into my cup.

"You don't have lips, Sass," I said.

"Not those lips," she purred.

I clenched my stomach and gagged. "I think I just threw up a little."

Saskia shook her head, walked to the end of the counter and gazed out of the window. "Oh please. You don't know what it's like being trapped in this body for centuries trying to be normal." She looked so stoic and wise with the sunlight washing over her. "What I wouldn't give for a good dicking."

"Gods, I need out of this flat. I'm gonna kill my cat and she can't even die," I muttered as I reached for my salvation.

The aroma of the coffee gave me some sort of comfort and normalcy.

"Was that what you were like when you hung out with Oliwia?"

Saskia's head sagged and she sighed. "I miss my gal pal."

Oliwia had been so much better than me. Not only was she a better szeptucha than I ever would be, she'd been a better witch, a better friend, a better human than most.

She'd saved so many lives working at the hospital. And even though she was more than paying her dues as a nurse, she'd still moonlight as a healer for the Polish Coven too. She shouldn't have been the one to die.

But then again, no one should have died that day.

"I miss her too."

"Morning!"

I jumped out of my skin. My cup almost slipped out of my hands. And when I turned to face the demon god standing before me my heart nearly gave out.

"I startled you. I'm sorry. Are you okay?"

He squeezed my shoulder and I had to remind myself to breathe. To breathe and ignore the heat of his touch or what it did to me so early in the morning.

Although, would it have a different effect on me any other time of the day? I doubted it.

"It's okay. I'm fine. I'm fine."

"I'm not," Saskia swooned.

I ignored her.

"What did she say?" he asked.

I grimaced. "You don't want to know. Trust me. Coffee?"

"Sure. I'll give it a try. You make it look...tasty!"

I ignored the remark and the heat on my cheeks and I poured a cup for him. While he drank his coffee I excused myself to the bathroom for my morning shower.

I didn't want to leave him alone with Saskia, but the only saving grace was that he couldn't understand a word she said so what was the worst that could happen?

A few minutes later, I was dressed and ready to go.

Saskia stayed behind to have a lazy day. We made our way to the nearest clothes shop to get Loki new clothes.

"You seem a lot more at ease today," I told him an hour later as we were on our way to Paternoster Square so I could start my shift.

He smirked. "My body...it has a way of adjusting to the world. Usually we have the host's soul to guide us, but even without it, the body has a way of helping us adapt," he said.

"I don't think I'll ever grasp that this isn't your real body. I bet it's weird always having a different body."

Loki shrugged. "It has its benefits but believe me, it's weird for me too."

The Java Jinx sign loomed ahead and I stopped to take a big breath. "That's my workplace. I'm hoping my boss can help us find Heimdall. He works for the High Council and is very connected."

"I doubt a witch will be able to find him, but if you think he can help..."

"Believe me, he's no ordinary witch. There's rumors about him," I said.

"What sort of rumors?" Loki grinned and his golden eye twinkled.

Wait. Was the god of mischief a gossip?

"That's not important right now. He led me to Mother Red Cap so he knows I want to find my family's killers, but it's probably best if he didn't know you were a demon. I don't know the High Council's or the Angel Guard's stance on demons and I'd rather not find out."

If there was even a tiny chance of either stopping me from getting my vengeance I didn't know what I'd do. How I'd survive. When Caleb had told me about the witch under Camden Lock he'd given me the impression she could cast a spell or give me a potion that would help me in my search. I didn't know if Caleb knew she used demons.

"Angel Guard? What the Hel is that?" Loki asked.

"Oh, it's like witch law enforcement. Well, witch and Nightcrawler law enforcement. It's relatively new. They've only been around for three years, but trust me. You don't want to cross them."

"'Nightcrawler'?" he asked.

"Yeah. That's all the supernatural creatures that aren't witch—"

"I know what they are, boy. I'm just surprised you're still using the term. It's so old-fashioned. So derogatory."

"Why derogatory?" That was the first time I'd heard that.

"That's what Christians would call them when hunting them. Among other things. Devil spawn was another."

That was strange. I was so used to the term being... just a word. To be honest, I'd never really thought about it. It was just a term everyone used.

"Language evolves, I guess," I answered him. "Anyway, when we're in there, try to avoid touching Caleb. He's an empath and the less people know about you, the better."

Loki nodded and his golden eye glimmered.

"We're all good. He won't even know what I look like," he said.

I cocked my head and waited for an explanation.

"I just glamored myself. He'll think I'm an old man."

"You don't look like one."

Wasn't that what glamored meant? That it gave others an illusion of something else? Or was that another word that meant something different to him?

"Not to you. But to everyone else. My master can't be *fooled* by my tricks." He hissed at the word "fooled".

"Oh. I'm sorry."

I started walking again and Loki followed me but it was only when we got to the front door that I noticed him staring.

"What?"

"You apologize a lot, you know. Even when nothing's your fault," he said and I couldn't tell if that was pity or admiration in his expression.

I probably shouldn't know the answer to that.

It could set me down the wrong path.

Like a path where I cared what Loki, the demon god of mischief and tricks, thought of me or about me.

And I definitely didn't need that.

LOKI

Tomasz stared as his boss came around the bar and even helped me to one of the tables before taking my order, although like Tomasz had warned me I didn't touch him.

Not that touch mattered to empaths unless they were lower-level witches, in which case that was the only way they could use their powers.

Dangerous creatures, empaths.

Dangerous and rare.

Probably rarer than szeptuns, so it didn't surprise me that he worked for the High Council.

He was a unique creature. Nothing like I'd ever seen before, what with his flowing silver hair and the numerous piercings. All neatly packed into a small package of a man who didn't appear the least bit intimidating.

And yet, anyone would be a fool to mistake him for a weakling.

"Here's your water, sir. Can I get you a coffee? Tea?" the empath said when he returned with a bottle of water and a glass.

"A coffee thanks," I said.

His eyes narrowed.

"You're such a kind young man," I added to supplement the illusion of the elderly person he was seeing.

He nodded and turned—not too bad of an ass— but didn't go very far as he turned to Tomasz who was still staring.

"Are you okay, Tomasz? Is he a friend of yours?"

Tomasz jumped and shook his head with a flustered look. "Erm, no. No. I'm sorry."

There it was again.

He was apologizing for no reason.

It was so strange to hear and even stranger to witness. It was as though he went about his life apologizing for even existing. And yet, when it came to his revenge, he was truly unapologetic and devious.

Was that the real Tomasz?

Or was the one apologizing all the time the real guy?

Which was the truth and which was the mask?

"I'll go get changed," he said and his boss followed him.

Moments later, the young empath served my coffee and Tomasz was behind the bar, hard at work.

And it all looked so complicated.

Cappuccinos, babyccinos, lattes, macchiatos, non-foam, extra shot. It was like its own special kind of alchemy and mixology, intoxicating to watch.

A couple of times Caleb walked to the back room with a customer and a few minutes later they'd both come back out all smiles and gratitude.

"What is going on back there? Don't tell me you have to give hand jobs as part of your duties," I told Tomasz when he brought me a fresh coffee half hour later.

His eyes widened and he blinked several times before he answered.

It was so cute to see him so flustered.

That was the other thing about him.

He blushed so easily as if he had no experience in life. As if his sexuality and his needs were something to be embarrassed about.

I wanted to learn more about him, why he was that way, what made him tick, but I knew what a dangerous path it had been in the past, having that kind of interest in my masters.

"Of course not. Are you crazy? It's a spell shop. Humans get coffee in the front. Witches get spells in the back. Wait, that sounds naughty." He bit his lip and looked up and out of the floor-to-ceiling windows into the busy street.

"It didn't sound naughty to me. Unless you want to make it naughty, in which case I can help." I offered him my cheekiest grin and I couldn't help noticing the knot that had formed in his throat.

"I'm all right, thanks," he muttered and marched off behind the bar again.

He's the most innocent master I've ever had.

And yet I was still bound to him.

He's not innocent. He's just like any other. Never forget, Loki.

I did my best to keep that to front of mind, but the more I watched him, the easier it was to forget.

Like the way he smiled at each customer as if they were dear friends.

Or how the creases around his eyes would intensify whenever he laughed at some joke.

And even when he turned his back to them and whispered things to the drinks before serving them.

"You're going to have to switch to tea or juice soon because this is your fourth coffee and Caleb is starting to look at you funny." He put down my cup and barely moved his lips when talking.

"Noted." I used both hands to bring my drink to my lips and after a sip I let out a long sigh. "Is that better?"

He rolled his eyes. "Nope. If you were old you'd have had a heart attack with all this coffee."

"You don't know how old I look to him."

"*I'd* have a heart attack with all that coffee." He

held the tray flat to his stomach, hugging it as he pursed his lips from side to side.

"Have you asked him yet?"

A sigh escaped him and his shoulders sagged. "I did. He doesn't know anything about demons. I'm sorry. I thought he could help. But I'm sure we'll find him another way."

There it was. Sorry. Was it a defense mechanism? Or a way to disarm others with an air of innocence?

I set my coffee down and scratched my chin.

Was he lying? Had his boss given him the information we needed and he'd decided to keep it to himself?

That was exactly what I'd do in his place.

"I need to get back—" He started to turn his back to me and walk away.

"What do you whisper to them?"

He paused. Then he spun back around. "Huh?"

"The coffees. You whisper things to them."

"Well, yeah. That's my power."

I crossed my legs and adjusted in my chair until I was turned toward him. "What sort of things do you whisper?"

"I don't know. Random things. Things that'll make their day. Maybe the day looks shinier to them, or work is easier, or their chest a little lighter. It depends on the customer, I suppose. Usually I just put some good luck spells in them. One guy won the lottery a while back. One million pounds, if you can believe it."

He gasped with a chuckle. My lips quirked into a smile without my permission. Sometimes he sounded so young. Too young.

A memory rose to the surface. It was only yesterday. When I'd tried to slice his neck open at the old witch's cave and instead had ended up almost bleeding to death.

He'd whispered something to me. A healing spell, if my Polish was still up to scratch.

And when it hadn't worked he hadn't seemed the least bit surprised.

"It didn't work. I'm useless," he'd said. But why did he believe that when he could control his power?

"Of course I can believe it. You're a szeptun. Your whisperings can cure illnesses. I'm sure they can make people win stuff."

He shrugged. "I'm not so sure about the curing part. I haven't been able to cure anyone yet. Or even heal a headache. I'm hopeless. And now that my family is dead I'll never find out how to come to my full power," he said.

I loathed the doubt and defeatism in his voice. It didn't suit him. And neither did the meek posture and lack of confidence.

Was it an act? It couldn't be. No one was that good an actor.

No one but me of course.

"Now, now. I'm sure there are other szeptuns who can help you and if all else fails..."

The image of me deep inside him blasted its way through my corneas and my chest tightened at the intensity.

"If all else fails, what?"

The sensation of me coming inside him, the strain in my body and the weight of my groan as I filled him.

Demon cum was potent. It could make even the weakest creature the most powerful of its kind.

But I didn't think he was ready for that.

Or maybe I could use it to tempt him into falling in love with me and freeing me, but that also ran the risk of me falling for him too and we couldn't afford that now, could we?

"Nothing. We'll figure it out," I said and brought the coffee to my lips.

I wondered if he'd whispered anything to it. Not that he needed to. He could ask me to do anything he wanted. He didn't need a spell.

Unless...

"Do you think you can...whisper good luck to my drink?"

He stared at me with narrow eyes, chewing his bottom lip.

"Maybe all we need to find your parents' killers is a little...*luck*." I added an extra flare to my last word, even though it was hopeless.

My powers didn't work on my masters so that meant I couldn't compel him either.

Tomasz froze, his eyes darting side to side, the

chewing of his lips accelerating and I watched him get lost in his thoughts for a few moments. "That could work. It could." He snatched the coffee from my hands and raised it to his lips. He whispered something with a single breath before he offered the cup back to me.

It didn't smell any different. It didn't taste any different. And yet the distinct feel of his magic infused the drink and myself.

He stared at me as I put the empty cup down and focused on the object in front of me.

Admittedly, it felt good having his eyes trained on me. I knew he was only staring to see if his whispering had any effect, but I liked to pretend that he found it impossible to pry his eyes off me instead.

"H-how do you feel?" he asked after a few seconds.

"Fine."

"Feel any different? Got any ideas? Inspiration?"

I shook my head and saw the disappointment overtake his posture.

"I knew it wouldn't work."

I lurched up and grabbed him by the arms. Whether it was an act or not, this whole hopeless act was infuriating.

It didn't suit him.

He should be standing tall and proud of himself. He should appreciate his power that had been passed through the generations and bestowed on him.

Szeptuns were one of the very few lines of witches

who all had the same power and who passed those powers to their children.

He was special.

Unique.

And he should act like it, damn it!

"No one said it was going to work straight away," I told him with as calm a manner as I could manage. "Stop putting yourself down. You're strong."

He raised his gaze slowly and I got a glimpse of those grey eyes with the golden flecks that never seemed to stay still and my body pulsed, my heart pounded like a trapped wild animal and my dick throbbed.

"Tomasz, are you okay?" someone said from the bar.

We both turned to Caleb staring at us with concern.

Tomasz straightened his back and took a step away from my hands.

"Yeah, I...just felt light-headed and this guy-erm kind man stopped me from falling."

The lie slipped out of his firm lips with an ease I couldn't help but be proud of. Even if it meant he could've been lying to me, this was more fitting for him.

Caleb went back to the till to serve a customer and the front door opened. A woman with fire-red wavy hair stepped in and greeted the empath. When she turned to greet Tomasz, she paused and winced.

She sniffed.

Then sniffed again and looked around.

"Lorelai? Everything okay?" Tomasz asked.

She didn't answer him. She continued to sniff around the café before she beelined for me.

"You! You smell rancid," she said.

"Lorelai!" Tomasz exclaimed.

"Thanks, I guess?" was my response.

"You smell...I've never smelled anything like you. You smell old."

"Again. Thank you."

Now that she was close I could smell her too.

A familiar.

A fox shifter.

"Lorelai, you're being rude," Tomasz told her.

She turned to him. "I...I can't place his smell. I can't recognize it, Tomasz. He feels different. Dead and yet ancient."

She was right on the money there.

Tomasz glanced at me with furrowed brows and a hard knot in his Adam's apple that he attempted to swallow.

The boy didn't want anyone knowing I was a demon.

I better sort this out before he makes me.

I raised my hand in front of her.

"*I'm an old man. Just an old man. All you see is an old man. All you smell is an old man who hasn't bathed for days.*"

I snapped my fingers and her pupils dilated.

The fox named Lorelai stepped away, winced and walked to the back.

"What did you do to her?"

"I compelled her."

"You can do that?" I nodded. "Have you done that to me?"

"I thought about it," I admitted.

"Oh."

"But like I said. My powers don't work on my master."

"Oh," he repeated, this time with something that almost resembled a pout.

The boy went back to work and soon the fox shifter joined him behind the bar.

I watched for hints of my compulsion wearing off but it seemed to hold strong.

That had been...unexpected.

If she could smell me, perhaps...

An idea formed in my head. A plan. But I would need to be very careful how I put it into action.

If I played my cards right, it could even lead me to my freedom.

"Are you okay?" Tomasz asked me when he served my next drink.

"Yes," I said. "I want you to take me to your house. Where your parents were murdered. I think your whispering worked after all."

Tomasz

"Have you done that to me?"

"I thought about it."

How foolish of me to think, even if for a second, that the reason he hadn't compelled me was because he liked me, or respected me too much to do so.

No. Of course he didn't.

He just...couldn't. That was all.

And why did I care?

Gods, I'm starting to sound like Saskia.

I don't need Loki or his approval. I just need revenge. That's all.

And he could get it for me.

That was why I asked Caleb for the next day off and took Loki to my family home in Ealing.

It was a classic Edwardian house my parents had slaved away to get, working two and three jobs, using their powers for every little gig that came their way, saving every penny and eating tinned spaghetti and frozen vegetables to make their dream come true.

And it had been snatched away like that!

Blood. Cold. Death.

The memory of what had taken place hit me as soon as I crossed the threshold, as vivid as if no time had passed.

Why? Why had they done it here? If they wanted to kill them, why not do it somewhere else? Why taint their dream with this nightmare?

I didn't know that I'd ever be able to step into this house without thinking of the terrible thing that had happened. And yet, I couldn't sell it. I couldn't give the home they'd built for us to a stranger.

"Are you okay?" Loki asked and squeezed my shoulder.

I nodded even though I wasn't. I probably never would be.

Maybe if I got my revenge...

But even that wouldn't bring them back. That I knew.

It didn't make me want it less.

"Do you think you can show me where it happened?"

I winced at his soft tone, his caring words. This man had so many sides. And yet they were all as strange as the next one. It was as if there were different people living inside him and only one could come out at a time.

Or he's just acting.

He wasn't the god of mischief by accident.

It was so frustrating, not knowing whether I could trust him or not.

I guessed the one saving grace was the Hofund. With it I had some sort of security at least. Even if I hated that I held such power over another creature.

I didn't answer him.

Instead, I walked past him, brushing against him. A wave of...of something. Something strong and torrid vibrating with intensity through me. Like a patch of light in absolute darkness.

It made me almost lose my balance, but I dug my nails into my palms, forced a breath out and showed Loki to the kitchen.

I wanted to explore it more, to drown in it, to suffocate myself with it, but I couldn't. That wasn't the time nor the place. Besides, it was probably all in my head because we were here.

Where my life had turned upside down in an instant.

I showed him where I'd found them. Mom sprawled over the back door threshold. Dad's guts inside out in the middle of the room and Oliwia...part of her in front of the basement door and part of her beside Dad.

An image I'd never get rid of no matter what.

Even if I could blank out Mom and Dad's bodies, Oliwia's would haunt me for the rest of my life.

Loki crouched down, touched the surface where each had been found, brought his fingers up to his nose, rubbed them together with an exasperated expression.

I could only watch him for so long before it happened again.

The blood. The cold. The death.

How sweaty I'd been after a trip in the oven that was the London Underground and rushing home before I was criticized for being late for dinner.

The weird looks I got talking to a cat running beside me.

Mrs. Wójcik from next door waving at me with the same pitiful expression they reserved for the useless whisperer of the family.

The key getting jammed in the lock as it always did because Dad refused to fix it when there were far more pressing expenses and matters to attend to.

How I'd started I apologizing the minute I was through the door and taking my coat off, while Saskia rushed ahead of me.

The coldness washing over me before I'd even stepped foot in the kitchen as Saskia's terror bounced off my own body with the limited connection we all had to our domowik.

Running to check on her, slipping on something.

Blood.

Their blood.

I leaned against the wall, tears streaming down my face, trying to keep it together as Loki was back on his feet, opening and closing cupboards.

I didn't have the strength to ask him what he was doing. Even when I wiped my face, I couldn't tell what he was up to. It looked like he was playing with herbs and a bowl.

What the hell is he doing? Can't he see my world is ending? Why the fuck is he playing with herbs and spices?

As if he could hear my judgment, he turned around. His hands glowed green. The bowl broke. A dark gem was clasped between his fingers.

I opened my mouth to ask him what and how but all that came out was a dry heave as Loki held out the gem and smoke burst from it, enveloping him. Me. The room.

What has he done?

A scream splintered my ear drums. A growl.

"*Igor. No. No!*"

"*Dad!*"

More screams. More growling.

"*Mom, run. Go. Run!*"

Something snarled as the smoke cleared and a wolf jumped into the air across the room toward the back door.

The wolf bit down into nothingness and a piercing

wail made my eyes burn again and the tears covered my face.

"What is this?" I asked, not sure if I could be heard through the pain and noise enveloping us.

"An echo spell. It can help show traces of the past by the...*invisible* evidence left around the room. Things we couldn't collect and analyze. Like residual energies and magic," Loki answered, now standing in the middle of the room. Right where Dad's body had been.

I attempted to wipe the moisture from my eyes but a third deafening scream cut through the air and the wolf jumped at the cellar door.

The sound of jaws gnawing, bones cracking, skin tearing.

And then silence.

And then death.

My stomach caved and my eyes prickled as I relived the past and walked into the kitchen. But I didn't see Saskia.

No, I couldn't see her at all even though she had been there.

I took a big breath but very little air reached my lungs.

My dad, dead.

A stab at my pounding heart both felt now and then.

All the things I had never said to him. All the things I'd kept from him for fear of rejection. All the fights we'd had because he couldn't accept I'd never amount to much no matter how much he believed in me.

Tears streamed down my face and my lungs inflated and deflated with increasing difficulty.

My mom, dead.

Another stab in the heart that made the oxygen I breathed feel like acid.

When was the last time I'd told her I loved her? What was the last meal I'd had with her? Had I told her how good it was? Would I ever again taste such magic as that of her cooking? Who would defend my choices even if she herself didn't understand them.

My lips quivered and my hands trembled.

What was that by Dad's feet?

It wasn't a ball.

Oliwia, dead.

Her head, here. Her body, there. Always the defender. Always the shining light.

A final stab through my heart that tore it in a million pieces. My knees gave way.

Who would I share my secrets with? Who would tell me there was nothing wrong with me? Or tutor my hopeless ass in hopes I could one day heal? Who would love me when we both grew old and I alone?

"Tomasz? Tomasz?" Loki was crouched in front of me shaking me with both hands. "I'm sorry. I shouldn't have done it with you in the room. I'm sorry."

I wanted to tell him it wasn't his fault. He hadn't killed my parents. But before I could I felt breathless again, but only because I was trapped in his arms, my face pressed to his chest so tightly I thought he was trying to kill me.

But the hand rubbing my back registered a moment later and I realized he wasn't trying to kill me. He was trying to comfort me.

"I'm sorry. I'm sorry, Tomasz. I'm so sorry," he whispered on and on.

He didn't stop. He didn't let go. He kept going and going until breathing became easier, my tears dried out and the memories faded.

The more time I spent in his embrace, the more details from the present I started to register.

The warmth radiating off him was so strong it made me feel feverish.

His rough beard scratching the top of my head.

His manly musk soothing the trembling.

We stayed like that for minutes. Or was it hours?

I didn't care. The longer I stayed there, the stronger I felt.

I didn't know how or why. He told me he couldn't use his powers on me so either he'd lied or this wasn't a power. But whichever it was, I appreciated it. It made being in this space easier, less formidable.

"I'm so sorry..."

I looked up and pulled slightly back to watch the demon god apologizing to me and my guts twisted.

He was white as a sheet, sweat beaded his forehead and his eyes so red and wide it was like he'd been crying.

"I'm okay," I whispered.

He didn't seem to notice.

"Loki. I'm okay. I'm okay, I promise."

Slowly, as if he was coming back to life or waking up, he looked down and his breathing halted.

His lips were mere inches from mine. I could breathe in the air he breathed out. I could almost taste them.

"I'm sorry," he said once more, staring right down my very core.

"I'm okay." My words were barely audible, but we were so close he didn't need to hear them. He could feel them.

"Will you ever forgive me?" he asked with the same intensity and volume as me.

"I already have." I attempted a smile, but my muscles were so numb I didn't know if it even resembled one.

I stared into his eyes, trying to see my reflection in them as he dipped down and gave me a real taste of his lips.

Ample. Soft. Hesitant. As if he was waiting for me to reciprocate.

I didn't think, I did.

I raised my head and deepened the kiss, opening up

for his tongue as his arms tightened around me, holding me close.

As if he didn't want to let me go.

I didn't realize what was happening at first. And when I did, I pulled back and put an end to it.

"I'm sorry." It was my turn to say it.

If it weren't for me, we wouldn't be making out on the floor of my family's crime scene.

I apologized for it, but it didn't mean I was sorry for it.

I wasn't at all. I was sorry I had to put an end to it, but I couldn't let him kiss me. I couldn't let a demon god kiss me like that. I was a nobody and he was fucking Loki. I had to end it. Before he realized what he was doing and did it himself.

I may have ended it but that didn't mean I could forget about it. Or the way he tasted.

Sweet. Salty. Manly. Improper. Powerful. Sinful.

How can one person, even a god, be all those things?

Tomasz

"So, a...a wolf killed my family?"

We were on the train, on the way back home.

I still had goosebumps from the kiss I'd shared with him, but I couldn't dwell on that. I had to dwell on the painful things that had happened back there.

Like the fact that I'd seen an echo of who had killed my family. A ghost.

And that ghost had the shape of a wolf.

"It looks like it," he said and gave my hand a squeeze.

"That makes no sense," I said as the train doors closed and another station blurred past, only to be drowned by the darkness.

"Did...did your family have any enemies?" I shook my head. "Any grievances? Anyone they pissed off?"

"My father was a healer and repairman. My mom was a kitchen witch and a social worker. Who could they have possibly pissed off?"

Everything they did was help the community stay safe, healthy and happy.

Why would anyone want to snuff that out?

"Anything or anyone they were protecting?"

I started to shake my head but a cold shiver ran down my spine.

That was why they'd died. I was sure of it. They'd died for that fucking egg. The question however was who knew about it?

The egg was our family heirloom and secret, passed down from szeptucha to szeptucha and szeptun to szeptun, a legacy that would die with the last of us.

And that was why we were strictly forbidden from ever talking about it or sharing it with anyone. Even my mom hadn't known about it until I was at least ten years old. If she had been alive she'd probably still be pissed with Dad about it.

"Tomasz?"

His voice broke me out of my thoughts and I blinked back into reality. I turned to him.

His brows were knotted, his eyes, big, watching me. "Are you okay?"

"I'm fine. Sorry. I...I must have spaced out. What did you say?"

His gaze narrowed but if he had any thoughts about my response, he didn't share them.

"I asked if they were protecting something or someone? Did they have a lot of money? Powerful spells?"

I pursed my lips with a big puff and shook my head.

"No. Nothing that I know of."

I could see in his face that he didn't believe me, but once again he didn't say anything about it.

"So, that wolf familiar? How do we find them? Why didn't Angel Guard or the High Council find them yet? They've got wolves in their hierarchy. Surely they could have traced the bastard and caught him by now."

Loki crossed his legs and hands and rocked his head from side to side. "They could have. Unless the wolf used Wolfshadow."

"What the hell is that?" I asked.

"It's a potion that can cover a wolf's tracks. Very popular with less favorable packs or solitary wolves. They're very territorial creatures as I'm sure you know already, so Wolfshadow was heavily used a lot in territorial wars and assassinations," he said.

"If they did, then we're doomed."

The train doors opened again and I realized it was our stop.

"Come on."

I jolted from my seat and ran out of the train and looked back for Loki but he was nowhere to be found.

"Where—"

The fucking bastard. Is he trying to run again?

Someone tapped my shoulder and my heart nearly leapt out of my chest when I found Loki standing right behind me with a smirk on his face.

"H-how did you do that?"

I was sure he'd still been sitting when I rushed out of the train.

Loki shrugged and winked at me.

"Reflexes," was all he said and spun around, following the exit signs.

"I assumed—"

"That I ran? I can't blame you. But no. I didn't. I can't run now. Especially now."

He stepped on the escalator and turned to face me.

"Why especially now? What's changed?"

I craned my neck up to keep my gaze trained on him. The light reflected off his back giving his silhouette a gentle rim light. It bounced off his hair making it resemble a halo.

I bit back a chuckle.

Loki is no saint.

That much, I know.

"Because for starters, we made a deal," he said.

I grimaced. "Are you trying to tell me you didn't attempt to leave the flat last night? And the night before?"

He didn't even look guilty when he shrugged. Just smug.

"You know it's in my nature to try. I wouldn't be the trickster god if I didn't."

"Yeah, yeah, yeah. So you keep saying."

"But that's not the only reason why I wouldn't run now. There's another."

I crossed my hands and watched behind him as we slowly came to the top of the escalator and waited for him to trip.

Just when I thought it was going to happen, he toed back around and stepped off as if nothing had happened.

Damn it.

I'd love to have seen the smug bastard go down.

Yeah, go down on me.

I slapped my face while he wasn't looking and fell into step beside him.

"What's the other reason? Are you going to tell me? I'm dying of anticipation," I said in my blandest of tones, matching my glare perfectly.

He raised his finger as if he had a lightbulb moment and smirked. "I know who can find the wolf."

In that instant I forgot about the pompous god and his mischievous ways and I stepped in front of him. "You do? How?"

His arrogant expression melted away, replaced with sincerity. As much sincerity as Loki could have.

"We-we need to find my children."

I rolled my eyes and walked away, tapping out of the turnstiles and getting out into the streets.

When I turned the corner, Loki was there.

"Jesus! Stop doing that." I clutched my chest and ignored the stares I got, walking past him.

"I know what it sounds like. I'm not a fool. I know you think I want to find them first because I'm an egomaniac or only think about myself—" He ran after me.

"Well, don't you?"

"Yes. Of course. But! Your whispering worked. It gave me the idea for the echo spell. But would you believe me if I said our fates are bound? I believe that now more than ever."

Empty words. That was all they were. Everything that came out of his mouth.

All he cared about was himself and his freedom.

About hurting me. About tricking me.

"Don't tell me. It's cosmic and we're meant to be together," I said before I even thought about how it sounded when it came out of my mouth. "I meant—"

"Tomasz, I'm serious here. My children can help us find the wolf. My son in particular. He's the god of wolves."

"And?"

"That means he can track any wolf on this planet whether they've drank Wolfshadow or not."

Had he just said what I thought he'd said?

Had he just given me hope?

———

"I knew he was amazing. You can feel it crackling in the air even before you see him," Saskia said when I recounted everything to her.

What happened at Java Jinx. What happened at the house. And what happened on our way here.

Everything but the kiss, of course.

She didn't need to know about that because it was nothing. It had been nothing.

A nothing I could still taste on my lips, but taste it I could.

Besides, I was pretty sure if I told her, she'd kill me considering how thirsty she was for him.

"But can we trust him? He tries to trick me every chance he gets."

Saskia let out a long, drawn-out yawn as if making a point. "He wants to save his children. And I'd be a great mama to them, just saying, but he's a father who wants to free them. And it just so happens that his son can help us find that fucking wolf that killed my family. *Our* rodzina. Why can't you believe that fate sent him to you for this exact reason? Surely that Mother Red Cap could have chosen any other god to help you, but it was Loki she invoked," she said.

"I think you're giving too much credit to fate and not enough credit to master of mischief right there."

I'd crawled to the bedroom upstairs to talk to Saskia and put some music on so he couldn't hear us but I could still hear him downing those beers downstairs like there was no tomorrow.

"Okay. Let's say for a moment he's lying. What harm would it do if you found his children first? You told him it's a partnership. Why do you have to find the killer first if that's the case?"

I huffed. "Whose side are you on?"

Sass narrowed her eyes and licked her muzzle.

"Yours. Of course. Although I wouldn't say no to being on his side. You know. As he took me—"

"Yeah yeah yeah. We get it. You're horny for him. Now shut up."

Was Saskia right?

Could I trust him?

Well, I already knew the answer to that.

But that didn't mean I couldn't help him. Even if we found his children first, he'd still be under my control. He'd still be required to help me.

"Did you tell him about the—"

"The egg? No. Are you crazy?"

"How is he supposed to help us if he doesn't have all the facts?"

I shrugged. "What if he tries to use it on me?"

"There's the stupidest question of the century. Did you really just say that?"

I tried to take it back. To say I hadn't been thinking, but Sass kept mocking me.

"You...you think he's gonna use the pisanka against you? Oh my Gods that's so stupid. Only a szeptun can use it. Oh my, I don't think I'll ever forget what you said."

She cackled to herself and I waited for her to join me back in Serious Central.

"He can't use the egg, idiot. No one can. And even if he could, he'd still need the zawlanie."

The zawlanie.

The other family secret.

The spellword, the word of power, that activated the pisanka, the egg.

This one we guarded with our lives.

"I know. You don't need to tell me," I said.

"So tell him!"

"I don't know if...if it's safe."

"Well you need to tell him something. He needs to understand why they died and what they died protecting."

I didn't want to admit it, but Saskia was right.

"Fine."

I took the stairs back down to join Loki at the dinner table. He was chewing an entire pizza slice when I pulled out a chair and sat opposite him.

Saskia climbed on my lap.

Had hell frozen over? There was a god across from me—a god she desperately wanted to shag—and she was sitting on me?

"There's something I need to tell you."

Loki tore the pizza from his face and looked up. "What is it?" he asked, the grease on his chin reflecting the kitchen light.

Even with that, he barely looked like a slob. Instead, he looked like sin on a plate. A very hot plate.

Focus, Tomasz.

"I lied to you earlier. When you asked me if my family was protecting something?"

"What is it?" He leaned forward, a shadow crossing his gaze and a glint in his eye.

Was he enjoying this?

"I can't tell you what they were protecting, but I can tell you it's very powerful. And if it falls in the wrong hands, it can be catastrophic. That's why they died. That's what they were trying to protect. I'm sorry. I didn't want to lie to you, but it's a family secret. We're not meant to share it."

He reached for my hand and covered mine with a forceful warmth that made me feel even shittier for not telling him the truth earlier.

Why?

I didn't even know if I could trust him and now I was feeling guilty for lying to him?

Maybe whatever was wrong with Saskia was catching.

"You don't need to apologize. Please, Tomasz. Don't ever apologize to me. I don't deserve it," he said and if there was a knife digging in me, he'd just driven it deeper and twisted it.

"Awww, swoon," Saskia meowed.

Maybe he wasn't a bad person. Maybe he didn't mean to be devious. Maybe he wanted to be a good guy, but no one ever trusted him long enough for him to change.

Maybe that was all he needed. For someone to believe in him.

"And thank you for sharing that with me. It helps knowing what they died for. I've been thinking about what happened today myself. I know Fenrir can find the wolf from the spell. If there are enough traces for an echo spell then there must be more than enough for my son to track him."

"I-I believe you," I said.

And you know what? I did.

"The problem is, how do *we* find *Fenrir*."

I sighed.

"I know," I said.

Loki raised his finger with a glint in his eyes. "But then I had an idea. Remember what happened at the café yesterday?"

I went back to the morning before and I tried to think of what he could be referring to, but so much had happened today, I couldn't even process what happened yesterday.

"I'm too tired for quizzes. What happened?"

Loki smiled. "Your colleague. Lorelai. She smelled me," he said.

"What? The fucking bitch! He's mine. Can you tell her that? Tell her that please. Next time you see her, tell her hands off or I'll scratch her pussy," Saskia said.

"She might like that," I mumbled at my cat and

remembered Lorelai's behavior when she'd come into work.

She'd called Loki rancid. Old. Dead. Ancient.

She'd smelled the death of his human body. But more importantly, she'd smelled the demon inside him.

"Oh my God. You're right. She might be able to track Heimdall. And your children."

Loki nodded and sat back.

"We need her."

"And I need to cast a curse on that manky fox!" Saskia said.

"Easy tiger," I told her.

"One of these days you'll have to tell me what kind of things she's saying to you," Loki said, grabbing the slice of pizza he'd dropped earlier.

I looked down at my cat and sighed. "Believe me, they could even give demons nightmares."

"Who says we don't get nightmares anyway?" His face dropped, but a second later he was grinning again as if it had never happened.

What kind of nightmares does a god like Loki have?

"Are you off tomorrow? We can go find Lorelai and ask for her help. I can compel her if needed—"

"That won't be necessary. I'm sure she'll help me if I ask her, but..."

"But?"

"Yesterday was her last shift. She's away on a mission for her pack or the High Council. She didn't say," I said.

Loki's jaw tightened.

"When is she back?"

"Hard to tell." I shrugged. "Her missions take as long as they take. It could be a day. It could be a month."

"Damn." He brought a fist down to the table and everything on it bounced.

"Here come the fanny flutters again," Saskia said.

I pushed her off me and she yowled, running away cursing me in Polish, English and gods knew what other language.

"I'm sorry," I said when Loki and I were all alone.

"What on earth for?"

"Because I'm useless. Because I brought you to Midgard and I don't even know what I'm doing. Because everything seems to be going wrong. I'm sorry."

Loki jumped off the table, leaning over it and grabbing me by the lapel, pulling me to him.

It all happened in a flash. One moment I was sitting down. The next, I was mere inches away from Loki's angry face.

"I told you before, and I'll tell you again. *Never* apologize to me."

I wanted to make a snide remark about the unnecessary aggression, but I was fighting with my bladder for control from the scare he'd given me so I just nodded and he let go.

He sat back down, grabbed the can of beer and brought it to his lips.

"Now, what do humans do for fun in this century?"

LOKI

I needed some fun.

To release all the anger inside me. All the guilt.

Tomasz's eyes still haunted me. The taste of his tears still lingered on my tongue. The horror of what I'd caused.

The echo spell had been necessary. I just wish I'd thought about the effect it would have on him before I'd cast it.

But I wasn't thinking. Tomasz was right. I was an egomaniac. I wanted results that would bring me closer to freedom and I didn't care about the price.

Not until it was too late.

And I almost broke him.

I hate this. I hate myself.

Tomasz was innocent. Despite everything he was

innocent, and pure. If I wasn't so certain before, I was now. And my actions had caused him great pain.

As if he hasn't suffered enough.

I wanted to slap myself. Punch myself. Gut myself for what I'd done.

I did what I had to do.

Yet that offered me no solace from the guilt riding my brain.

"You can't be serious. You want to have fun after what happened today?" he said, mouth agape and brows raised.

His lips were glossy and inviting under the muted lighting created by the moonlight peeking through the windows and the LED strips under the kitchen cupboards.

"After what happened today."

What had happened was that I was no longer curious what he tasted like, because his flavor blazed inside me, a wraith that clawed at me, at all my resolve and determination and threatened to make me risk it all.

"What happened? Did someone switch you off? We can do that?" Tomasz said.

He was smiling but the sadness lingered behind his eyes. No mask could hide that.

"Yes. We need fun!"

After what I'd put him through, I had to at least try and fix the trauma I'd caused him.

"It's been the shittiest day of my life in recent

memory. I know it was not fun for you either. You've been cooped up in here dreaming of revenge for however long and you've been working your ass off to, I'm sure, try and dull the pain. We need fun. Especially you. You deserve it."

Tomasz pursed his lips and inspected his flat as if it was the first time he was seeing it.

"It *is* Saturday, I guess."

An indeterminate smile crept across his face and I had to pry my gaze from him before I gave away the wildfire he'd started inside me.

He got up and started going through his clothes with a focus I'd only ever seen in him when he'd been working yesterday.

Saskia joined him moments later and he started answering her questions absentmindedly while she helped him pick his outfit.

His wardrobe was muted and limited to mostly one color. Black. Even though Tomasz was a rainbow himself.

Or he could be. If he had more confidence.

Saskia sat on a crop top with pink sequins that spelled gay and meowed.

"I don't think so," he answered her and rolled his eyes, picking a plain black blouse instead.

"Why not?" I asked him.

He froze as if he'd just remembered I was there or something and offered me an awkward smile.

"Uhm I don't like it," he said.

Saskia turned to me and meowed.

"What did she say?"

"I'm not lying," he said to her at the same time.

"So you do like it?" I winked at Saskia before I returned my attention to Tomasz.

"Well, yeah. But...I don't know. I've tried it before. I don't think I can pull it off."

The cat went off again.

I only needed to raise an eyebrow before Tomasz translated for me.

"She's saying I only tried it in the house."

The cat dropped her head and sighed.

It was funny how human she appeared when you knew what she was and paid closer attention. It was a shame only the family she was bound to could understand her. She sounded like a riot, judging by the way Tomasz responded to her.

"So why do you think you can't pull it off if you haven't tried it outside?"

Tomasz shrugged and turned away. "I don't know. It'd be embarrassing."

"Why?"

He rubbed his arm, still refusing to return my gaze. "Because..."

He appeared so vulnerable, standing in the middle of the living room, holding himself.

I didn't like it.

There was an urge—a need almost—to go over, lift his chin, hold him before me and tell him there was absolutely nothing embarrassing about him, nor would there ever be, and that was exactly what I did.

Even though I shouldn't.

I shouldn't even have been touching him, let alone looking into his gorgeous eyes and telling him things only lovers were supposed to say.

This is dangerous.

This need I had around him, a need that grew stronger by the day, hour, minute in his presence.

It was the kind of need I had been afraid of. The one I'd tried to stomp down before it got me hurt once more.

Tomasz blushed at my words but to my surprise he didn't pull away. Not for a long time and when he did, he hugged himself again.

"I've spent my whole life thinking there was something wrong with me. I wasn't like other boys but every time I brought it up I was reassured I would be. I never did."

I tilted my head to the side and narrowed my eyes. "Not like other boys in what way?" I asked. I didn't understand what he was talking about.

He took a deep breath and stared at the fruit bowl on the coffee table. "My parents were great parents but they weren't exactly progressive. It's not their fault really. They were a product of their time. They never told me anything, but I knew their views and beliefs. I heard them talk about others.

"I guess in my head I still see myself through their eyes and don't want to be a person they'd...judge."

I watched him, I listened, but I still had no clue what the hell he was talking about. "I'm not sure I follow. Judge what?"

"Me."

"Why would they judge you? They loved you."

He fell back on the sofa and sighed. "I know, but I don't know what they'd think of me if they knew."

This was getting ridiculous. It was as though he was speaking in riddles for the sake of torturing me. "If they knew what?" I almost gritted through my teeth but I restrained myself and sounded a lot more pleasant.

"That I'm gay," he said.

I stared and waited for the rest but it never came. "Is that it?"

He nodded. "Well, it is kind of a big deal. For some people."

"Is it? Since when?"

I'd spent so much time over the centuries in Midgard and I'd never felt that it was. What the Hel did it matter what preference of partner did one have in bed?

"I don't know, since forever ago?"

I called nonsense on him and he explained it all to me. Not that I could believe it. Apparently humans had been made to believe that gay people or those who weren't heterosexual had always been persecuted and looked down on.

"What a load of crap. And is that why you don't want to wear that top?"

Tomasz nodded with some hesitation and Saskia said something but Tomasz didn't need to translate to understand the tone.

He was talking rubbish.

"Because someone older or stupider might judge you or look down on you?"

"I guess."

"Well yeah. And it's also a safety issue."

I raised an eyebrow. "I'd love to see anyone try to tamper with your safety."

Tomasz pursed his lips into a hint of a smile, but it wasn't enough for me. I wanted more. I wanted that familiar blush on his cheeks. "Now let's see you in it," I said.

He grimaced.

"You said you looked embarrassing in it. I'd say, let me be the judge of that. I am old and conservative after all."

There it was. The flush on his skin. Paired with a disarming, airy eyeroll. "Please, you're not even close to a conservative guy."

"But I *am* old. I've lived through all sorts of wild ages, seen all sorts of different crusades against cultures, communities, creatures. I have pretty high standards for 'embarrassing.' If I don't find you embarrassing, then you're not."

He stared at me and we breathed in unison. The memory of our kiss came to the forefront, the way he felt against me. The tenderness of his lips. The intensity of his desire.

These are some dangerous familiar waters.

I didn't know what I was doing and why but if I didn't stop to control myself I'd be in deep trouble again.

Oh screw it. After what I put him through, he deserves some attention.

I picked up the crop top and handed it to him.

"O-okay," he mumbled and took it from me.

He glanced at it, at me, at his cat for a moment and then he disappeared into the bathroom.

"He's unique, isn't he?" I turned to Saskia.

I'd never seen a cat roll her eyes until then. And it was as disturbing as it sounded, but equally entertaining.

When the door opened and he emerged, I caught my breath.

Even though he bit his lips and stood with his hands in front of him as though he was shy or something, he looked every bit as adorable as I'd imagined he would be in it. And not only because wearing that particular garment gave me a very sexy preview of what hid under those dark clothes he always wore.

"It's awful, isn't it? See, I told you," he said,

stretching his arms to his sides as if to make a point, although if he was making one I failed to see what it was. Because he was wrong in every sense of the word.

He trained his eyes on me as I walked toward him and took his hand to spin him around.

"Oh gods. You h—"

"You look...delectable," I said, just about able to tame the growl that threatened to come out.

His lips stayed parted and his chest stopped expanding.

"R-really?"

I leaned forward and inhaled his scent, peering into his eyes before glancing at the rest of his body. "Very much so."

The urge to kiss him, to retaste, relive that moment of bliss amidst chaos at his family house overtook me.

And as if he could read my mind he froze and watched. Or waited.

"Anyway, I'm not sure about..." he said seconds later, pulling away from me and breaking whatever spell I'd been under.

Spell. That was it. That was all it was. A spell. An enchantment caused by my binding to him.

Maybe he'd even commanded me to...to feel this way.

That was all.

Yeah. Let's go with that.

Because the alternative would make me the stupidest god on Midgard.

Tomasz

As if the memory of his kiss wasn't haunting enough, now I had the memory of him calling me delectable terrorizing my mind.

The worst part was, I didn't think there was anything I could do or say to erase either.

And even if I could, would I want to?

With a hesitant move, I glanced up to find him staring at me and despite the fact we were surrounded by people—squashed by them, actually—it felt as if it was just the two of us, in my apartment, held by him as he admired my body.

He raised an eyebrow and I apologized to him.

"Here we go again. What are you apologizing for now?" he asked in his normal voice, caring very little about everyone else around us.

Gods, I hate the tube on weekends.

Everyone and their mother were packed like

sardines trying to make their way to the hippest, coolest club in the city.

"Because. It's so busy," I said.

Loki laughed whole-heartedly and more than a few people leered at him, probably having similar thoughts to Saskia.

I couldn't imagine anyone not finding this man—this god, really—attractive and want him to fuck their brains out.

"If it's your fault then make it go away," he ended up saying and I noticed a couple of smirks from girls beside him.

"You're right."

"I usually am."

I hated him when he went all smug like that. It made me want to wipe those stupid grins off his face with a slap or two.

The train came to a stop at Liverpool Street and gave us a chance to breathe as passenger stepped off the train.

"What did Saskia tell you before we left, by the way?" Loki asked as I watched the train get eerily empty.

Only to fill up with fresh groups of vivacious people.

I turned to Loki and chewed on my lip.

"You bitch!" she'd said.

"What did I do now?" I'd asked.

"You've been playing all innocent, pretending you

don't care about him, but you've got the hots for him, don't you? You've got the hots for my future demonic vibrator!"

"*I don't know what you're talking about.*"

"*You little shitbag. You know he's mine!*"

The audacity of that cat! To even suggest I was attracted to Loki. Which, of course I was, but that was beside the point.

"*You know, technically, I saw him first,*" I whispered to her and watched my domowik gasp before I joined Loki at my front door.

"*You're dead to me Nowak. If you suck his demon cock, we're done. Over. Koniec, dupku,*" she'd yowled.

"Oh really? Then I might just do it so I can get some peace and quiet for a change!" I'd told her and pushed Loki out of the door.

"What? Oh that? It was nothing," I answered him just as we got to Tottenham Court Road.

Loki followed me as I got off and made my way to the escalators and closer to the surface.

"You know. One of these days you're gonna have to tell me what gets you so worked up when you talk to her."

Yeah, I didn't see that happening anytime soon, but even a demon god could dream.

"She just...she has a crush on you." That was putting it mildly. "And she got kind of jealous."

That was it. That was all I was going to say. Nothing more.

"Huh."

That was the only thing *he* said until we got to Soho, a short walk from the tube station. "I don't know if I should worry that this feels no different than it did a hundred years ago, or to revel in it."

I took in the dirty streets, loud people, the pumping music coming from every club, bar and restaurant and tried to look at it through his eyes.

"Would it help if I told you everything is probably twenty times more expensive?"

Loki chuckled. "That's no bother."

"Really? How come?"

Before I'd even finished, he held out a wallet and I frowned. "Don't tell me. You've got Demonic Express. Is it limitless? Do you get air miles?"

He stared at me with a confused expression but instead of asking me to explain what I was talking about he shrugged and opened the black leather wallet. "I don't know. Let's find out."

Seconds later he took out a large wad of cash from it.

"What do you mean you don't kn— Wait. That isn't your wallet? Whose wallet is it?"

I caught a glimpse of a toddler in the photo slot and gasped.

"Does it matter?"

"Did you steal that? Of course it matters."

Loki just waved me off and walked further into Old Compton Street. "You're no fun," he said.

"Because I don't condone stealing?"

"But murder is okay? Because that's what you want me to do to your family's killer, right?"

I opened my mouth but whatever I said, if there was even anything, refused to come out.

"Fine. Point taken. But don't steal anymore wallets!" I wagged my finger in his face and he grinned.

"Is that an order?" His golden eye glimmered for a moment and I got lost in its light.

"Yes. It's an order. Don't steal anything!"

His chest rose and fell and he huffed in agreement.

"So, where do we start? My treat." He flashed me that wad of cash and, considering payday wasn't for another week and I'd already spent this week's budget on Loki's new wardrobe, the offer didn't sound so bad.

"It's not like we can return it, right?" I said.

"I think there's a card here—" he started to say, taking out a business card.

I whipped out of his hand and threw it behind me. "No there isn't. Where should we start? Where should we...How about Craft Royale?" I pointed to a pub on the corner with a black exterior and golden signs, and we dove inside to a buzzing atmosphere.

"Or maybe somewhere else?" I scanned the compact space and sighed.

"What are you talking about? This is perfect," Loki answered with a pleased expression.

"But there's nowhere to sit..."

And really there wasn't. Except for a few tables at

the back but they were all taken by several big lads with, like, a hundred shot glasses and beer in front of them.

"You need a table to have fun? Boy, sounds like you have the wrong kind of fun," he started. "But if a table is what you want, a table you shall get. You get the drinks."

He held a few twenty-pound notes in front of me.

"What do you want?"

"Surprise me." He winked at me.

I snatched the money to go wait at the bar. It didn't take long to get served despite how busy it was. It seemed like everyone already had their drinks.

"What will it be?"

"Well, if my rubbish bin is any indication, beer, beer, and more beer," I told the bartender. "Four lagers, please."

Three for him. One for me.

"Is that what you call fun?"

I could picture him criticizing me already like he'd had so many times tonight. I knew it should irritate me, drive me up the wall, anger me, but all it did was make me stubborn. To prove to him I was no wallflower even though I most likely was.

"And two shots of tequila," I added when the guy turned around.

The man set the drinks down in front of me and once he was done gave me a smirk.

"Would you like a tray?" he asked, piercing me with his dark gaze as if he liked me.

Pfft, why would a tall, buff guy like me?

I nodded and he prepared the tray for me and his eyes trained on me.

He had soft but manly features and when he smiled he looked like a teddy bear. He brushed a hand through his short, black hair and when I tried to give him the payment he shook his head.

"On the house, cutie." He winked.

"Really? Why?" I said before I could stop myself.

He'd just told me why. Gods, I was hopeless.

The guy didn't look down on me, however. If anything his smile deepened. "The 'cutie' should have been a clue," he said.

"No, that's too much. I can't let you pay for all this." I ignored his remark.

"Don't worry about it. We gotta watch out for each other anyway, don't we?" Before I could ask him what he meant the bar and everyone in it came to a halt and the music died down. Everything trapped in time. And in a flash it all started up again.

"You're a..." I started.

"Yes, I'm a..." he copied me with a chuckle.

"H-how did you know? That I was a..."

He shrugged. "I've got my ways." He reached over the bar and shook my hand. "Drew. Nice to meet you...?"

"Tomasz." I shook his hand and even though I

expected the butterflies, the tickles—anything—there was nothing.

"See you around." He winked at me again and turned to the next person waiting to be served.

I had no idea what had just happened or how, but if there was ever further proof there was something wrong with me that was now.

I should have been flattered by Drew's compliments and gesture. I should have felt...something when he touched me, but all I thought about was how much warmer Loki had made me feel. How big of a fire he'd started inside me with a kiss.

"Who was that and why did he touch you?" Loki growled when I approached the table in the back. The big, loud lads were nowhere to be seen.

"Nothing. He just introduced himself. Did you do something to those guys? Did you hurt them?"

He snatched one of the beers and glared at me as he raised the glass to his lips.

"I merely suggested they might have more fun elsewhere," he said and tipped the glass back, finishing the pint in two, three gulps max.

"When you say elsewhere?"

He shrugged. "They may or may not be using the black rubbish bin bags outside as a trampoline. Now what did he say to you, because you're lying. He didn't just introduce himself to you."

I tried to kick the mental image of a dozen guys making it rain rubbish everywhere out in the alley and

focused on the breathy tone of his voice and the deep
frown that formed in an instant.

"He just called me a cutie, that's all."

"And then he stopped time to impress you."

"How do you know?"

"Because he didn't stop time for me. I'm gonna go
have a word with that guy!" He slammed his pint glass
to the table and got up, but before he could advance
on the bar, I stepped in front of him and put my hands
to his chest.

Boy, are those muscles tight or what?

"Don't cause a scene." And then I realized I had no
idea why he was even making a big deal out of this.
"And why are you acting all macho anyway? It's not
like I'm your boyfriend."

That seemed to give him pause and he shrunk back
to his seat. "I just...well, I thought he...I don't...you
know, he might have insulted you or something."

Was Loki, the god of fucking mischief flustered?
Over me? Did I believe that? Was it an act?

His taste—sweet, salty, manly—rose to the surface
like my beer had his flavor.

That was real. It had been. I was sure of it. So why
couldn't this? This babbling version of the demon I'd
come to spend day and night with?

"Ready to hit the next bar?" he asked merely half
an hour later.

I nodded and he led the way.

As she we made our way to the door, a woman

kissed a guy at the bar, his arms wrapped around her waist before she pulled away and walked off toward the bathrooms.

Loki passed by the man and stopped.

"Wh—"

Before I could finish, his hand came up, snatched the slender man's neck and pulled him into a kiss.

"Loki, what are you doing?" I said through gritted teeth, unable to believe what I was witnessing.

What the hell is he doing? Why is he kissing a stranger? Why isn't he kissing me?

I shook my head and bit hard on my lip, looking away.

Numerous empty pint glasses sat on the table we'd just vacated.

Maybe he's drunk.

Although the idea of Loki being drunk sounded crazy, even to me.

No, he was just a wanker.

Why so sour, Tomasz? Jealous?

I couldn't be. Why would I be jealous of him?

I didn't want to be messing around with Loki anyway. I had too much to lose.

Loki giggled and forced my gaze back into him, as the girl who had just walked away stormed back screaming and shouting at him.

Loki put his hands up, turned to me, smirked, and walked out of the bar. The girl however continued fighting with the space Loki had occupied only seconds ago. And when she had enough of talking to thin air, she slapped her boyfriend's chest and started going off on him.

The door closed behind me to a roaring pub egging the girlfriend on as she fought with her boyfriend and whatever illusion Loki had cast.

"Mmm, it's so good to be back in Midgard. I forgot how much fun it can be." He stretched his hands out and tilted his head back, shouting at the dark sky.

"You think breaking up a couple is fun?" I told him.

"Anything can be fun. If—" He wagged that forefinger in my face. "If you put your mind to it."

It was all a joke to him, wasn't it? It was all just one giant game of Cards Against Humanity and he was the highest scorer. Creating chaos with words, tricks, emotions.

"You are—" I started to say.

He draped his hand over my shoulder, hugging me close to his chest, the strong musk drenching his clothes encompassing me, and my whole world toppled upside down.

Maybe it was the alcohol inside me, or maybe I'd lost my freaking mind, but whatever I wanted to say was lost in the heat washing over me and threatened to erupt like a volcano.

"I am...? Great? Fun? Perfect?"

His breath got heavy like mine and his face tightened, giving his skin a roughness that stole the air from my lungs and forced my gaze to him.

"Delectable," he murmured and snatched me by the back of my neck like he'd done to the guy at the bar, and closed the gap between us.

His tongue nudged my lips and I parted them, letting him claim my mouth as his. He could claim my body if he wanted. My very soul.

He tipped me back and I held onto his shirt for dear life, my own tongue darting back and forth. The taste of sin and impropriety seeping out of him shot straight to my temples, making me drunk, and to my groin, making me horny.

As if he sensed my desire throbbing between us, he slid his hands down to my butt cheeks and pulled me tight against him.

Someone whistled. Several someones. And my hardness pressed against something large and pulsing.

I gasped. I opened my eyes—the stars twinkled in the night sky—and pulled back.

Our mouths separated and Loki watched me, panting, lips bruised from the intensity of our kiss.

From the edge of my vision I noticed the spectacle we were making with several groups parked around us, cheering, shouting or taking videos.

What are you doing, Tomasz?

I steadied myself. Loki leaned forward, lips first but I put my hand between us and pushed him back.

He smirked and as soon as I put it down made another attempt to kiss me.

"Don't do that!" I whispered before I lost my mind again and succumbed to whatever this was and walked away.

Stupid, stupid Tomasz.

What had I done? Why would I kiss him again? Why would I let him kiss me?

He wasn't interested in me. Why would a god like him ever be interested in me? He was thousands of years old and I was barely twenty-four. There was nothing I could offer him.

He's only doing it to rattle me. Because it's easy. Because he can. Because he's the god of lies and deception.

But he made one big mistake in his big plan of trickery and mischief.

He called me delectable and I'm most definitely not even remotely so.

LOKI

Had I pushed too far? Had I stepped out of line? I thought he wanted my kisses as much as I wanted his.

"Don't do that!"

And for a change I was thankful for his order because it sobered me right up.

The way he'd said those words was as if I'd hurt him. As if he were disgusted by me. As if he didn't want it, when I was pretty sure he'd kissed me back.

But how far would I have taken it if he hadn't ordered me to stop? How far would I have gone if I wasn't bound to him? I dreaded to think.

"Tomasz, I'm sorry." I ran after him, knowing the night—and the fun—was about to end prematurely.

It was all my fault. This obsession with having fun at all costs was too much for normal humans. It must have been intolerable for a guy like him. Soft-spoken. Delicate. Pure.

Everything I wasn't.

He power-walked down the alley and came out into the main street, making his way back to the underground station.

I ran after him. "I fucked up, didn't I? Are you never going to talk to me again?"

He shook his head and wiped his face before he spun around. "Let's just forget it happened. I'm tired. I want to go home."

He didn't utter a word the rest of the journey back to his place and I didn't know what to do with myself.

I'd hurt him. I'd gone too far and I'd hurt him.

Why do you care? He's your master.

As much as I wanted to listen to the voice in my head trying to reason with me, I knew it was already too late.

I'd fallen for the trap again.

I'd fallen for my young master.

I was hopeless. Even after all my resolve, all my determination, I'd still allowed it to happen.

What was it about me and bonds anyway? What was so intrinsically wrong with me that I always fell for that person holding my leash, like a stupid dog?

Had I not learnt my lesson? Had I not been through enough of this kind of trouble?

I couldn't give my heart to them because all they did, all they would ever do, was crush it into a million pieces before they sent me back to Hel to rot for another century or two.

And rinse, repeat.

I watched the whisperer lost in his own thoughts, his upper body jerking left to right in accordance with the movement of the train and tried to find all the reasons why I should hate him.

He was my master.

He kept me chained to him despite what he'd said about this being a partnership.

He...

There was nothing else.

He was different. I didn't know why or how I even knew that, but he was.

He was sweet and considerate.

He was excruciatingly shy and insecure.

He carried the weight of the world on his shoulders and despite everything, he made it look easy.

And he was beautiful. Simply beautiful.

I'd fallen for much less.

It was much later, when we were in front of the front door of his flat that he turned and spoke to me again.

"Do you think we can use any other familiar to find Heimdall? Caleb knows a raven. He could help. Although he is a Guardian Angel."

His voice was music to my ears. As if I'd been deprived of it for a thousand years and I'd finally been allowed the honor of hearing it again.

There's something seriously wrong with me.

"I don't know. I don't think so. I think the reason she could smell me was because of your whispering."

Whether that was true was yet to be proven, but in all the time I'd been to Midgard, now and before, I hadn't had a shifter smell me.

"But all I did was ask to give you a clear path. I don't know why that would have made her smell you. Man, my power is so weird."

His gaze dropped and he hunched, turning back to the door to slide in his key.

"Your power is not weird." I leaned into his ear and I noticed the way the hairs on the back of his neck rose as I spoke.

He moved his head to the side, took a breath and his Adam's apple bobbed. His bottom lip quivered and there was nothing I wanted more than to catch it between my teeth. To pin him against the door and feel his body on mine.

But he'd asked me not to do that so I couldn't.

Or could I?

He hadn't been specific enough so maybe...

"Then maybe I'm the weird one." His voice was barely audible. "My sister and dad could do so much with their power. My babcia could literally reverse death and put protective shields over people. And here I am, useless and stupid, and I can't even get a simple charm—"

I snatched him by the shoulder and spun him

around, pressing him to the door with a thud. He froze, eyes wide open as I put my hand on his chest and leaned into his ear.

"You're not useless or stupid, you hear me?" I grunted and I felt his exhale on my neck and his heart pounding against my palm.

He still smelled of apples and lemons with a hint of alcohol that hadn't been there before. And also a trace of something else. A trace of lust.

He wanted me and I wanted him. So why resist me?

I could pin him. I could lean over him. I could touch him. But could I kiss him?

I slipped my hand lower, allowing my fingers to trace over bones and muscle. Fabric replaced by skin. That crop top was more than cute on him. It was useful. His abs trembled under my touch but I felt their seismic effect all the way down to my core.

I stopped when I reached the waistband of his jeans and he gulped.

"May I kiss you?" I could risk trying it and having my body control stolen from me under the effect of his previous order and I didn't want that.

I didn't want to steal more kisses from him.

I *wanted* him to want them.

His lips parted and his stomach clenched.

"You...you can."

Using my other hand, I cupped his face and looked into his eyes as I brought our mouths together, witnessing ecstasy taking over him. I trapped him against the door, and slipped my hand under his pants. He gasped. His cock hot and hard pulsed. He pushed out as I cupped his balls and rubbed his length with the heel of my palm.

Tomasz's hands stretched against the doorframe, steadying himself as if he were trying to balance on a tightrope. His keys dropped to the floor. A door opened somewhere in the hallway, but I didn't care and neither did Tomasz as he closed his eyes and thrust his hips against me.

I swallowed down his groans one by one, savoring each and every one, each becoming kindling for the fire burning bright inside me.

My dick throbbed, desperate to be touched, licked, fucked by him, but I knew any sudden movements might scare him away from me again and I couldn't bear that.

I carefully peeled back my lips and pressed them to his cheek, then his nose. Over his eyes. With each gasp of approval I claimed a different part of his face before I dropped to his ear and bit down on his lobe.

"Don't stop," he moaned and bucked his hips against my touch.

In my need to taste every part of him I could, my grinding had slowed almost to a halt. A smothering wave of compulsion blasted through me, encouraging my hand in his pants and my lips on his neck. Even if he hadn't told me, I wouldn't have stopped for the world.

The coercion eased inside me, but not without leaving an effect. The command reverberated through me, shot straight to my groin, and the more I repeated it in my head, the more aware I was that he'd commanded me whether on purpose or by accident the more my cock throbbed.

I couldn't let go of him. I couldn't stop stroking his raw manhood or kissing his beautifully freckled skin. I wasn't allowed to. I was his pawn. His puppet. His pet.

It was my turn to growl the pleasure pumping inside me.

In response, he caught his breath. "Kiss me," he said.

The order torched my body, stole the oxygen from my lungs and tightened every muscle in me.

I connected our mouths, lashed at his tongue, tasted his sweet flavor and my balls seized.

A searing wet heat struck my wrist once. Then once more. And then over and over again until my fingers were slick with his seed. Tomasz wheezed, chewing on his bottom lip and my heart skipped a beat. My cock strained and cum pooled in my own underwear too.

My knees buckled under my weight and I fell against him, panting on his shoulder. After a moment our breaths synced so much that when he breathed in I breathed out and vice versa.

And as spent as I was, I kept stroking, I kept touching him, even after his erection eased.

"Don't stop."

That had been his command and that was exactly what I was doing.

Not that I wanted this moment to be over. What I wanted was to keep going and going and going until we were both hard and desperate again. He didn't seem keen to let go either as he rested his cheek on my chest and his wild heartbeat slowed to a gentle rhythm.

A ringing ruptured the sanctity of the moment. Tomasz's eyes popped wide open and he bent out of my touch, reaching for the phone in his jacket.

"H-hello." His voice was hoarse. "Oh hi, Ciocia." He cleared his throat.

Despite him pulling away from me I still had the urge to please him so as he gazed at the ceiling talking on the phone trying to breathe, I got to my knees and undid his jeans, slid the zipper down and lapped on his soft dick, tasting the spend on his crown.

"I told you, before...no arrest, no funeral. I don't know why you can't—" He groaned.

He brought his hand up to cover his mouth and glared at me. If he looked gorgeous at eye level, he was positively divine from all the way down here.

I didn't get the chance to tell him because he blinked, and shrank away from me to redo his trousers.

"Because that's my decision and it's final. Stop being a bitch about it and accept it!" he shouted before shoving his phone back into his jacket.

I grabbed him by the hips and pulled him toward me.

"Stop it!" he said and the relentless urge inside me tamped down to a sizzle. "Gods. Oh gods. What have I done? What did you do? Why—" he mumbled and bent down to pick up his keys.

He barged into his house before I could say anything. Before I could even get back on my feet.

Saskia sat by the door and watched me with big kitty eyes before she ran after her master. I remembered what Tomasz had said.

She had a crush on me.

If she knew what we'd done, Tomasz was about to get an earful.

Maybe it was better that I couldn't understand her. I just wish I could understand her master.

My master.

"Tomasz?" I knocked on the bathroom door. "Tomasz, are you okay?"

The shower came on seconds later and he didn't come out for another half hour. Saskia waited for him the whole time while I grabbed myself a beer and ran the moments—our moments—over and over in my head.

I couldn't help it that I got hard again.

But I also couldn't help but get confused by the

mixed signals he was sending.

He wanted me and then he didn't. He kissed me and then he didn't.

What was that all about?

I fought with myself and my compulsive habit of falling for my masters, but I didn't let that influence how I treated him.

What was going on with him?

He didn't say anything when he emerged. He barely even glanced at me as he made his way upstairs to his bed. Saskia stalked after him but a few seconds later he shouted something in Polish and the cat yowled, running down the stairs and out of the window. It was more than a two-floor drop. But when I looked outside she walked the jump off as if it had been nothing.

Tomasz came downstairs a few minutes later and grabbed a bottle of water. As he made his way back toward the stairs again, I grabbed his hand.

He stared at it and his breathing slowed but he didn't say anything.

"Are you okay?"

Nothing.

"Did I do something?"

Still nothing.

"Why aren't you talking to me?"

"I'm going to bed." He slipped his hand from under mine and started climbing those stairs.

Had he said it before, when he was gasping under

my touch, I would have taken it as an invitation, but it wasn't. Not this time.

"Can you at least tell me what I keep doing wrong? I must be doing something wrong. You seem to want me but then you push me away. What is it?"

He stopped at the top of the staircase and turned to look at me. "There's nothing wrong with you. It's me who's wrong," he said.

"Bollocks. There's nothing wrong with you. I'm doing something and you're too afraid to tell me."

Tomasz sighed. And I climbed several of the steps.

"You're not—"

"You're lying. What is it? What is it I do?"

A few more steps and I managed to grab him again. Tomasz's Adam's apple bobbed as he swallowed. "You make me want you," he mumbled.

"Is that...bad?"

I was so confused. What was wrong with wanting me?

Let's not open that can of worms, Loki.

"It-it's is," he said.

"Why!" It came out as a growl and I didn't even care anymore.

"Because," he answered. "I'm a virgin, okay? I'm a twenty-four-year-old virgin and I don't want my first time to be with a demon who's been with hundreds of people better, and more experienced than me."

And with that strike, he yanked his hand away and turned his back on me.

He was a virgin? How was that possible?

Then I remembered our conversation the day before, when he'd told me he was too embarrassed to wear the crop top and I wondered if it had anything to do with his insecurities and his parents' acceptance.

"I'd like to sleep now, if you don't mind," he said. "Alone."

I respected his wishes and made my way back down.

He was a virgin.

He didn't feel like a virgin. Not the way he ground against me or the way he moaned as I stroked him.

Innocent, yes. But a virgin?

So much of him made sense now.

He was a virgin.

I was a god.

And he was terrified of comparing to my other lovers.

Wait a minute.

He said he wanted me. He said my attention made him want me.

And he'd said he didn't want his first time to be with a demon.

Which meant he'd thought about it. Probably fantasized about it.

And if that didn't make me want to pop his cherry, then I didn't know what would.

Challenge accepted.

Tomasz

"I'll go gentle on you."

Why would I say that to him? Why would I tell him any of it?

"Can you stop?" I told Loki as he walked beside me.

"You can even control me the whole time. I won't be able to do what you don't want me to," he insisted.

It was so surreal hearing him talk about taking my virginity as if it was the biggest prize on the lottery or something.

"Don't tell me you didn't enjoy yourself last night."

Oh boy, didn't I.

I had more than enjoyed myself. From the moment he'd slipped his hand into my pants I'd had to fight the urge to come and remember how to breathe.

All night, he'd been impossible to take out of my mind or the way my body reacted to. And I'd be lying if the idea of having him do to me what I wanted and only what I wanted sounded more than appealing, but...

"Can we focus on the task at hand?"

"I can multitask," he said.

He sounded like a teenager begging me. Nothing like the demon god I'd come to know.

And who I want to fuck my brains out, apparently.

"Look, it was your idea to visit the Polish coven and find out the latest gossip, so can you focus on that and not my...forget what I said last night."

Loki stopped in his tracks and leaned over me.

I braced myself for the kiss. I balled my fists and steadied my stance.

"As if I could forget your...." he whispered in my ear instead.

I slapped myself mentally. How had I gone from wanting to use that man for revenge to being desperate to use him to punch my V-card? I tried to whisper some strength for myself, but I knew already that was going to fail considering the kind of control I had over my power.

Anything more than ambiguity and things went haywire.

I should just stick to "good luck" and "good fortune" and accept that I'd never be half the szeptun my family members were.

"So what's the plan exactly?" I asked even though I knew it very well already, but I needed anything to take my mind—and his—from my purity and being desperate for his sin.

Loki straightened his jacket over his torso, rubbed his beard and huffed. "You go in, socialize like you always would—"

"Sitting in a corner and shoving food down my throat. Got it!"

Loki chuckled and shook his head. "And then I'll come along, glamor and compel the Hel out of everyone until someone spills what they know about your family."

I nodded and inhaled deeply.

Everyone loved gossip. That was the perfect way to use it to our advantage.

We turned the corner on Park Square in Fitzrovia to find the long line of prim and proper white houses with the big arches and Greek columns. For the umpteenth time I felt like dirt just walking down the expensive street and that feeling would only multiply when I walked through the coven center.

"I'll meet you inside." Loki's gold eye twinkled and I knew he must have disguised himself as someone.

I wished I could see the illusion he'd created for himself.

"Or not, most likely."

I pushed the door and passed the security crystals. Familiar nameless faces greeted me, but unlike my sister I wasn't a social butterfly. I didn't know them, or their histories, not even their powers.

If only I'd paid more attention, if only I'd been more like Oliwia, maybe I'd have a clue where to start finding her killer.

"Witaj, Tomaszu," said a woman I'd seen several times when helping Dad with his work, but whose name escaped me.

"Witam. Witam," I replied and rushed through the foyer to the refectory where the food was. Where most witches gathered to socialize.

I passed several. Some greeted me, most watched me go past with raised eyebrows and an attitude.

"Tomasz, what a surprise," Mrs. Kaczmarek, Oliwia's mentor at the coven, said as soon as she spotted me. "What are you doing here?"

I worked my way through the buffet and tried to not look hungry or homeless in my eagerness to get out of the conversation. The last thing I needed was for them to pity me.

"My family has always been so close to the coven, I thought I'd try to keep that connection alive," I answered, feeling the lie seep through me.

Most witches didn't like me, or the fact I worked at Java Jinx, an English high council business. I'd had so many people approach me when I'd taken the job to offer me ones in their cafés and restaurants and I'd declined each and every one.

I wanted to find my own way into this world and learn from other people. Since my szept was so tame in comparison to the rest of my family, I thought maybe working with Caleb would help me master spellwork, but I was just as hopeless at it, although that wasn't my fault entirely.

Szeptuns couldn't use spells most times. We had our szept. There had been szeptuns who had been able to utilize spellwork, but they hadn't been around for generations. I had foolishly thought maybe that would be my calling instead, but it had quickly turned out to not be the case. Nowadays, I begrudged spending the money on gemstones I couldn't use.

But working with Caleb, I'd learned more than I'd ever learned living at home and frequenting the coven. Most importantly, he'd shown me there was a way to be gay and happy even if there didn't seem to be much hope for me to do the same.

"That's fantastic, Tomasz. I'm so glad you want to do that. I think it will be great for you. And you know the coven is always here for you. What happened to your family is terrible, terrible business and what's worse is that they haven't caught who did it yet. Of course if the investigation was done by our boys—"

"The high council is doing everything they can to find them, Mrs. Kaczmarek."

Even I didn't believe that lie, but the last thing I wanted was for her to brag about how much better our coven was in comparison. No one was stopping them from collaborating to find the culprits, but stubbornness and pride were strong in both circles.

When I turned around, plate in hand, Loki was there, in the room. A group of people had already gathered, talking to him.

He spotted me and winked with his golden eye, yet his stare didn't linger as he turned his attention to those in front of him.

It suited him having a flock of people fawning over him, but then I remembered they weren't seeing the man I was seeing.

Big, tall, muscular.

Strong.

My butt-cheeks clenched as last night's front door incident and the *strong* way he'd held onto me whiplashed before my very eyes. I had been so tempted. So *freaking* tempted. I'd been tempted to pull him closer, take him to my bed, and have him touch me— taste me. Do everything to me I'd ever dreamt of and more of the stuff I hadn't.

Mrs. Kaczmarek kept yapping on but I tuned her out while Loki worked his way around the room, keeping a healthy distance from the black sheep of the Nowak family.

Eventually Kaczmarek handed me over to her husband who had his own views and ideas of what I should do with myself and my family's fortune.

Resisting the urge to tell him to shove his views and ideas up his arse proved a task in and of itself.

I pretended to listen while I topped up my plate with all the different kiełbasy and I couldn't help but wonder which sausage closely resembled that rock-solid mass I'd felt in the streets of Soho.

It couldn't be the kabanos. It was too long, thin and flimsy. The slaska was too short and stubby. No, if it looked anything like a sausage it was probably closer to a biała, big, thick and juicy—

What am I doing? Why am I comparing Loki's penis to sausages?

Good god, I'm thirsty.

I'd always craved touch, a man's touch, and had come so close to succumbing to temptation but I came to my senses before I acted on it.

My sister thought I was a prude.

Saskia thought I was an idiot.

All I was was scared.

Scared of doing something I'd regret. Scared of choosing the wrong guy. Scared of the pain. Scared of what it would mean for my manhood.

As if not having sex with a guy made me more manly.

I knew it was a silly hangup and my thoughts and fantasies were more than gay enough, but something about the whole ordeal made me clench and run away in fear.

I hadn't run from him yesterday.

I searched for Loki.

A guy was pinned against him. Loki draped his hand over the guy's chest like it had with me last night. He laughed and so did the guy as he leaned into his neck and took a deep breath.

He was a natural. And I was anything but.

He'd been with so many people. I was sure he had. Loki the god of mischief must have been with hundreds if not thousands of people.

Hell, he had children. He'd been with more than enough men and women to populate the earth twice over.

What could he possibly want me for? I'd only ever be a disappointment. Gods didn't sleep with weaklings like me.

I picked up a piece of kiełbasy but the kabanos flopped in front of my mouth, mocking me.

I dropped it back to the plate, dumped the plate in the bin and walked out of the center, back into Park Square.

There was no reason for me to be there anymore. I'd done my part, gone in and given Loki the chance to strike up conversations about the surviving Nowaks. He could handle the rest on his own. Probably fuck some people while he was at it.

I turned on Albany Terrace and a big mass of a man collided with me.

Loki.

I fell back and looked at him, but it wasn't Loki staring down at me. It was a hairy, buff man, whose eyebrows seemed to have no beginning or end and who didn't appear the least bit apologetic for knocking me over.

"I've been looking for you," he said as he bent down and lifted me as if I was a ragdoll and not a human being.

"What? Who are you?" I shouted.

I tried to push him off me, but whatever punch I managed landed like a slap. He didn't even flinch as he flung me over his shoulder and started to walk away.

People stared but no one cared enough to intervene. It wasn't like Londoners, especially the kind of posh people that lived around Fitzrovia, to get involved in anything that didn't concern them. Why get into trouble over nothing?

"Put me down you stupid wanker."

I kicked and pushed and screamed but the guy didn't care.

He headed straight for a van parked illegally on the pavement and I knew the second I ended up in that van, I'd be good as dead. I whispered three times. I whispered six times, but no matter how many whisperings I did, I couldn't harm anyone, nor could I make anyone do anything.

Wait a minute.

"Loki, save—"

"Excuse me. I think that's mine," he said as he appeared in front of me.

How had he even gotten there so fast? How had he heard me? Was he even there because of my command?

The guy turned to face Loki and let out an inhuman snarl.

Shifter.

Was he a wolf? Was he the man who had killed my family?

"Run away, old man. This doesn't concern you," he said.

"This...is mine and you better put it down if you value your life."

It? It? I'm not a fucking object.

Not that it mattered at the moment. What mattered was I didn't want to die.

I kicked and punched at my assailant to no avail.

But then, something did make contact.

My foot on his groin.

"You like that, murderer?"

I kicked again and he dropped me on my head. I put my hands up before I met the ground and as I scrambled to get back up, Loki was onto the wolf familiar's throat.

"If you even touched a hair of his body," he snarled, wringing the man's thick neck with both hands.

The familiar punched Loki's stomach and he flew back several feet, landing with a thud.

"Shit. Loki!" I shouted but the familiar spun and hoisted me over his shoulder again.

He slammed the van door open and flung me inside. I banged my head on the edge of the tailgate and then again on the floor of the inside of the vehicle.

I rolled to my back as my temples pounded with blood and pain. My eyes started feeling heavy. The wolf familiar stood in front of me for a moment, his silhouette illuminated by the daylight behind him.

I couldn't believe I was being abducted in the middle of the day, in the middle of London, right outside the coven with a demon god by my side.

"I thought I said—" Loki said, appearing behind the man. He was okay. He wasn't hurt. He was still breathing. "—he's mine."

My eyes closed and when they opened again, the familiar swiveled around, aiming his fists at Loki's face.

Loki disappeared and appeared right in front of the guy, crouched inside the van, and kicked the wolf. The wolf stumbled back.

I blinked again and again, each time feeling it a little more difficult to come to.

I caught Loki throwing another punch at the murderer. The murderer elbowed Loki and sent him flying again. Loki stepped back and watched as the murderer fought with nothing.

The more I blinked, the more of the action it felt like I missed. But what I didn't miss was when Loki snuck behind the man and twisted his neck. The crack of bones echoing through the interior of the van was the last thing I remembered before everything went dark.

The crack and Loki leaning over and whispering "I've got you. I've got you now," in my ears.

TOMASZ

Darkness.
　　　Pain.
　　　A man tried to snatch me, to take me, to kill me.

A man turned to two. The two turned to four. The four turned to millions.

They all wanted me. They wanted to hurt me. They wanted to make me feel pain. Just like they'd done to my parents. The same way they'd done to Oliwia.

They fed on fear and the more I was afraid, the stronger they became until they were invincible.

No one could help. I couldn't help myself. No one could save me.

Darkness.

Pain.

Him.

Just when everything was grim, hopeless and certain, a light.

His light.

A golden light that seemed to originate from his eye glowing brighter and brighter before it burst in the darkness and defeated it.

He slayed the men, a demon of immense power taking lives as if it meant nothing to him. As if their lives were nothing if it meant saving me.

Darkness.

Pain.

Him.

"I've got you. I've got you now."

His words rang in my ear, a soothing tickle that multiplied, it grew and moved from my head to the rest of my body.

"You better wake up, you bellend! I may be pissed off with you but I'll be damned if you die on me too, you cunt!"

"Saskia. Charming as always," I croaked.

I opened my eyes. Light flooded my vision but I fought it despite the thrumming it caused in my temples.

"I don't know what she's yapping in your ear, but she hasn't left your side since I brought you home."

His voice boomed inside me, but instead of adding to my headache it calmed it.

Loki appeared before me, dressed in nothing but a

vest and pajama bottoms, his hair ruffled and his frown a permanent fixture.

He extended a hand and offered me some water. I took the glass but when I tried to lift my head off the couch a sharp pain made me whine.

Within seconds, Loki was by my side, one hand underneath me, the other easing the glass to my lips, and that was the exact moment my body chose to go still.

"Speaking of not leaving your side, guess who also hasn't stopped faffing over you? I'll give you a hint. Tall, dark, lip-quivering sexy, goes by the name of Loki —oops, I've given it away, haven't I?"

He had?

Saskia stared at Loki's hand holding the glass for me and if possible with half-slitted eyes and a grin.

I looked up at him, and found his intense bicolored gaze. He barely twitched as he helped me, focused on my lips and with every sip I took, he allowed himself to blink.

But then he noticed me staring, or he simply glanced at me and I forgot how to drink, how to breathe, how to swallow. A lump formed in my throat and the water suffocated me, dripping from the sides of my mouth and spilling all over my clothes—

No, not clothes. Pajamas. I had on my dark black T-shirt with moons, stars and cats all over and the matching shorts.

That's not what I was wearing before I passed out.

I shot straight to my feet, the wetness on my shirt cooling my chest before the room started spinning and I fell back...back in his arms.

"Easy there, pudding. Where do you think you're going?" he whispered in my face and I didn't even register the pet name with his breath warm on my skin, bringing back the familiar tingle to my cheeks. "How are you feeling?"

He helped me back down and I rejected the glass he tried to pass me.

"Twisty," I mumbled.

"I'm feeling horny. Oh, he wasn't asking me? Okay, I guess," Saskia said.

I didn't even have the energy to glare at her.

"I can help with that. I would have done it sooner, but it's a bit dangerous to try a healing spell when someone is unconscious." He rose to his feet, walked over to the table, picked up a green gemstone and returned to my side.

"How do you do that?" I asked him.

"Do what?"

"The spells. You created one from scratch back at my house. I'm assuming you created this one."

He smirked and held the stone between us.

It was a raw crystal with bright edges and a dark core. It kinda looked like a sea urchin but it was far too refined and shiny for that.

"All demons can create them. Unlike witches, we

can harness pure energy and concentrate it to form a power stone. Or spells as you call them."

I nodded with a smile, but all I kept thinking was how powerful they were in comparison. Most witches couldn't create spells. That was why places like Java Jinx existed, so regular witches could buy them.

Having the power to create spells from scratch gave demons—gave Loki—an unfair advantage. Which made me wonder, why couldn't he free himself? Why couldn't he find his family? Why did he need me?

Maybe his power had its limits, but if he had any, I hadn't noticed yet.

That wolf familiar had pushed off with such ease. He'd landed a few strikes before Loki had snapped his neck.

"The guy!" I shouted. "The guy who tried to take me—"

"He's dead now," Loki answered before he closed his fingers around the spell. The thing exploded in his hand, the dust covered me with a glistening film for a moment before it disappeared and with it, my headache.

Who needs painkillers when you've got a demon with insta-spells.

"But...but he's the one who killed my parents, right? He's the wolf that—"

"Wolf?" Loki asked, confusion across his expression. "You think he was a wolf?"

Why was he so dismissive of that? It had been quite obvious.

"What else could he be? He was big, strong, hairy..."

Loki opened his mouth and laughter bounced off the walls, making the hairs on the back of my hands rise.

"You think because he was big and hairy he was a wolf?"

"If not a wolf than what—"

"He was a squirrel."

"A squirrel? But how—"

"He was a half-breed. I'm assuming his power was strength."

A half-breed?

That meant he was both a shifter and a witch, born of parents who weren't soulmates.

Familiars were the soulmates of witches. For every witch out there, was a familiar destined to protect them. Their offspring were usually either witches or shifters.

However, finding a soulmate amongst however many million witches across the world was a pretty rare occurrence. Which was why witches often hooked up with familiars regardless of their soulmate status. The children born out of those unions were considered half-breeds and dangerous because they had both parents' powers and as such they were often looked down on.

At least that was the case in the UK where the high council with its perverse politics and crazy ideals had reigned supreme for decades. Thankfully, the high council had been rebuilt from the ground up, thanks to Caleb and his friends.

"What the hell did he want with me?" I asked.

I didn't care about his status. I cared about what he wanted to do to me or with me.

"That, I do not know. I know I should have kept him alive and tortured the truth out of him, but he was berserk and he hurt you. All I wanted was to check on you and get rid of the scum."

His head dropped and his chest expanded when he inhaled.

"Hey, it's okay," I said, laying my hand on his leg without thinking. "I appreciate it."

"Awww, isn't he cute? He wanted to save you!" Saskia swooned on the coffee table.

"I thought you hated me," I told her.

I still hadn't forgotten how she'd stormed out because I'd let Loki touch me.

"Oh well, it's pretty clear he's not interested in me, so I can be fucked vicariously through you," she answered.

I gagged. "You're pretty gross, you know that?"

"You just don't like a truth-teller."

I flipped her the bird, but Saskia focused on my hand still touching Loki's leg.

Oh. I didn't realize I was doing that.

"What did she say?" Loki asked, staring at the hand too.

Something large and hard snaked under his trousers and I caught my breath as I felt its effect also snaking through my body.

Last night had been so hot. He'd made me come undone with a stroke and it had changed my entire world.

And he had said he wanted to...*pop* my cherry.

Was it wrong that I wanted it too?

I knew I didn't deserve it. I knew he didn't want me, he wouldn't choose me if it weren't for the dagger, but...I no longer cared.

The way he'd come for me, the way he'd snapped that man's neck, the way he looked after me, made sure I was okay—probably because he didn't know what would happen to him if his master died, but still.

"Truth-teller, leave!" I said to Saskia. "You either leave or I lock you in the bathroom." I added when she didn't budge.

I didn't even glance at her, I just stared at my hand, and his leg.

"You're so cruel. I hate you," she whined, but she did turn and jumped out of the window.

Those big leaps would kill a regular cat, but she couldn't die, so they barely affected her.

"Why did you send her aw—"

"Did you mean what you said earlier?" I asked.

"What did I say earlier?"

"That you wanted to...*be* my first?"

The frown that had been there since I'd come to lifted and he turned to me with a mix of bewilderment and satisfaction.

"I did."

I felt my heart pumping louder and louder until its drumming was all I could hear.

Am I really about to say this?

"I...I want you to do it. To me. Erm, with me. I-you know what I mean."

Could I sound any more pathetic than I did already?

"Uhm...I don't think I do," he answered and closed his legs, trapping my hand between them.

My dick throbbed.

"Are you going to make me say it?"

He leaned into my ear and whispered to me. "Oh yes."

His voice was quiet, and drawn, and rumbling and it caused a storm inside me.

I swallowed, tilted my head, feeling the shape of his lips like a ghost inches away from mine, and opened my mouth.

"I want you to fuck me."

Loki bit his lip with a moan. "I want to fuck you too," he said.

He covered my face with his hand, and my soul might as well have left my body.

Am I really about to do this?

"Not that I want to shoot myself in the foot here, but...why the change of heart?" he asked in the same sexy tone, still only inches away.

"Because you might be my last chance."

He pulled back and his brows united in a frown. "What do you mean your 'last chance'? Why would it?"

The way he questioned me, I felt stupid for even saying it. As if it weren't true at all.

I shrugged. "Because. Look at me."

"I *am* looking." The sensual tone returned to his voice.

"Who would ever want to fuck me? Who would ever want to be with me?"

Loki snatched my hand away from his legs.

That was it. I'd done it. I'd blown my chance at losing my virginity. I knew it was stupid. Ambitious, really.

Who am I to be taken by a god?

"You're cutting yourself extremely short," he said and brought my hand to his mouth. "You're gorgeous." He popped my index finger into his mouth and sucked.

A ripple of want washed through me.

"You're sweet." He bobbed his head and took my middle finger in his mouth too. "You're strong."

I barely had the presence of mind to laugh, but it was laughable. Me, strong? But he added another finger in his mouth and licked before taking them out again.

"And most importantly, you've got a genuine heart."

His tongue lashed at the tips of my fingers before he slid them down his chin, to his throat.

"It'd be an honor for any man to take you."

I knew it wouldn't, but in that moment, the way he held me, the way he spoke to me, I believed it.

With my hand wrapped around his neck he bent down for a kiss, his golden eye glimmering.

"One second," I said before he kissed me and I lost all control. "Before we do this, I need to know you're telling the truth."

"I am. But if you don't believe me...command me," he said.

He couldn't be lying. He wouldn't, if he was asking me to force the truth out of him. I didn't even know I could do that—it hadn't crossed my mind— and he had willingly given that to me.

He hovered in front of me, waiting.

I should trust him. I should believe him.

But then one look at the golden eye and I remembered who he was. God of mischief. God of tricks. God of deception.

"Tell me if I can trust you," I told him.

"No," he answered without hesitation. "But you can trust me with your body."

I bit my lip. "Tell me if you're hiding something from me."

He took a deep breath and smirked. "So many things. I'm a very bad man."

I knew he kept aces up his sleeve. I knew he hadn't shared everything with me.

What else should I have expected from a god like him?

"Tell me if you really think I'm gorgeous."

Again, he didn't miss a beat. "Yes. I do. I find it hard to resist you."

He did?

How was that possible?

I wasn't anything special. I couldn't even control my power.

"Tell me if you like me."

Loki huffed as if struggling with himself.

"What's wrong?" I asked.

"That's a difficult question to answer," he said.

"Why is it difficult?" He kept his lips shut so I added, "tell me."

"There's no single truth. I hate that you have control over me, but I like it at this moment. I hate that I'm stuck with you, but I love that it's you. I don't like that you won't set me free, but I admire you for it."

I understood. And even though I'd forced the truth out of him I appreciated that he told me and that

I knew. "Tell me if you really want to...take my virginity."

"Yes."

Again, no pause, no hesitation.

"Then do it," I said. "I-if you want."

I didn't want the whole thing to be a command I'd given him, even though his answer was definitive.

His mouth collided with mine, his tongue slipping into me with a little force and a lot of desire and I put all the rest of his answers—the answers that should worry me—to the back of my mind.

He squeezed under my back and under my knees and within seconds I was in the air, in his strong arms, leaning against his big chest.

He climbed the stairs to my bedroom, never breaking our connection, not until he laid me on the bed and crouched in front of me. "How are you feeling?" he asked.

I gulped, trying to tame the heat crawling under my skin. "G-good."

He dipped down and claimed my neck while his fingers tickled my sides and I had to choke down my laughter. Before I knew it, he yanked my T-shirt off and kissed my exposed collar bone, the dip in my sternum. His teeth reached my nipple and a sharp gasp left my mouth as he bit down.

I glanced beside me, where the Hofund was still lying on the bedside table, where it had been for days now.

"Are you okay?" he asked again and caught me staring at the dagger.

I nodded.

"You can use it if you want."

"It-it's fine," I said, focusing on him.

"You can control everything I do to you, how I do it, how long I do it."

My throat clenched and I stopped breathing.

That sounded...exciting.

"It's okay," I said.

Loki climbed back up to my face and stared me down.

"I'd like you to use it," he said.

"I-I thought you hated the thing."

He smirked. "Not always. It's got its uses," he answered.

The excitement threatened to pool in my pants. He wanted me to control him. To command him. To make him navigate my body on my terms.

"Okay," I whispered.

He smiled. "Where do you want me to start?"

Tomasz

I looked down at my nipple, hard and red from his bite and my cock pulsed.

"D-do the nipple thing again. That was...that was nice."

He wasted no time as he returned to my chest with a smile and hooked my nipple between his teeth again. He flicked his tongue back and forth and I arched my back. His hand pushed on my stomach settling back on the mattress and then continued its trail south toward my groin.

"Don't touch me there yet," I said and the hand stopped its journey.

"You're enjoying this, aren't you?" he asked, raising his head.

"And you don't?"

"You got me there," he said and then dipped down to bite my other nipple.

I leaned back, closed my eyes and focused on the pleasure he was bringing me and not stressing about what was going to happen or how alien these sensations were. "Kiss my belly," I said.

He obeyed, kissing wet trails all over my abdomen while he stroked the small of my back, making me feel all warm and fuzzy.

"Take the rest of my clothes off."

My cock sprang out of my briefs as soon as he slipped them past my hips and he stared at my nakedness with a hunger I'd only seen in him the night before when he'd had me pinned and under his thumb.

But I felt exposed. Way too exposed. Because even last night he hadn't seen me at my weakest. He'd only felt me. This was different. I was vulnerable. I was completely stripped and he wasn't. I was ugly.

"Take your clothes off."

Maybe that would level the playing field and make me feel less insecure.

It didn't, but it gave me something to focus on. Something new to worry about—his enormous length.

He was big and terrifying. The veins running along his cock appeared venomous. Dangerous.

How was I ever going to take him? How was I going to do this? I'd made a mistake. He shouldn't be my first. Even if he was my only chance, he couldn't be my first. He'd break me.

"Don't be afraid, little szeptun. I'll go easy on you."

I didn't know how easy he'd have to go for me not to tear apart, but even if I didn't believe him, I had no power to stop him. We'd gotten this far. I was naked in bed with another man, a demon god. There was no turning back now even if I wanted to.

"Suck me," I commanded him and watched him spread my legs and lower himself over my length.

His lips wrapped around me and as he eased me into his mouth he made me feel huge even though I knew I wasn't. But Loki either didn't care or didn't know because he worked up and down my cock with increasing hunger, spittle flying the faster he went, growling, moaning, staring at me as I stared at him.

This is beyond crazy.

I never thought I'd have a literal god sucking me off, especially a god who looked like the porn star of every man's dreams.

"Stop!"

The need inside me had dropped to the pit of my stomach and if he kept going it'd all be over before I'd even done the thing I was scared to do.

Maybe I should ask him to finish the job and stop here.

"What do you want me to do next...*master*?" he asked in a low snarl as a drop of spit ran down his chin and dropped onto my cock.

I wanted him to fuck me, but...

"I want to suck you," I said.

He offered me his length all too eagerly. He sat over

my chest, his big cock bouncing off my face, looking every bit as terrifying as I thought it had.

I wrapped my fingers carefully around him and guided him into my mouth, catching a sweet bubble in his slit, and I salivated.

He was large and sizzling and even though I went slow he was soon at the back of my throat.

I gagged. Loki held my head with both hands pinning me to him even though I couldn't go anywhere near fitting him all in like he had me.

I coughed and choked and panicked, but before I started to lose my faith in him, he pulled out and I was able to catch my breath.

He didn't look apologetic or smug about it, but he wiped the dribble off my mouth. He pressed his thumb on my teeth and I bit him.

Loki growled. "Again?" he asked, cock dancing before my lips again.

I didn't answer, I lifted my head and tightened my lips around him, feeling the rumble coming out of him right down to my core.

"You learn fast," he panted when I let him go.

I offered him one of those smirks that were usually his signature. "I'm not that innocent," I said. "I've watched porn."

"And? Does it compare to the real thing?"

"Not even close."

I took him again. And again and again. I took him

until he crumpled over me, gasping and groaning, subject to my mercy.

He collapsed beside me, taking deep breaths, and I took the opportunity to admire his hairy chest and the definition of his body.

"Are you okay?" I asked him.

"I should be asking you that."

"I'm not the one out of breath."

He chuckled and put his hand under his head, turning to me. "Ready for...more?"

I pursed my lips without meaning to. "I'm...I'm scared."

"I told you, you can trust me with your body." He ran a finger over my chest.

"That doesn't change how big you are," I said.

"I'll go easy."

That was a tough statement to believe. Even if he did, he was still huge. My mouth was hurting from how much he'd stretched it. How could my poor little hole handle him?

Granted, I'd used my toys before, but that didn't mean...

"Oh," I said.

"What?" he asked.

"Open the first drawer and take everything out," I commanded him.

He rolled over to do as asked.

Soon the side of my bed was filled with dildos of

various sizes, butt plugs, anal beads, a collar with a chain, cock rings, and enough lube to drown in it.

"You are a virgin?" he asked when he was done.

"What?" I shrugged. "I didn't say I was a blushing virgin."

He narrowed his eyes. "Have you seen yourself in the mirror? You're blushing right now."

I probably was. I hadn't shown my toys to anyone, and with Saskia living with me the last few weeks, I hadn't dared take them out, other than the butt plug that lived in my bathroom.

"Want to stop?" I asked.

"Do you?"

"Hell no." I shook my head and picked up the small, bulbous butt plug. "How about you start with this and work your way up?"

Loki took it and examined it. "I'm sure you can start with another. The one in your shower was bigger than this," he said.

I gasped. "I knew you'd seen it!"

"Seen it? I used it," he said.

I caught my breath. He had?

"And before you start, demons don't get or carry illnesses," he added.

I tried to picture him with my toy inside him, but I couldn't.

"Okay," I said, a naughty idea forming in my head. "You put that inside you and start with something bigger for me."

Loki smiled and obliged as he squirted a generous amount of lube into his hand and smeared it over my toy.

Then he stretched his legs and slipped it between them. I watched as my black butt plug disappeared behind him, in him and my cock jolted in response.

"You like that?"

"I do. Do you?"

"I can barely feel it," he answered. "Now what is this?"

He raised the collar in his hand and the chain rattled.

"It came with one of the toys. Sometimes I liked putting it on and tying myself to the bedpost and pretending I'm a prisoner, or a puppy, or something."

Loki turned the collar in his hands, unhooked the buttons in the back and smirked. "Do you want me to be your...pet?" he asked.

That was definitely not what I expected him to say. "Do you want to be my pet?"

He nodded with a zeal I hadn't seen in him before. My balls tensed and my hole clenched.

Gods, this is hot.

"Then put that collar on and be my pet," I told him.

He wrapped the collar around his neck and closed the clasp. The leather fabric was tight, redness already shading his skin. He felt the thing on his neck and moaned. A moan which rang through me, desperate for release.

"Master," he said and offered me the end of the chain.

For the first time in forever I felt powerful. I knew I was, at least when it came to him and controlling him, but holding his leash made me *see* it.

I never expected to like that.

"Pet. Did you forget what I asked you? Find a toy to fuck me with."

Loki inspected the collection before him and picked up the pink vibrator. It was about four or five inches and perfectly smooth. "Will this do, master?"

I nodded.

He pumped lube on it and opened my legs, pressing the tip against my hole. With his free hand, he used his finger to dab more slick around my muscle.

My body stilled, my teeth sank into my lip, and I kept back a groan as I waited for him to insert it.

I had done this so many times before, on my own but never had it felt like this. Never had my body felt more alight than now. The explosion waiting to rage inside asphyxiated me.

"Ready for the next one, master?"

"Y-yes," I said, swallowing the groan and fighting with my own body for control. "Ne-next one."

The next dildo he picked up was a rainbow seven-inch veiny cock, a replica of Ari Grand, the giant porn star of a man who had dominated my fantasies until Loki had come along.

Once again, he lubed it up and eased it inside me with the same attention and care he'd done so far.

He paused when he met some resistance, but then he pressed on and on, until I'd taken it all. He slid it in and out slowly at first, then faster.

Moments later something larger pressed my hole and I opened my eyes to find the black ten-inch dildo I'd bought when I was feeling aspirational.

I bit back a cry and trusted him as he stretched my hole like it had never been stretched, but when the pain got too much I pulled at his chain and he looked at me like the obedient puppy that he was.

"Easy, pet," I managed to articulate before he pushed on and I realized it wasn't the ten-inch dildo that was inside me anymore. It was him.

I hadn't even realized he'd switched. When did he do that? How did he manage it? Had he used his powers on me?

No, that's stupid. He can't use his powers on me.

But he had been fast before. Sneaky. Deceptive.

"Okay?" he asked.

Was I okay? I was being fucked by a Norse god who was under my control. Of course I wasn't okay. I was great.

"Fuck me, pet. Fuck me, Loki. Fuck me and don't stop until you fill me with your godly seed," I said.

It started as a plea and it ended as a shout while

Loki obeyed and halfway through my sentence pushed inside me and pounded me like a madman.

I bucked my hips, arched my back and allowed him easier entry, which he was all too content with. Yanking his chain, I forced him to tower over me and wrapped the leash in my hand until he was close enough to kiss.

He tried to.

"You don't get to kiss me until you do like I asked."

He panted mere inches from my lips, the glimmer in his golden eye inhuman and terrifying. The glow in his green eye innocent and pleading.

As if Loki could ever be innocent.

I used my free hand to stroke my strained cock and groaned in his face, louder and louder, as he groaned in mine until we were both a pair of loud screaming idiots.

I didn't care.

I didn't care if we were being loud, or insensitive, or wild. All I cared about was the ticking bomb inside us both and how it thrummed the faster he fucked me.

It thrummed and pulsed and beat until heat filled my insides and sprayed my skin. I couldn't ever remember a time when an orgasm had felt so good, when its effect lasted so long it made me weak at the knees.

Loki kept going even after he'd come, sweat beading his forehead and a rasp rolling from his lips before I loosened his leash and he collapsed on top of me, claiming my mouth just like he'd claimed my body.

And despite the mighty orgasm sucking on my core, depleting me of everything, I didn't feel tired. I didn't feel exhausted. I only felt stronger and stronger with each breath.

I never imagined my first time being like this, but by gods I wouldn't change it for the world.

"We're doing that again," I whispered.

Especially if every time felt like I was feeling now.

"Whenever you want, master," Loki whispered in my ear and rolled beside me, his left hand and leg wrapped around me still, binding me to him.

It probably wouldn't be long before I could go again.

I opened my mouth to tell him.

But there was a knock on the door.

And then the knock turned into erratic banging.

Loki

The pounding was relentless, not even when Tomasz shouted he'd be right there.

He fled the bed and the warmth he offered my body and got redressed with the pajamas I'd only just taken off him. Or so it felt.

The time we'd spent together, the time I'd spent inside him had felt as if only seconds, no more, not enough.

I watched him slip everything on, wanting him to turn around and command me to claim him again, but he didn't.

I was lost. I was so lost. I'd lost myself to Tomasz and his sweet voice, the tight shape and feel of his body, and the gentleness with which he did everything, even order me around. It didn't matter what I said to myself, what kind of lies to convince me it wasn't what it was.

Deny it as I may, I had fallen for Tomasz.

Just like I'd fallen for every other master in my long, tortured life.

The thing I'd dreaded from the moment I'd awoken in this body in Midgard and yet now that it was apparent, I knew it was different. That Tomasz was different.

Or maybe it was the most comfortable lie. The lie that meant I wouldn't have to face how weak I was in resisting the people who held my leash.

"Tomasz, open up," someone kept shouting.

Tomasz groaned. "Agh. Gods, help me. Not her."

As soon as he said that, I rose to my feet and came to his side. The worst part was I didn't know if it was a command or if I did it naturally.

"Who is it?" I asked.

"Oh it's fine." He put his hand to my chest and smiled. "Don't worry. I can handle her. But you might want to get dressed."

I nodded and reached for my vest as Tomasz stuffed the toys back into the drawer.

The chain of my collar fell in front of me when I bent down and I looked back at Tomasz. Was it stupid that I didn't want to take it off?

"I don't think I even want to explain this," Tomasz said and reached behind me to undo the collar for me.

As soon as it broke free I came to my senses.

I was a god. No matter what happened during sex, I had to be freed. I couldn't be subject to a human, to a witch for the rest of my existence. I deserved my freedom. Not to be bound to eternal servitude.

The realization sobered me up even if I didn't like the sharpness with which it took over my body, especially after the bliss that was Tomasz's orgasm.

You're forgetting why you're here, I told myself over and over until I remembered this trip to Midgard was no holiday.

This was my chance to finally be free.

"Finally, Tomasz. What the hell have you been do—" a woman said in a shrieky tone, marching into the flat and stopping short when she saw me walking down the stairs.

Her blonde hair was tied up in a bun and her eyebrows were thin, almost non-existent. But it was the faded green gaze that put me on edge.

"Who the hell is this?" she asked with no regard for formalities.

"Oh. Ciocia, that's Lo—erm, Locke, a friend," he said. "Locke, this is my aunt."

I didn't extend a hand and neither did she. She gave me a fleeting glare and then turned her attention to her nephew.

"Why aren't you answering my calls? Why aren't you replying to my messages?" She stood in front of him with crossed arms, her bag hanging from one elbow.

"I told you. I'm not having the funeral until—"

"Yeah, yeah, yeah. I know about that. I don't agree with it—"

"It's my decision," Tomasz said.

There was an extra quality to his voice, to his tone. It wasn't like it had been before. It was louder, clearer. Stronger.

My cum was already making him more powerful. It had filled him with a confidence that hadn't been there before I'd fucked him, and I'd be damned if that didn't turn me on.

"That's not why I'm here. I...are you okay?"

"I'm fine. Why?"

There it was again. The extra pep in his voice. It probably wasn't noticeable to anyone, but I could feel my power coursing through him like I could feel it inside me.

"I had a vision. I saw someone attacking you, putting you into a van and then...and then..." The aunt hunched over herself and sniffled.

Tomasz relaxed his stance and embraced his aunt.

I'd met several witches with the power of precognition or premonition and I was highly aware of the strong impact it could have on the witch physically and emotionally, but this felt...off somehow. I couldn't quite put my finger on why, however.

"I'm okay. See? Nothing's happened."

"But...but it's gonna happen," she cried.

"It's not, Ciocia. It happened already. Someone tried to take me, but they weren't successful."

The sniffling stopped and her back straightened. "H-how? I thought you couldn't use your power to harm anyone."

Tomasz pursed his lips and looked behind her, at me. "It wasn't my power that saved me."

The force of the events of this morning came back at me. The squirrel shifter's punch knocking the wind out of me. The manhandling of Tomasz. The bang of Tomasz's head on the van. The rage that burst inside me. The snap of the squirrel's neck.

I was no saint, but I didn't want anyone harming Tomasz. I didn't want anyone laying a finger on him. He didn't even need to ask me, I'd save him every time. No one should harm the kid, but me. And I couldn't unless he asked me to.

"You? And who are you exactly?" The aunt examined me from top to bottom, a certain crookedness to her mouth as she took all of me in.

I didn't know what kind of impression I was making on anyone, or what kind of assumptions people were making about me but I only needed a hint of her feelings to manipulate them. Maybe she thought I was intimidating, so I'd make myself small and weak to ease her guard.

Or maybe she thought I was dressed like a slob, in which case I'd make her see a well-dressed man.

Or maybe...

Was she one of those family members who had

made Tomasz believe there was something wrong with him all these years?

"Like I said, he's a friend."

"What kind of friend? I've never seen him before. Czy ty jesteś Polakiem?"

"No, I'm not Polish," I told her.

"Are you a witch? What are you?"

"Does it matter, Ciocia? Come on. Leave him alone."

Tomasz pulled his aunt toward the door but she didn't budge much.

"What? Is it a crime? I'd like to know how this *friend* of yours saved you. It's not unreasonable."

No, it wasn't, but like Tomasz had warned me with his boss, we didn't know what people would do with the information about my true nature.

"I am. A witch," I told her with a wink.

My golden eye reflected in hers and I shaped the illusion and molded her mind until all she ever remembered seeing, all she saw right now before her, was a smaller, uglier man in a dark Angel Guard uniform.

It didn't matter I'd never seen those "Guardian Angels" as Tomasz liked to call them. She had and it was exactly what I wanted her to see, so that's what she did see.

The worry in her changed into suspicion and then into acceptance and her sour grimace turned to just a disapproving glare.

"I'm so glad you're okay. Thank you for saving

him, officer. You should be careful, Tomasz. Do you want to come stay with me for a while? Until we figure out what the hell's going on?"

Tomasz stared at me, frowning, but he didn't say anything.

At least not to me.

"I'm okay, Ciocia. I'll be fine. I can...take care of myself."

Yet again he pulled her toward the door and unlike before, she let him.

"Call me if you need anything. And if you change your mind about the funeral. She was my sister too, you know. I don't like the idea of her frozen in a morgue. What if they never catch who did it? We have to bury them. It's the right thing."

"I'll tell you as soon as my mind changes," Tomasz said through gritted teeth and slammed the door shut.

I watched him take a deep breath before he turned around.

"Finally! What did you do to her?" he asked with a smile.

"How do you know I did anything?" I feigned innocence, but it dissolved to nothing as he sauntered toward me, dripping sin.

"For starters, she called you officer." He put his hands around the straps of my vest and pulled me closer to him. "And for mains, I saw the change in her. You did something."

Oh damn it.

How could I keep my wits about me when he was being so cute and so sexy?

"I just made her see what she wanted to see."

"Good, because what she was seeing before would have had her weeping," he said, his gaze dropping to my neck and I felt around it. "She's a raging homophobe. Even the fact I have another man in pajamas in my flat could have driven her insane."

"Is she the reason you don't feel like you can be yourself?"

He shrugged. "Part of. But my dad wasn't any better. He wasn't as vocal, or as rude, but I knew what he thought of people like me."

"Of people like us," I corrected him. "We are the same."

He laughed. "We're so not. I'm...me and you're a whole-ass demon."

"And don't you ever forget it." It was both a warning and a reminder. For him. And for me.

"How could I?" He pushed me back and we fell onto the sofa, Tomasz climbing into my lap with grace and no humility.

Yeah, this was an entirely new Tomasz. A cum-infused Tomasz who knew what he wanted and how to get it.

Sexy.

"So tell me something, Tomasz."

He hummed as he got busy with my neck.

"If your father hated what you were, why do you mourn him?"

The kisses stopped. He leaned back and tilted his head to the side. "Why wouldn't I? He was still my father."

"But he hated you."

"He was a flawed man, and I was too much of a coward to tell him because I was afraid he'd stop seeing me in the same way. But that doesn't mean he wasn't my dad and I didn't love him."

"So you love flawed people."

"Aren't we all flawed?"

I didn't answer him. I didn't know how.

My only flaw was my chains. And maybe that fact I still yearned to hurt him if it earned me my freedom.

But would he love me if I told him that? Or was that too much of a flaw even for him?

"Do we have to talk about my dead dad? It's killing my boner and I'm trying to get you to fuck me again."

I cleared my head and focused on his words ringing so loud inside me. "Well, well, look who's not a blushing virgin anymore," I said and leaned forward to kiss him.

"No, wait." He put his hand in front of my lips and smirked. "I like our kisses better when you have a collar around your neck."

The little shit *had* changed.

I really shouldn't fuck him, let his system use up my cum and wear out so he could go back to the meek, shy whisperer I'd first met. I was sure that version of Tomasz was much easier to manipulate.

But when he said things like *fuck,* or *collar,* how could I *not* fuck him?

"Yes, master," I said and carried him back upstairs so we could pick up right where we'd left off.

The change in him grew more apparent the more I came inside him, the more malleable he became under my touch.

And the more we fucked, the more I forgot about my purpose and mission here.

So did he.

But a week later, his phone pinged and we both crashed back to reality.

CALEB:

Hey, just letting u know L is back.

The time for fucking was over.

It was time for action.

LOKI

"Are you sure?" he asked for the fifth time.

And yes, I had been counting.

He'd been relentless all week. More confident. More gutsy. And not because when Saskia wouldn't leave the apartment he actually picked her up and locked her in the bathroom as he'd threatened her before.

He was also questioning me a lot more. Questioning everything. Maybe I should let him fuck me for a while if it meant he settled a bit, but as he was, he was dangerous.

Dangerous to both my plan and my resolve.

"Yes, I'm sure," I told him. Also for the fifth time.

He pinched the skin of his puffy, freshly kissed lips, and mulled over my response as if it was the first time he'd heard it.

"And it won't hurt her?"

"No," I said. "All I'll do is cast an illusion so she thinks I'm just another witch in need of something, we'll ask her to guide us to Heimdall and then I'll make her forget everything. She'll be fine." My words didn't seem to soothe the worry lines on his forehead, though.

"But she'll know I lied to her," he said.

"No. She'll just know she can't trust her memory of the incident."

"Which is as good as lying."

"If you're that concerned about your friend, why don't you tell her the truth? If she is your friend, she'll be happy to help you."

He shook his head as emphatically as he refused the plan the first time, the movement of the train making it even more pronounced. "No. I can't risk that. I know she's a friend, but I don't want to put it to the test."

I narrowed my eyes as the pride swelled in me. Not afraid to use the people closest to him to get what he wanted. It was a rule out of my playbook, if I had one, but a trickster knew better than to keep one.

And yet, as proud as I was, I was equally worried.

Would he keep his word? Would he let me free once he got his revenge? Or would he keep me because he liked having a weapon of mass destruction in his arsenal?

Hopefully, the answer would soon not matter.

Hopefully, Lorelai would lead us to my children

and this would all be over.

"Then we stick with the plan."

He studied my face for a few moments. I'd done the same over the last few days, I'd memorized every square inch of him in immaculate detail.

So much so it didn't matter if I closed my eyes or not, I could see him as clear as day performing every scandalous act I hadn't thought possible before I'd claimed him. The taste of his skin and the vision of his orgasm was etched onto my soul like nothing I'd felt before.

I'd been with my masters in the past, with many of them, many times and yet none had felt like he had. I didn't know what made him unique but I felt it to my very core, as if it had been written there since the beginning of time. If I was one to believe prophecies and predetermined destinies I might believe he was the one meant to set me free, but I was wiser than that.

But there was no other explanation I could find for why he was different.

Different or not, I'm sticking with my *plan. Even if it'll pain me to do so, I had to.*

"We stick with the plan," he finally answered and for a minute I thought he'd read my mind before I remembered there was a different plan he was referring to.

He leaned forward in his seat opposite me and stretched his shoulders as if to make himself appear bigger and more determined.

Caleb was there when we walked into Java Jinx and he was busy serving customers. He looked up and smiled.

"She's at the back, waiting for you."

Tomasz marched over to the almost hidden section of the café and I started following him when I noticed Caleb staring.

His eyes were dark and wary, his body still. I didn't know what had come over him. I was a harmless petite witch as far as anyone was concerned.

Unless he was a stronger empath than Tomasz or he let on and he could see beyond my glamors.

"Are you all right?" I asked him, popping the imaginary gum all innocently just for him.

The bubble popped.

He jerked back to motion.

"Y-yeah. I'm-I'm fine," he replied, but I couldn't help noticing the circles under his eyes.

The silver-haired empath turned back to his customers with half the enthusiasm he'd had before as if he'd been drained of all his energy.

I hopped to the back of the café and popped my gum once more for Tomasz's boss's benefit.

Go on, little empath. Try again. Try to see beyond my tricks. You'll only hurt yourself.

"What did I miss?" I asked as I approached the comfy sofa and table Tomasz and his colleague were sitting at.

Lorelai, unlike her boss, brightened the moment

she saw me, extended her hand, introduced herself, and patted the seat beside her, eager to get to know me.

It was a striking difference to the first time I'd met her when she'd called me old, ancient, and rancid.

"So, how can I help you guys?" Lorelai twirled the end of her ponytail around her fingers.

Tomasz's stare burned the side of my face and I glanced at him for a moment before I took a deep breath, put the imaginary chewing gum down on the table and looked at Lorelai, woman to woman.

"I'm looking for my friends. They were taken by a stupid-ass witch, and I can't find them."

Lorelai hummed and drank her coffee. "Okay. Okay. I can help with that. Do you have any clothes, or items that belonged to them? I can't promise anything, you'll probably have better luck asking a wolf, but I can try."

I shook my head. Lorelai glanced at Tomasz and he did the same.

"Without a possession of theirs it'll be impossible for me to find anything. I'm not a witc—"

"See, that's where you're wrong. I was actually here the other day, getting a coffee and a spell, and I was talking to Tomasz about my predicament."

"That's right." He picked up his cue, getting her attention. "I wanted to help her so I did my thing with her coffee and then—"

"And then you came in!" I said and looked Lorelai straight in the eyes.

I winked. The reflection of my golden eye in hers glimmered and I manipulated her memories from our first meeting so she remembered the little bubble-gum-popping witch I was presenting as now.

"Oh yeah, I remember," she said with a pleased smile.

Tomasz put his cup down with a *thud*. His chest rose and fell with increasing speed. His expression darkened.

"Are you okay?" I asked him.

He nodded, casting a concerned glance at Lorelai.

"You do? You remember...her?" he asked her.

"Of course. Please don't tell me you could smell that foul smell. I hope it's not a dead rat because I ain't picking it up," she answered.

"Aren't you a fox?" Tomasz asked her.

"It doesn't mean I like rats. Or dead things. Or hunting them because of who I am. Shut up." Lorelai put her hand in front of Tomasz and turned to me. "So what do I have to do with it? How do you think I can help?"

I crossed my hands and turned on the shy mannerism I'd seen Tomasz use, which had become almost extinct since I'd started fucking him. "Well, I think his magic made it so that you were the only one who can track him. Those words you used to describe the smell—'old, ancient, rancid'—they perfectly describe the bastard who took my friends."

"Oh." Lorelai paused, squinting. "I've been

wondering why that stench was following me. I'm telling you it was impossible to do my job all week. You really think it's Tomasz's magic in action?"

"I do. I really do."

"Then I guess we need to go find that witch," she said.

"You'll help us?" Tomasz asked, looking surprised at his friend's determination.

"Of course. I don't think I have a choice."

"Why?" Tomasz snapped his head around and raised an eyebrow as if questioning what I'd done to his friend.

Something pinched my chest and I caught my breath. I felt my magic waver for a moment.

Had he done something to me or...

Is this guilt?

"Well, yeah, if I ever want rid of that smell I think I have to help you."

"Oh." His gaze dropped. "Okay."

I inhaled deeply and worked my magic on Lorelai again, ignoring the pinch that had turned into a claw in my chest.

I hadn't done anything to influence his friend's decision other than what we'd agreed.

Despite everything he'd said, he still felt bad for lying to his friend. And from the looks of it, he still didn't trust me. Which was exactly what any sane person would and should do in his place. I'd even told him he couldn't trust me when he asked me all those questions before I'd taken him to bed for the first time. He'd be a fool to forget my answer, and innocent or not, he was no fool.

I watched him. He kept throwing fleeting glances at his friend and glancing down at his coffee as if he wanted the cup to pull him right inside. He hated lying to Lorelai, I knew that, but there was barely anything we'd told her that wasn't true. The only thing that was deceptive was my true nature and that of my "friends." I didn't understand why he looked so guilty. And yet, despite it all, he still went on with our lie.

What was he so afraid of?

That his friends would turn on him, that he wouldn't get his revenge, or that he would be stopped before he got it if he told them the truth?

Maybe it was all three.

A person could battle with more than one fear.

Like I was.

I was close—so close I could taste it—to getting my children back, but the closer we got, the more I wasn't sure about my plan and whether I wanted to go ahead with it.

I wanted my freedom and I wanted Tomasz.

Can't I have both?

"Right." Lorelai set her cup down and got up. "Let's go."

"What? Now?" Tomasz asked.

"There's no time like now. Besides, you have no

idea how bad the smell is and now that I know what it is, I can't suppress it."

She walked around the table and we followed her out of the café. Caleb barely looked at us as we left.

The hustle and bustle of the area was hectic. It was gorgeous. If only I wasn't bound, I'd go around and cause more trouble to revel in, watch everything turn to chaos. Feed off it.

Lorelai sniffed the air.

"How close is it?" Tomasz asked.

"I won't know until I shift. Let's hope animal control doesn't get to us before we find them." Lorelai undid and redid her ponytail and straightened her jacket.

"Don't worry about that," I told her and cast a trick around her.

She winked at me and her eyes glowed.

Smoke erupted out of her, covering her completely. There was a flash of light and a bang and a second later when the smoke disappeared a large red fox stood in Lorelai's place.

She sniffed Tomasz's feet, then moved up his legs. He raised a hand in an attempt to stroke her soft fur, but she snapped away from the touch and turned to smell me.

It wasn't long before she was rubbing her cheeks against my hips, my waist, my stomach.

"Uhm...what the hell?" Tomasz muttered under his breath.

His voice seemed to pull Lorelai away from spreading her scent on me and back to the task at hand.

"So basically, every animal turns into a whore around you," he commented as we followed the fox down the road.

I didn't know why she wasn't repelled by my scent the same way she'd been last week. I had no explanation for that.

Was it possible she never thought I stank but it had always been Tomasz's magic in action?

"Apparently, I smell good now. I don't know what to tell you." I was as confused as he was.

He didn't comment on it and soon even I forgot about it as Lorelai took us north, hot on the demons' trail.

We followed her side-by-side, the backs of our hands brushing every so often. The need to touch him battled with the logical part of my brain, the one telling me there was no future between us so I might as well quit now.

But how could I? How could I when every other part of my brain, every other part of me, wanted him. To kiss him. To taste him. To fuck him. To love him.

It didn't matter what happened before and how many times I'd been betrayed. My body and soul wanted him.

But if I was going to be successful, I had to use my brain, my logic. Nothing else mattered.

Nothing else should *matter.*

Tomasz took the choice out of my hands as he joined ours and reminding myself about my freedom became even harder.

"Are you—is this okay?" he asked me.

I didn't have the heart to tell him no. "Of course," I told him, and it was. It was more than okay.

Lorelai didn't stop once. She kept going and going and going.

Was she going to find them? What if the whispering hadn't worked? What if all that waiting had been for nothing?

The longer it took, the more I dreaded what we'd find, if we found it.

All this time, I hadn't allowed myself to think about my children and what Heimdall could have done to them. What was the point in stressing about something I had little control over? But now, I allowed myself to worry. I allowed myself to think about the man who'd taken my children. Whatever Heimdall had done to them was bad enough that Hela wasn't able to return to her realm.

If he'd hurt them...

My children were both strong and powerful, but that didn't mean they weren't vulnerable. Especially if the bodies they possessed couldn't contain their power.

And if they died in their human bodies, they died for good. Ceased to exist. Not even the goddess of death could come back from that.

Was I already too late? Had I wasted a week

succumbing to human pleasures while my children were both dead?

No, he wouldn't dare.

I was playing right into Heimdall's game. He knew I'd come for him the minute he stole my children. It didn't matter that I had little choice in crossing the realms, he knew I'd come. Even if it took a lifetime.

He knew there would be nothing I wouldn't do to get them back. Just like he wouldn't rest until he fulfilled his purpose.

We thought we could avoid it once but apparently we couldn't. Everything led to this.

Either I killed him or he did.

"What are you thinking?" Tomasz asked me with a sliver of sweat forming on his forehead.

We'd been walking for over an hour now and Lorelai was showing no sign of stopping. Tracking was such a mundane job.

"Nothing," I said.

Tomasz leaned closer. I thought he was going to kiss me, but he didn't.

"You're lying and you're not even trying to hide it."

I shrugged. What was the point of keeping it from him?

"You're thinking about Heimdall, aren't you?"

"He's a dangerous man," I told him.

And that was the absolute truth. He was a single-minded, extremely powerful god who had charged into war many times. He'd won every single one.

He also hated me with passion.

"So are you," Tomasz said.

"I am. But my danger is contained and his is not," I said.

Once upon a time, Heimdall thought we could avoid the fate foretold. How could we kill one another when we had been in love?

But that all over when he bound me to his sword and I...took my revenge.

"Why does he hate you so much? What did you do to him? He...he wasn't your lover, was he?"

"No." I lied.

I didn't know if Tomasz believed me and for the first time I didn't care. It was all too painful to think about.

"Then why does he hate you?"

"Because *I* hate him. Because *he* hurt me. He should be glad I didn't rip him in two."

Tomasz's gaze darkened but if there was anything on his mind, he didn't get to share it with me.

"We're here," Lorelai said, back to her human form.

And as I took in our surroundings, I felt it. The surge of power around me.

Heimdall was there.

And he was waiting.

TOMASZ

As we stood in front of the magnificent Victorian mansion, a striking black gate, though rusted with time, perfectly framed the estate. The iron bars were adorned with cobwebs and dirt, only adding to the eerie charm of the decaying structure it protected.

The two-story brick house stood tall, its once vibrant red hue now darkened by time. The ashy bay window, with its intricate gothic details, stretched across both floors, and its slimy chimney added to the number of them extending into the darkening sky.

Smoke rose from one of them.

"Spooky." Lorelai whistled. "Can't believe anyone lives in that shithole."

She chuckled and I pursed my lips in an attempt to smile.

I'd lied to my friend. One of only two friends I had left in this world. Saskia didn't count. She was stuck with me and I was the only one who could understand her now.

I didn't like lying to her, but what other option did I have? Telling her the truth was too risky. She worked for the high council. She had connections with the Angel Guard. Her and Caleb might be friends, but they were law-abiding citizens. Hell, Caleb's boyfriend even was a Guardian Angel. One of the founding members, in fact.

What would they do if they found out I'd awakened a demon to help me find and kill the wolf that had murdered my family?

"Thanks Lorelai. You have no idea how grateful I am." I stepped into her arms and kissed her cheek.

"That's what friends are for, silly," she said. "Oh, and would you look at that, the fucking stench is finally gone! I guess you were right. It was your whispering."

I gave her an extra tug before I let go and looked at Loki.

"Fantastic. Now, *forget* where you took us. *Forget* what we asked you to do. *Go* back to work and if *anyone* asks, you helped a witch connect with an old lover from your pack." Loki snapped his fingers in front of her face.

Lorelai's expression went blank and emotionless. Without another word, or glance, she walked away, leaving the two of us in front of Heimdall's residence.

I took a deep breath, staring at the well-worn path leading to the house. Only four—five weeks ago I was on my way to my parents' completely oblivious to the world of demons and murder, and now this was all my life had become.

"Don't worry. What she can't remember can't hurt her," Loki said and squeezed my shoulder.

I turned to him and shook my head. "That wasn't...I was just thinking we're so close. You're about to take back your children, and I'm about to find the wolf who murdered my family."

He swallowed a tightness in his throat and gave me a sad smile.

"There's no need to be afraid," he said.

I cocked my head and frowned. "Scared? Who said I was scared? I'm ready. Are you?"

And it was true. I'd done enough sitting and wallowing. It was time for action.

He huffed. "Scared or ready?"

"Either."

He raised his glance to take in the mansion that felt like it existed in the middle of Nowhere, Finchley.

"Both," he said, taking me by surprise.

Loki was afraid of something? In all the time I'd known him, which granted wasn't long at all, he'd always carried himself with confidence and pride. Nothing was too much trouble or too depressing.

What was so scary about Heimdall that had him feeling so unlike the guy I knew?

Was he scared he'd hurt him again like he had before? I couldn't even imagine anyone hurting a guy like Loki. Anyone even having the power to do so.

Loki took a step forward and rattled the gate. The chain keeping it shut snapped in two.

I followed him onto the path leading to the house and felt the energy around me seep out, and my hairs raise all over my body.

I should have been scared. I should have been trembling walking into an abandoned building not knowing what to expect, but the shiver passing through me made me feel...stronger.

This was weird. Why wasn't I scared?

Could it have something to do with Loki's seed inside me?

It couldn't be. He'd said it'd make me more powerful, not fearless. And even that hadn't worked, because for all the sex we'd had, I still couldn't rely on my whispering for anything other than serendipity and not for lack of trying.

Loki stood by the front door. He straightened his hunched shoulders and inhaled before he turned to me.

"I'll be out as soon as possible. Whatever happens, whatever you hear, *don't* come inside!"

His golden eye glimmered. I didn't know why he

was trying to compel me when he knew it wouldn't work on me.

"What are you talking about? I'm not staying out here."

"Yes, you are," he replied and cupped half of my face.

I'd become so used to him holding me like that in the past week, when he was in bed, inside me, or standing in the middle of my flat kissing me. It was starting to feel like part of me and I missed it every time he removed it.

It had the ability to both light up my body and put me at ease.

But this wasn't going to work here and now.

"Are you forgetting who's the master and who the slave?" I told him.

His lips parted and closed as his expression darkened. "You are to stay back and *not* to get involved in whatever happens in there. Heimdall is dangerous. Do you understand?"

I nodded and he turned to the door that was already cracked open. I put my hands into my pockets and wrapped my hand around the Hofund. It had changed into a Swiss army knife as soon as I attempted to put it in my coat. I hoped I wouldn't need it, but it was the only weapon I had and while I didn't need to be carrying it to command Loki, I could always use it to protect myself.

The floorboards creaked under his weight but Loki didn't lose his composure. He navigated the hallway slowly, carefully and when we came to the first entryway, he jumped inside.

I tried to do the same. I crashed into his big mass of chest and muscle.

"I thought I told you to step back," he growled.

As if that would scare me. He was forgetting I'd seen him fall apart under my rule.

"Don't make me make you shut up." I raised an eyebrow and smirked.

Everything turned into a blur before I crashed into a wall, my shoulder blades digging into the rough exposed bricks, knocking the wind out of me.

Loki's lips hovered mere inches from mine, but he wasn't threatening me with a good time.

"Do you not understand how serious this is?" he growled.

I attempted to fill my lungs, but he slapped his hand over my mouth.

"Don't try it, little one. This is dangerous. It's not time for games. No silly commands, no stupid jokes. You understand?"

He kept his hand pressed until I nodded and he eased off me.

"What? No apology?" I asked, straightening my clothes.

"You deserved it."

That was probably true. And I'd think of the

implications and possibilities of what had just happened, later, when all this was over, because that was fun. But like he'd said, now wasn't the time for snark and boners.

He went out, back into the hallway and I took a moment to inspect the front room. There were broken wooden units everywhere, and a torn-apart sofa with a colony of rats scampering inside, but no children.

Someone growled and I followed the sound. I found Loki in the next room—a larger reception area, probably a dining hall—crouched over two figures illuminated by a rainbow spotlight.

"Motherfucker!" Loki spat.

The two figures, one a young girl who couldn't be older than six, and one an adult man, were lying on the floor, eyes closed, hands clasped at the chest as if they were being put to rest in caskets.

I crouched down beside Loki.

"Are they okay?" I asked.

Loki inhaled and exhaled several times before he answered. "No. The bastard has them trapped in Bifröst."

I narrowed my gaze and studied the rainbow spotlight. It encompassed both figures and illuminated the floor around them but when I tried to find where the light was coming from, I couldn't. There was nothing on the ceiling. The light disappeared before it reached it.

"I thought that was a bridge," I said.

Loki extended his hand toward the young girl, but his hand went through her.

"It is. It bridges all the realms. But the fucker is keeping them suspended on it. Suspended between realms so neither body nor soul can do anything," he explained.

That was so freaky. This was worse than a coma. At least when people were in one they could still recognize the voices of their loved ones. These two didn't even know their father was here.

"I knew you'd come," someone said.

A chill ran down my spine.

Loki sat back and his face creased with unnatural harsh lines that made him look like an animal.

A handsome, imposing white man with wavy golden locks, dressed in leather, stood with a blank gaze and a grim smile in the doorway.

"It must have killed you not knowing when," Loki said without turning to him.

The man, Heimdall, crossed his arms and huffed. "You think it's funny?"

Loki glanced at me. Sadness rippled over his face. He turned to look at Heimdall, who stepped into the light created by the Bifröst. "A little," Loki told him. "I mean, think about it. The god of foresight losing his sight is quite poetic."

"You stole more than just my eyes!" Heimdall shouted.

I noticed the cloudiness in his gaze. How was it

possible? This wasn't even Heimdall's real body, just like Loki's didn't belong to him either. Had he been invoked into another blind man's body by someone, because that would be quite sadistic.

"And I would do it again after what you did."

"And so would I!" Heimdall snarled.

"Believe me, Heim, I'm still suffering the consequences of your curse, just like you are of mine."

Heimdall's face twitched and he brought his fingers to his lips. "Heim, huh. No one's ever called me that in millennia," he said and approached Loki, his eyelids fluttering. "Tell me, Loki, did you miss me? All these years without me did you ever think about me?"

The man who had sounded pissed as all hell two seconds ago was all sultry now, his voice just short of a purr.

What was going on here? Was Heimdall an ex-lover?

Why wouldn't he tell me?

Any time I asked about Heimdall, he always said he was an old friend turned foe but he never elaborated.

And when I'd asked him if he was an old lover earlier, he'd denied it. Why would he lie to me? Why wouldn't he tell me the truth?

Why does a Loki do anything a Loki does?

Maybe he was still in love with him and he didn't want to admit it to his latest fuck toy.

Or maybe it had been a one-sided relationship and

Loki never saw him as anything but a sexual transaction.

Was that how he saw me?

Would he also take something from me like he had Heimdall's eyesight?

"Oh I thought about you," Loki whispered and my guts twisted.

Heimdall hung onto his words with the same desperation I probably had when I asked him to fuck me.

I'm such a fool.

"I thought about how much I hate you with every fiber of my existence."

Heimdall's face dropped. "You're a monster!" he shouted.

"That didn't stop you the first time!" Loki kept his composure despite Heimdall's outburst.

"Well, we all make mistakes." The fair-haired demon shrugged.

"Is that why you took my children? To punish me for mine?"

"What?" Heimdall said, transferring his fingers from his lips to Loki's. "No, no, no, Loki baby. I didn't take them to punish you."

I watched in silence as the person who was obviously Loki's ex hovered over my demon, barely able to prevent himself from kissing him.

"I thought he hated you." I also couldn't stop myself.

Loki had lied to me. Or kept the truth hidden, which was just as bad. He had no difficulty lying to Lorelai. He had no qualms about deceiving my friends and twisting their perception. Why did I ever think he was being truthful?

Why did I ever think he could be trusted?

And why did it matter? It wasn't as if he was my boyfriend. He was my key to revenge and that was all. When in hell had I forgotten that and had started believing he was more to me, I didn't know.

"Oh I did. I hated him so much," Heimdall said, not bothering to look away from Loki.

"The feeling's mutual," Loki gritted and my insides plummeted.

I'd let the trickster god into my life, I'd let him be my first, I'd given him more than I ever thought I could. Was he going to turn around and hurt me too? Was he going to do it with a smile on his face because he'd never felt anything for me?

"I know. You always hated me. And that hurt, Loki-boo."

Loki's face hardened as if he didn't like facing the truth. "Is that what you think?" He snatched Heimdall's hand away from his face and held it over his head so that they were both so close they could've kissed. "After everything, do you really believe that?"

"Are you calling me a liar?" he whispered. "He hates me, really." He glanced at me, the first time he'd acknowledged me since he'd walked into the room.

Loki looked at me too and the stony expression turned into a grimace. He pushed Heimdall off him and Heimdall skidded across the floor. "Truth hurts, doesn't it?" he said as if he hadn't felt a thing.

And he probably hadn't. Did demons even have feelings?

"The truth? What truth? You've been spouting lies ever since you walked in here. You're the liar, not me," he screamed, towering over the fellow god who appeared tiny and weak under his shadow.

"So you did love him?" I asked before Heimdall could.

Loki snapped his head around and he studied me as if in battle with himself.

"Come on. Answer the boy."

Loki inhaled and exhaled but he held my gaze. "I did. I...I loved him more than anything."

I shouldn't believe him. I shouldn't even listen. But the way his lip quivered, the way his voice carried across to where I was standing it was impossible not to.

"What happened?"

The gold in his eye dimmed, and for a moment he looked almost human. "I gave him my heart, my body, my soul and he took everything from me."

His words reverberated through me, the hurt in his tone so jagged it made my own eyes sting while his glistened with the threat of tears.

Was it possible I had it all wrong? Was it possible

the trickster god was no trickster but a broken-hearted man?

"Yes, because you were going to destroy everything! I did it to save the world. I did it to save you," Heimdall said.

The man was still on the floor, and looking at him I'd have never believed he had the ability to not only invoke two demons but the cruelty to trap them in a cruel magical coma.

"And how many times has your foresight been wrong?" Loki barked. Heimdall didn't answer. "I'm waiting."

"You slaughtered the elves. An entire race of creatures gone. The signs were there," Heimdall said.

"Is that true?" I asked.

Loki could barely glance at me. "They took my children. They deserved it," he said.

I glanced at the two bodies trapped in a rainbow and the harshness in my breath eased. He was just a father who would do anything to protect his kids. Wouldn't anyone else do the same?

"If I hadn't stopped you, you would have burned the whole world to the ground." Heimdall crawled back until Loki was no longer over him and got back to his feet. "I had to do something to stop you from hurting yourself."

I watched the god regaining his composure like a literal transformation from a weakling to a super-human sure of his conviction.

A vision. An entire race slaughtered. The earth burnt to the ground.

"You bound him to you." The realization slapped me in the face. "You're the one who enslaved him."

Tomasz

Loki's silence was answer enough, but that didn't cut it for Heimdall.

"Why can't you understand I did it to protect you? I've forgiven you for using me. I've forgiven you for blinding me. I've forgiven you for sending me to Muspelheim."

"How did I use you? How—you took advantage of me, you enslaved me, you treated me like your toy—"

"Don't pretend you didn't enjoy *that*."

"I had no choice!" Loki shouted, his voice bouncing off the walls and echoing long after he stopped talking.

"And was that reason enough to blind me? To gift me to Surt, like I was an object?"

Surt. I remembered watching a movie once with the fire giant going face-to-face with a Norse god. If

Surt was anything like in that movie, that sounded painful.

"Isn't that what you did with him?" I asked. "How is it different?"

Heimdall turned to me and for the first time I saw something sinister in his expression.

"I did it to protect him. What danger was I to the world? To him? Everything I did was because I loved him."

"I thought you'd forgiven him," I said, seeing through whatever facade he was trying to present.

I wasn't buying it anymore.

"I have," he replied and turned back to his ex-lover.

"Is that why you are hurting my children now?"

"Hurting them? They can't feel a thing."

"Why did you take them?" Loki snarled. "What did they ever do to you?"

"Because. You'll do everything for them. I knew you'd come for them," Heimdall answered.

"Everyone knows that," Loki said.

"Yeah, especially after you wiped out the Dark Elves," Heimdall muttered.

"You want something."

"Don't we all, Loki-boo?"

"What?" *Loki-boo* snarled.

"To be a family, of course. To all be together like you always wanted."

I laughed.

Heimdall glared.

"Are you serious?"

"Very."

I turned to look at Loki. He wasn't as amused as I was.

"You took my children for that? Tell me, did Surt fuck your intelligence as well as your body?"

Heimdall huffed. "You loved me once. And I love you still. If I could forgive you for what you did to me, why can't you forgive me?"

"Because you're crazy," I said.

"Shut up, witch. No one talked to you."

"I'm afraid I have to agree with the 'witch'," Loki said and stepped up to Heimdall.

"Now, Loki-boo, don't be rash. Think about it. Think about what we had. You used to look at me as if I hung the moon and I would have, if Máni hadn't already done it." The man rubbed his hand in front of his chest with wide eyes and a quiver in his lips.

"But that wasn't enough for you. You wanted to control me."

"I wanted you to be mine and only mine. Is that so bad?"

"Yes!" both Loki and I said at the same time.

"So you admit your vision had nothing to do with why you bound me."

"One doesn't negate the other. I saw an opportunity to be the hero and save my lover, I took it."

"You wanker!"

Loki swung at him making me jump at the sudden

movement and change in mood, but when his fist collided with Heimdall's face, nothing happened.

The god didn't stumble or fly across the room, in fact he didn't even flinch.

"What the..." Loki muttered.

Heimdall closed his eyes, lowered his head and pursed his lips. "And here I was hoping for a loving reconciliation." He pouted. "I guess war it is."

With that, Heimdall pushed his hands out, and crushed them into Loki's stomach. He went sailing, passing through his children and crashing into the darkness behind them.

When Loki emerged he stared at his ex with a perplexed expression.

"You like?" Heimdall asked. "It wasn't all bad with Surt. He taught me a thing or two. Like how to feed off vengeance. It's intoxicating." He spoke with such indulgence as though he was talking about new attire.

"So much for love," Loki growled and bolted for Heimdall.

Heimdall ducked out of his way, spun around, grabbed him by the collar and threw him to the floor between his son and daughter.

"I guess the vision will have to come true," he sighed, towering over Loki.

"What vision?" I asked.

"My very first one. I was only a babe when I had it, but I remember all my visions," he answered. "And in it, we both kill each other."

Loki wiped the spittle on his face with the back of his sleeve. "See? Now you're talking my language."

He kicked at Heimdall but he only ended up skidding back, but that didn't stop him for long before he was at Heimdall's throat again.

Heimdall moved around him like a sprite, dancing with ease and grace. "Yes, baby. Hit me. Hit me more. The more you want it, the stronger you make me."

Heimdall slammed his foot between Loki's shoulder blades and the crack of bones splintered in the air. I felt it in my body as if he had kicked me.

The god was feeding off Loki's hatred for him. The betrayal and hurt burned inside him and the more he failed to strike him, the brighter it'd get.

And Heimdall would only get stronger.

There had to be a way to stop him. To end the madness. Could I command Loki not to feel anything for his ex?

I wrapped my hand around the Hofund in my pocket and took it out. I almost fell to the floor as the Swiss army knife changed into a sword and clattered to the floor.

"My darling, I haven't seen you in forever," Heimdall said and immediately the Hofund flew to his hand.

I should have known. It was his sword after all. Did that mean he was Loki's master again?

Loki froze as Heimdall held the tip of the blade to Loki's chest.

"It still feels like yesterday," Heimdall hummed.

He inspected the blade with a bewildered face as if he could see it before he looked up at Loki.

"Let's see. What should we start with?" He clicked his tongue. "How about, kiss me, Loki-boo?"

I held my breath.

Loki remained still, staring at the blade threatening to stake him instead of his old lover. The command went ignored.

"I said kiss me!" he insisted but Loki didn't.

"It's not your blade anymore," Loki muttered. "It's his."

Heimdall's face dropped with a pout.

"Oh well. I can still kill you with it," he said.

"No!" I shouted.

Heimdall glanced at me and Loki took the opportunity to step away from the blade and smash his head against Heimdall's from the side.

Loki yelped in pain, stumbling backward, his head in his hands.

"You stupid, buffoon. You can't touch me. Unless you forget what I did and move on, you will never be able to touch me."

Heimdall swung at him again. Fabric flew, revealing a thin line running across Loki's chest. The line got thicker as the blood dripped. The demon yelped and his breathing hardened.

"Mmm, that feels good." Heimdall ran the blade across his tongue and tasted Loki's blood.

My nails dug into my palms. I ran toward him but

before I got to him, he turned and pointed the sword at me.

"You, darling, are delicious," he told me. "I mean his thirst for vengeance is strong, but yours? Yu-umm."

My thirst?

Shit. Of course.

He wasn't just feeding off Loki. He was feeding off me. For what I wanted to do to the wolf that killed my family. All the things I wanted Loki to do to that monster before he ripped him apart.

"Oh yes baby. Don't hold back," Heimdall continued with a satisfied grin. "Your vengeance is gorgeous. I could use a man like you."

He studied me from head to toe with the same quiver he'd had when he'd been begging Loki, while the man he'd proclaimed to still love was on his knees behind him, holding his chest, trying to breathe and not bleed to death.

"Wow. You move on fast," I told him.

Heimdall shrugged. "I had thousands of years to get over him. But I'm a new man. With brand new powers. And you...oh, you would be perfect by my side."

"And what happens if I don't want to? Will you subjugate me the same way you did him?"

Heimdall grimaced and seized my throat. Loki groaned.

"If I have to," he hissed.

I spat at him and he snarled. My feet dangled in the air, his hand digging into my carotid.

"Don't. Touch him," Loki shouted.

He rose from the ground, clenching his jaw and looked at me for a second before he crashed into Heimdall's back.

One moment I was in the air. The next I was rolling on the floor and out of his grasp.

Loki grabbed Heimdall by the hair and smashed his face to the ground over and over again.

Heimdall didn't flinch. With every attempt he laughed louder.

I got to my feet. I wanted to help. There had to be a way. To do something. But what could I possibly do?

The sword.

I went for the sword.

That was the only weapon around here.

I ducked to grab it.

Heimdall's hand got there first. He pushed back, shuffled around and stabbed Loki in the gut.

"No!"

He may as well have stabbed me. The pain tore through my body as if it were my own. The slash of flesh as Heimdall pulled the blade out made me wince.

Blood poured from him like a torrent. He was going to die. He was going to die and it was all my fault. Because I'd been obsessed with my family's murder, because I wanted revenge more than anything, whatever the cost.

I couldn't save them, and now I couldn't save him. Because I was useless. Weak. Powerless.

"I wonder if you taste as decadent as your hatred," Heimdall said, turning to me, completely ignoring Loki dying before him.

This man was deranged. There was no stopping him. And I was either gonna end up his victim or his prisoner.

Or both, like Loki.

"Tell me, witch. What is your power?" he asked, pinching my chin and lifting my head until I met his gaze.

My insides flared.

My power.

My power was useless. Weak. Like me. It was unpredictable. But maybe I could still use it. Or die trying.

I glanced at Loki staring at me pretending as if that wasn't his blood he was drenched in.

"*Ugasić pragnienie. Ugasić pragnienie. Ugasić pragnienie,*" I whispered.

My ears rang with my hushed plea. A wave of murmurs soared in the room and both Loki and Heimdall looked around, searching for the source.

A weight lifted from my shoulders and the back of my head tingled.

I felt fifty pounds lighter. Almost at peace. But still strong enough to push Heimdall off me.

"What have you done?" the god cried out, flexing

his fingers, turning his head from side to side as if someone was whispering in his ear.

"I just took our thirst for vengeance away. Now we're all equal. Now you don't have the upper hand," I told him with each step I took.

He stumbled back, confused and powerless until he almost tripped on Loki. "Take it back," he shouted. "Take it back now!" He waved the sword in front of me as if it meant anything.

I laughed and stepped into its reach.

My stomach spasmed. Pain erupted inside me.

What?

I looked down to find the blade piercing me, the blood painting my clothes red.

How was that possible? I was the master of the Hofund.

"What? Did you think it couldn't hurt you? My darling boy, that only works if he tries to stab you with it. I know it's a magic sword, but it's still a sword."

My mouth filled with the taste of copper. I tried to choke back a cough but the blood burst out of me anyway. My throat tightened.

Heimdall pulled the sword away from me and I felt my limbs go numb.

"No!" Loki shouted.

I stared at him, the beauty of his green and golden eye striking me as if for the first time.

My moments with him flashed before my eyes.

The first time he saw me and tried to kill me.

When he agreed to help me.

The time he used my shower and found my butt plug.

The first time he kissed me.

The first time he touched me.

The first time he fucked me.

At least I'm not gonna die a virgin.

At least I've lived a little since I met him.

I dropped to the floor as Loki rose to his feet and snatched the Hofund from Heimdall's hands.

My head crashed to the floorboard with a bang and as I looked up, blood rising in my mouth, I took pleasure in knowing that at least Loki would finally be free of a master and could save his children.

Loki screamed and as my vision blurred, he slashed at his ex-lover's neck.

Something clattered to the floor beside me and the headless body of Heimdall collapsed on Loki.

"*Be free. Be free. Be free, my Loki,*" I whispered and closed my eyes.

LOKI

"No!"

I pushed Heimdall's limp body off me just as my own convulsed. My insides turned. My muscles tightened. My head throbbed.

Heimdall's body fell to the floor with a thud and everything that was happening inside mine seized for a moment. Then another.

What the hell is happening to me?

And then the pain from the wounds I'd collected spasmed, bringing me to my knees.

But I didn't care about that.

All I cared about was Tomasz, lying still on the floor. It was a bloodbath. A fucking bloodbath.

What had he done to my Tomasz? How could I have let this happen? What was wrong with me?

"Why? Why didn't you listen, silly boy?" I pushed my hand on the wound in his stomach and wiped the sticky hair out of his face. "You should have stayed outside. You should have...I should have..."

It wasn't his fault. It was mine. I'd allowed him to come here. I'd lured us both in this trap with my lies and deception and I went and got him killed.

And even if Heimdall hadn't...

"Father!" someone said behind me.

I snapped around, closing my arms over Tomasz's body.

No one else was going to hurt him on my watch. I'd die before I let anyone near him. And I'd die soon.

"Father, you're hurt," a petite girl, with big bright green eyes and short brunette hair said.

She ran to me while the man crouched beside her watched me, the girl, Tomasz with a narrow gaze.

"Hela?" I said when the little girl touched my shoulder and ran her fingers over my wounds.

"The one and only. Miss me?" she said with a deep, genuine smile.

She was so small, so tiny. She didn't appear anywhere near her real age.

"My Helfire." My hand slipped from under Tomasz's head and I brought it up to her face. "Are you okay? Did he hurt you?"

The man towered over both of us and looked at me.

"Father. Kept yourself busy I see," he said, no expression apparent on his face.

"Oh, Finn, shut up and help me save him," Hela slapped his leg and Fenrir raised an eyebrow.

His human body didn't seem a day over twenty, twenty-five, and his blond hair was a striking change to his usual dark features. But his eyes were just as golden as they'd always been.

"Why should I, Helsie?" he cocked his head. "What did you do this time? What poor thing did you cheat, lie to and fuck this time?"

Well there was another thing that hadn't changed one bit. Not that he was wrong of course, but...

This time was different.

"You haven't changed—" I started but I fell back in Hela's hands who, despite her size, was able to take my full weight.

Fenrir sighed, dropped by my side and sniffed the air. "He'll bleed to death if we don't do something," he said.

"No shit, genius!" Hela snapped back at him.

Fenrir ignored her and scanned the room. "Who is that?" he asked, looking at the decapitated body.

"Heimdall," I said, straining every one of my muscles.

"Shit. So he escaped."

"Finn, can you fucking focus. Our father is bleeding to death. Be a dear and find the kitchen in this place. We need a spell!"

Fenrir flipped the bird at his sister but obeyed her like the good boy he was.

"What happened here?" she asked, glancing at Heimdall and Tomasz.

"You...you mean you don't know?"

How was this possible? Had he not even given them a chance to get used to their hosts before he'd trapped them in the Bifröst?

"No, no clue. I don't even know how long we've been gone, although I'm sure if I ask Elsa, she'll tell me."

"Who?"

"My host. She's a sweet, little girl," Hela answered.

I nodded, biting down a groan, and looked over at Tomasz. Hela pressed harder at my second wound, the one in my stomach and for a moment the pain stopped and throbbed quietly.

"Who's that?"

"He-he's Tomasz," I said.

But he wasn't just that, was he? He was more. So much more? And now he'd die, we'd both die, because I was too stupid to see it in time.

"He's on the brink. Should I help him?"

"He-he's what?"

My heart seized. My limbs went numb. My eyes burned.

It was one thing thinking it, but to hear her, the goddess of death, say it?

"No—stop it-don't." I coughed blood on my hand.

"I can't stop it. You know that. But I can help him. His family is waiting for him," she said.

"No!" I shouted. "It's not his time yet. He's not ready. He's...he's mine."

He was, damn it. His family had him for twenty-four years. I'd only had him for a little over a week and even in that time I hadn't been completely genuine with him. I'd been scheming and plotting and planning my freedom and his demise.

I couldn't let go of him. Not now. Not yet. Not before I made up for the way I'd hurt him.

"Save him," I shouted. "Save him no matter what it takes."

Fenrir returned to the room and shook his head.

"There's nothing. This place is old. I can run, find someplace else—"

"It won't do any good. He—they won't make it," she told him as he knelt on the other side of me and Hela passed me over to her brother.

She walked to Tomasz's side with bloodstained hands and dress and touched his face.

"Save him!" I screamed and my wounds retaliated.

It should be me. I should have died. Not him.

Hela looked at me and her eyes turned black like the abyss.

"It's his choice now," she said.

I shook my head and fell back.

I might as well die now too.

Who would choose to be with me? Who would

give up eternity with their family to spend their living days with someone they could never trust?

I'm sorry.

"I'm sorry, Tomasz."

I'm sorry I never got the revenge you wanted.

I'm sorry I couldn't give you the one thing you asked of me.

TOMASZ

"I'm sorry. The tube was packed again and those fucking idiots won't let people step off before they pile on. Hope you haven't started without me."

I hung up my coat as Saskia ran past my legs and into the kitchen.

I got goosebumps.

Why did this feel familiar? Like déjà vu, or something.

Saskia yowled. A shadow settled in the pit of my stomach and it only grew bigger and coarser with every step I took.

Yeah, definitely some serious déjà vu.

My temples throbbed in protest and I held my breath as I walked into the kitchen.

"Took you long, enough," Oliwia said and a collective sigh of relief put my pounding heart at ease.

"Oh shut up. As if you don't know how it is," I told her. "Oh, I'm sorry. You would but you don't because you never go anywhere."

"Pot, meet kettle."

Mom picked up a big tray covered in kitchen foil and carried it to the dining room, and even before she spoke I could tell exactly what it was as the yummy goodness hit my nostrils and made me salivate. "Oh stop it you two. Come on. I've made your favorite," she said.

As I approached the table, she turned and grabbed my hand, and her smile wavered. "It really is great to see you again."

I patted her and chuckled. "Gosh, don't try to guilt trip me, woman. I try to make it every week but it's not always possible."

Mom rolled her eyes and sat at the chair. Oliwia sat opposite her and I took the seat between them.

They both crossed their hands on the table and watched me lift the foil. Steam rose from inside.

The roasted pork loin looked more divine than it had any right to and I could barely contain myself as I placed a slice on my plate.

I cut a piece and opened my mouth when I noticed both women staring at me, smiling.

"What? I'm starving."

Oliwia smiled so much it brought tears to her eyes.

When I turned to my mom, she was crying too.

"What is it, you guys? I'm not waiting for Dad. He never waits for us," I told them.

"Nothing," Mom said and wiped her face. "I'm just so glad to see you, Tomek."

"Me too, little brat. Me too," Oliwia added.

I turned from one to the other waiting for the punchline, or an explanation, but they offered me none and despite wiping their tears, there were fresh ones rolling down their cheeks.

"You guys are acting weird," I said and made another attempt to eat the pork.

That was when he walked in.

"What are you doing here?" he shouted, towering over the table like a madman.

Oh, gods. What have I done now?

"Are you mad that I'm late because I already said I'm sorry."

"Late? You shouldn't have come. You shouldn't be here. You don't belong here," he said, making both Mom and Oliwia jump.

Damn, I was never gonna eat that fucking pork, was I?

I slammed my knife and fork down and pushed the chair back. "What's gotten into you, Dad? What have I done this time?"

Mom reached for my hand and squeezed it. "He's right, słoneczko. You shouldn't be here with us."

I turned to my only chance of sanity and answers around here. "Oliwia, did you let them smoke weed again? Because we've been through this. They act stupid when they do it," I told her.

Oliwia shook her head and buried herself in her hands, crying her guts out.

"You need to go," Dad said. "Now!"

"Will any of you tell me what the hell is going on and what you're talking about?"

"We don't have time, Tomek. You need to go before you end up here with us," Mom said.

I looked at the pork longingly. All I wanted was to eat this delicious dinner with my family and they were all acting insane.

I pulled my hair and screamed.

"If someone won't start explaining what the hell—"

I stopped.

What was I doing here?

No, that was the wrong question. What were *they* doing here?

They shouldn't be here. They should be...

I couldn't quite put my finger on where they should be but I knew this was wrong. This whole picture was wrong.

How had I ended up here?

The tube, before the tube, I walked. Had a little argument with Saskia—the usual.

But what had happened before that?

Had it rained?

I remembered a rainbow, but I was pretty sure it

hadn't been raining when I was making my way here or I'd be drenched. Oliwia always rolled her eyes at the fact I didn't carry an umbrella even though we lived in London, but who had space and patience to carry an umbrella around?

No, it hadn't rained.

So why on earth do I remember seeing a rainbow?

Rainbow.

Sword.

And there'd been a sword.

Where the fuck would I have seen a sword. For crying out loud it must have been a dream.

Rainbow.

Sword.

Blood.

There was blood. I knew that. It had been so much I could almost taste it.

Rainbow.

Sword.

Blood.

Loki.

My body thrummed and I collapsed on the chair.

Shit.

The memories rushed through me knocking the wind out of me.

I looked up at my family.

"Am I dead?" I asked them.

Heimdall. He'd stabbed me and I was bleeding.

Yeah, that was where I should be. Dying on the floor of some decrepit house. Not here.

Definitely not here.

"Not yet, sweetheart. But you will, if you don't hurry."

She pointed to the hallway, where a bright light was coming from the far end.

I took a step toward it but stopped.

"Wait a minute. If I'm almost dead, then...that means you are."

Mom burst into tears and Oliwia rushed to her side. It was Dad who stepped forward and grabbed my hands.

"We are, my boy, but you don't have to be," he said. "You. Need. To go! Leave us. Our fate is sealed. Yours isn't." Dad's eyes were red and his voice trembled despite how he held himself.

Wait a fucking minute.

What the hell was I doing? Why was I about to run off when...

When they were right here.

"I can't. I...I'll stay here."

"You can't!" Dad said.

"Why? I'm good as dead anyway. I'm bleeding somewhere in North London. What's the point of going back? I'll only end up back with you."

My father squeezed my hands and shook his head.

"Tomek, you're talking rubbish. You're a healer."

I rolled my eyes. Even in death my dad was in denial.

"We've been through this, like, a thousand times. I'm not Oliwia. I can do shit with my szept."

"Don't talk like that about yourself and your gift," Mom said.

"It's the truth."

"Only because you made it the truth," Dad insisted.

When would they realize I was hopeless with my gift? Why did they have to torture me about it both in life and in death?

"How? How have I made it my truth? It *is* the truth. I've tried everything. Amplifying spells, potions, training with Oliwia day and night. Hell, I've even fucked a demon and his seed still didn't make me any better with my powers!"

I didn't realize what I was shouting until it was too late and when I did, I slapped my mouth shut.

"Oh my Gods! Finally, Tomasz. I thought you were going to die a virgin." Oliwia cheered.

I glared at her.

Dad had frozen in front of me. Mom was frozen too, staring at my dad.

This was definitely not how I wanted to come out to them. Actually, I never wanted to come out to them.

What the hell did I do?

"I-I'm sorry, Dad," I said before I saw the disappointment in his expression, bound to come.

"Igor," Mom said.

Dad took a deep breath and frowned at me. "I knew the day would come," he said.

The day when he pushed me away. The day when he told me I was no son of his. Had it been written in the stars? Was that why he'd always been so hard on me?

"I'm sorry, Dad. I...I know I'm a letdown but...I can't keep lying to myself. I know you hate me but I hope you can find—"

"Hate you?" Dad huffed.

"We don't hate you, honey," Mom said, but I couldn't look away from Dad.

"You think I hate you?"

I shrugged. "Don't you? I know how you feel about...about gay people."

"And you think that makes me hate you?"

"Doesn't it?"

Thinking he would say anything other than yes was a pipedream. That was why I'd accepted I could never tell him.

"Tomek, you're my son," he said, tugging at my hands.

"Yeah, I know. And no son of yours can ever be gay, I've heard it all before, Da—"

"Tomasz, you're my son. And I love you."

Had he just said...

"What?"

My dad would never say that. I must have misheard. Death was messing with my hearing.

"I love you. And I always will. Even the parts of you I can never understand."

Oh, you know what? This isn't the afterlife. It's just a dream. Now it all makes sense.

"I'm sorry I planted so much fear in you that you thought I'd ever hate my own son. I'm a terrible father." He wrapped his arms around me and squeezed for dear life. If there was any life left around here.

"We do, honey." Mom embraced both of us and not a moment later, Oliwia joined in too.

I breathed in.

I didn't know if this was real or fake, or just an illusion but I didn't care.

It felt good and that was all that mattered.

"Who knew we all had to die to be a happy family, huh?"

"You haven't died yet," Oliwia said.

"You need to hurry," Mom added.

Dad broke the embrace and looked toward the hall and the light.

"I'll still die so why bother?"

Oliwia touched Dad's shoulder and he crossed his hands.

"What have we always told you?" he asked.

Things. So many things. Where did I start?

"That my gift is me and I'm my gift," I mumbled. As if shit like that would help save me.

"That's right. The more you deny that, the more you'll struggle," Dad said.

"Believe in yourself, Tomek. You've got to believe in yourself. That's the only way you'll ever master your szept." Oliwia poked my chest.

It was as if they'd just met me. Hadn't they been telling me the same thing over and over since the dawn of time?

But then again, I had tamed the vengeance in all of us long enough for Loki to kill Heimdall.

Surely that was just a fluke. One of those times when my gift worked instead of doing roundabouts.

"Even if I believe in myself, it still doesn't work," I told them.

And it was the truth.

The past week with Loki had been intense. I'd discovered parts of me I never knew existed.

But my gift remained like it was.

Useless.

"Then you need to embrace the chaos, little brother. Embrace it, and use it."

Embrace the chaos.

That was new.

Just like the chaos that had taken over my life since they'd been murdered. Since they'd been taken away from me.

And Loki had come into my life.

He was chaos personified. Everything he did, everything he said, everything he touched was full of his mischief.

Oliwia's eyes went bright.

They went so bright they blinded me, but before they did, she nodded and everything made sense.

Loki might be chaos, but so was my power.

There was no way to know how it would work, how the probabilities would fall in my favor. That was why when I'd asked for help, my whisper hadn't given me a sign, it had given me Lorelai.

The light dimmed.

It dimmed so much it was replaced by darkness. And a pair of green eyes staring right down at me.

A little girl smiled and looked at my stomach.

I did too.

My T-shirt was soaked. The puncture in the middle of my belly was swollen and a deep red almost black.

This was it.

Embrace the chaos. Believe in yourself, Tomasz and embrace the chaos.

"*Uzdrowić! Uzdrowić! Uzdrowić!*" Blood filled my mouth again, but not before I whispered.

And within moments the blood receded, my wound throbbed and my internal organs sewed themselves back together.

"Fuck me, it worked," I shouted. "Shit. Sorry."

The kid laughed and looked up.

"You're healed too," she said.

I turned to find who she was talking to but Loki appeared in front of me, and squeezed me in his arms.

"My little whisperer. You did it. You did it, Tomasz," he mumbled in my ear, rocking us back and forth.

A numbness overtook my body and my eyes went heavy, but when I closed them this time, I knew I'd be okay. We'd all be okay.

TOMASZ

I woke up in my bed, the aroma of coffee beans infiltrating my the room as though through my very pores.

When had Saskia learned how to use the coffee machine?

The bitch refused to try even though I was pretty sure her shadowy friends could press the right buttons for her. I'd seen her do worse things than the horror of making coffee with an Espresso capsule machine.

But when I looked over, Saskia was sleeping by my feet, which of course didn't last long as soon as I stirred.

She was up on her feet and in my face in no time.

This was how it used to be, in the *before* times. Sometimes I'd wake up with her in my bed, most times, I wouldn't. I'd get up, go to work, make lattes and cappuccinos with chocolate powder on top—an atrocity in and of itself—then came back home, chilled on my sofa watching soaps and trashy reality shows. Rinse. Repeat.

This felt like any one of those same, old, boring days.

Maybe it had been a dream, all of it, and I'd never nearly died, I'd never invoked Loki, I'd never even lost my parents.

But if I didn't know it in my head that it hadn't, the fresh smell of coffee would have been a dead give-away. That, and the fact the sky was purple instead of orange. Setting instead of rising. I never woke up in the evening.

I turned my head toward Sass. She was staring at me.

"What did I do now?"

"Nothing," she replied. "Why do you assume you've done something wrong? *Have* you done something wrong?"

I shrugged. "You tell me. You're the one that freaked out because I fucked 'your boyfriend'."

"Oh I'm over that. You can have your Loki."

"I can?" I asked.

"Oh yeah. It's not like I can erase seeing you two in bed fucking like bunnies from the back of my eyelids."

I rolled my eyes and sat up. It was good to know some things never changed despite how much my world had rocked from its core.

"Thank you, your Grace."

Saskia sauntered next to me as I got out of bed and put my slippers on and pointed a clawed paw at me.

"But hands off the son. That hunk is mine. You hear me?"

The son?

I'd forgotten about his son. All I remembered was Loki. And a little girl. But when I woke up from my near-death experience there had been no son there.

"You can keep him," I told her, dismissing her with a wave and started to descend the stairs. "You do know he's a wolf, right?"

Saskia huffed.

"He's not just any wolf. He's the god of wolves."

That didn't stop the fact that he could probably eat her in one go—and not in the way she fantasized— but I kept my mouth shut.

There were three people when I got down to my living room, all sitting around my tiny dining table with a cup in front of them.

A little girl, feet dangling from the chair, with a pair of piercing green eyes. A young man with blond hair and striking, gold eyes. And no other than Loki.

My Loki.

Everyone stared at me as I approached, which should have unnerved me, but it didn't.

"Morning," said the girl.

Loki pushed back his chair and got up to refill the coffee machine, placing my favorite mug—*I whisper my coffee*—underneath the pourer.

"How did you sleep?" Loki asked me as he waited for my drink.

"Me? How did you sleep? Or more importantly, where?"

I scanned my house but there were no clues of any sleeping arrangements.

"We didn't," the young man said before Saskia jumped onto the table in front of him.

She meowed and I fully expected him to growl at her, but he just narrowed his eyes and stared back at her.

"See what I mean? Look at those eyes. He can rip me a new one anytime as long as I can look at those eyes."

"Saskia, not now," I shouted at her and lifted her away from the wolf god.

She hissed.

"Either you shut your mouth and behave, or I'll whisper you to sleep." I wagged my finger in front of her face.

She grimaced. "You? Whisper me to sleep? Pfft, did you lose it while you were away? Since when are we throwing empty threats out there?"

I lowered my voice and leaned into her ear. "Who said they're empty?"

She didn't respond and I turned my attention back to the table, and Loki's children.

"Let me guess," Loki said, offering me a cup. "She has a crush on Fenrir?"

"Bingo." I turned to Fenrir and patted his shoulder. "I apologize in advance for any and every stupid, creepy thing she does."

Fenrir laughed and looked over to Saskia sitting on the coffee table and blew her a kiss.

I expected a remark from her, but there was nothing. She stayed still with wide eyes and a gaping mouth.

"You're tempting fate," I warned Fenrir.

"Two, Tomasz. I just had two orgasms back-to-back. And you don't even care," Sass said behind me.

I ignored her.

"Anyway." I offered my hand to both Fenrir and Hela, introducing myself. "You guys should have woken me up. I would have given you the bed, or made something up down here. You must be tired."

Hela tipped her cup back and then passed it to her father.

"Trust me. We've been asleep for three years. I can do two days without sleep," she said.

Loki refilled her cup with coffee and handed it back to her. It was weird to see a child downing caffeine, but I guessed the soul inside was thousands of years older so it shouldn't matter.

"You guys were trapped on the Bifröst for three years?"

That was incomprehensible. I couldn't imagine how the poor things felt.

"Wait, did you say I was asleep for two days? Fuck! Caleb is gonna ki—"

"I called him and told him you'd be out of work for a few days," Loki said.

I'd already missed so many days off work, I hated to miss more. Frankly, I didn't know how Caleb hadn't fired me yet. Maybe he was about to.

"Don't worry. He's got Lorelai back. He didn't have an issue."

The verdict was still out on that one.

"How are you feeling?" Loki asked.

"I'm feeling good," I answered. And it was the truth. I was still groggy from sleeping for two days straight, but I was physically and mentally great.

"You healed yourself," he said. "You healed us both."

I nodded.

Embrace the chaos.

The words still rang in my ears, as did the rush of my whispering. I'd just accepted that it might not work, I accepted that it might take a detour before working, or just not work at all. The only thing I could ever do was try and if it didn't work? Well, then it wasn't meant to be.

"Who knew accepting you're shit would make you *not* shit," I said.

"You're not shit," Loki said and embraced me, planting a kiss on my forehead.

I didn't realize how much my body had missed his until he did that, until I was cocooned in his arms. I didn't even care if his children were watching us.

"I'm sorry," he whispered.

The voice sent shivers down my spine and a deep, low groan built inside me that I managed to quench down to a sigh.

"What for? You warned me. I just didn't listen," I said.

"But if it weren't for me—" he started.

"Oh, stop it, Loki."

"It's the truth. I did something—"

"We both knew the road to revenge wouldn't be an easy one. So don't apologize. If anyone's to blame, it's me. And, hey it all worked out in the end anyway," I said.

Loki's eyes narrowed. "What did you say?" he asked.

"I said it all worked out—"

"No, not that. You told me to stop."

"Exactly, so drop it."

"But I can't," he said.

I sighed.

"You must," I insisted.

"No." He pulled away from our embrace and I no longer had to crane my neck to look at him. "That's what I mean. I can't. You keep telling me to stop and I can't. I don't feel compelled to."

As his eyes went wide I went back to the abandoned mansion where I'd almost lost my life. I had whispered something before it all went dark. But it had been in English, and English didn't work with my power.

Let alone the fact I wasn't a strong enough szeptun to free anyone from an ancient demonic spell.

"Give me an order," he said, with wide eyes and the beginnings of a smile.

If this was real, if I had freed him with my whisper. What would that mean for our partnership? Was he going to abandon me? Was he going to run away with his family?

Was he going to hurt me?

"Shut up," I told him.

He shook his head. "No. It doesn't work. Give me another."

"Sit down."

Again, he shook his head, his smile deepening with every failing order.

I should be happy for him. He wanted to be free and deserved it, especially after everything Heimdall put him through. And yet, I couldn't help but feel sad.

"Kiss me," I whispered.

Sad, because now he didn't need to be with me. He didn't need to stay, or protect me, or love me.

He snatched me by the neck with both hands and crushed me to him. A tingle buzzed in my head, warm and overwhelming.

Maybe it hadn't worked. Maybe he was still bound to me. Maybe there was still a chance...

"I wanted to do that," he said, when he let go. "I'm free. I'm free, my Helfire."

He practically danced around the table, laughing, grabbing his kids' faces and shaking them.

"That's great, Dad. Now calm the fuck down," Fenrir told him. "You're giving me a headache."

Loki stopped and glared at his son. "But, Fenrir, I'm free. After thousands of years I'm finally free." He looked up at me and his smile disappeared. "How exactly am I free?"

I shrugged. "I wanted to set you free before I died. I guess I whispered it true."

"That's impossible. That's crazy. That shouldn't work," Loki said.

"Neither should my healing whisperings, but they did," I said, although that I could attribute to something.

"What the everloving fuck happened to you while you were gone?" Saskia asked.

"I wish I knew. I just...It happened before I even saw my parents—" I glanced around the room, trying to find an explanation.

"You saw Igor and Krystyna?" Saskia asked.

"Yeah. And Oliwia."

Saskia jumped off the coffee table and ran to stand by my feet. When she looked at me again, her eyes were big and shiny.

"You saw Oliwia? H-how? Is she okay? Are they... are they okay?" Her voice was strange. Off.

It was human.

She missed them just as much as I did, even if she hid it very well most times.

"They're okay," I said. "I mean, they're dead, but they're okay."

"How? What happened?"

"I don't know how. Heimdall stabbed me and when I closed my eyes I was with them, at home. Mom had made a pork roast."

Saskia licked her nose.

"I know." Hela raised her hand.

I glanced at her and her shimmering green eyes and I remembered seeing the same glow in them when I came to after I'd woken up.

"Of course," I said.

She was the goddess of death after all.

"You were on the brink, so I thought seeing them would help you make your decision." Hela looked over her shoulder and smiled. "They said they're proud of you."

"You can talk to them?" I asked before I realized what a stupid thing I'd said. "Can you tell them I'm sorry I didn't stay?" Hela opened her mouth. "Tell them I'll get the bastard who did this to them."

Hela hugged her cup and a sad smile crossed her face. "They know," she said. "They're saying they want you to move on."

I shook my head. "Not before we find him." I turned to Loki and took a deep breath, afraid of his answer. "I know you're free now, but...will you still help me?"

Loki let out a long, deep breath and his shoulders sagged. "That's what I needed to talk to you about," he said, taking my hands in his.

It was already happening. He was already doing it.

Fuck, why hadn't he left while I was asleep? Why did he have to wait for me to wake up to break my heart?

"Please, Loki. I know you're a free man now, but... please do this for me. That's the last thing I'll ever ask of you. Please help me and then you'll never have to see me ever again."

He shook his head and cupped my face.

"Tomasz, I'd never—" he started but I couldn't face it.

I couldn't face the rejection.

"Fenrir, will you help me, please? Will you find the wolf who killed them? I know you don't have to do shit for me, any of you but I'm begging you."

Fenrir glared at his father before he turned to me.

"Of course, Tomasz. You don't have to beg. And just call me Finn."

I nearly choked the man when I wrapped my arms around him but I didn't care.

I couldn't blame Loki. I'd been his master, I'd enslaved him and used him for my own objectives. He didn't owe me shit, but...then again, I thought we had something. When he kissed me...when he fucked me... it felt like it meant something.

Maybe it was just an order and that was all it had been for him.

"Tomasz," Loki said.

I didn't need his rejection right now. I didn't want to have to deal with it or what it meant for everything that had happened between us.

But even if I avoided his gaze, he still forced me to watch him.

He stroked my cheek with his thumb and touched his forehead to mine with tears in his eyes.

"Of course, I'll help you. I'll always help you," he whispered.

He looked into my eyes and my heart skipped a beat.

"I'll never betray you ever again."

Maybe it hadn't all been a lie. Maybe it wasn't all fake. Maybe he did like me after all.

And he was a free man.

Didn't promises mean more that way?

LOKI

I couldn't stand it.

I couldn't stand what I'd done to him.

There was nothing I wanted more than to tell him the truth, but the way he looked at me when he thought I'd abandon him made me sick.

It made my insides turn. And my mind come up with all the worst case scenarios possible.

I didn't think he could handle it.

If he knew, he'd never forgive me.

And he'd soon find out the tale I'd woven to get what I wanted.

Oh, how things fast things changed. Only a few days ago I wanted to be free of him no matter the cost and now I wasn't ready to pay it.

"Are you sure we can leave her here all alone?" Tomasz asked me after he got washed and dressed, fresh as ever.

Not that his level of cleanliness would ever alter how beautiful he was.

There was just something about him being all free of blood and dirt and dressed for the night that looked so good on him.

It made him look different.

The ripped blue jeans, the roll-neck black sweater, tucked in to show the silver shiny belt buckle. The leather brown bomber jacket with the matching shoes.

It was as if he'd jumped straight out of a fashion magazine.

But that wasn't it. That wasn't all, at least.

It was the way he carried himself in those clothes.

The way he carried himself, full stop.

If he'd been confident after I fucked him, he looked fierce now. Like a flower in full bloom.

It was a sight to behold. Tomasz dripping with power. It was sheer joy.

A joy I was going to rob him of, sooner or later.

"Tomasz, I'm not really alone. Elsa is here with me," Hela replied to him.

Apparently, I'd been too busy staring.

"I know. But it still feels wrong," Tomasz said.

Hela patted his hand and smiled.

"I've got a lot of catching up to do, and Elsa is willing to teach me everything she knows. I'll be more than okay. But you guys be careful."

"Always careful, sis," Fenrir told her, punching her arm teasingly.

"I know you are. I was talking about Father. I can't trust him not to screw everything up," she answered.

"Again," said Fenrir.

Tomasz laughed. I didn't.

My children had every right to be distrustful of me. I hadn't exactly been a god to revere in my life.

I just hoped they'd believe me when they found out what I'd done and when I told them I regretted it.

"Let's go," I huffed in response.

There was no point lying to them. They could tell. They could always tell.

"So, what have you guys been up to while I was sleeping away like Sleeping Beauty?" Tomasz asked once we were both on the train to Ealing.

The train that took me closer to rejection and pain.

Damn it. This should be my time.

Freedom was everything I'd craved for all my existence. Why did it mean so little now I had it?

Because I'm about to lose Tomasz.

I'd fallen in love with all my masters in the past, to my detriment. I'd put my faith and trust in them. And they'd all used me the same way Heimdall had used me.

After the way they'd treated me, I wouldn't care about losing them. In fact, I'd kill them with my own hands if time hadn't already gotten to them already.

But with Tomasz, things were different. He kept his word. Not only did he keep it, he'd even let me go before I did his bidding.

Just like that, he'd given me the thing I'd craved my entire life. And he didn't demand anything in return.

Instead, he'd asked.

How great was it to be asked and not told.

"Nothing really." Fenrir answered, stroking the cat on his lap. Saskia appeared more than pleased. "Other than eat a lot and drink a lot. Pizza is my new favorite food, by the way. Why didn't we have pizza in Asgard?"

I shrugged. "Don't ask me. Ask Odin."

Tomasz laughed. A few passengers gave us weird looks, but neither Fenrir or Tomasz paid them any mind.

"Wait til you try Thai. It will blow your mind," Tomasz said, mimicking an explosion with his hand next to his head.

"I'll hold you to that." Fenrir winked at him.

Tomasz smiled before he rolled his eyes at Saskia and turned to me. He offered me his hand and as he tangled our fingers together I felt like the biggest wretch in the world. And I was.

He was at so much more at ease around Fenrir. Around both my children. So relaxed next to me.

He had no reason to be suspicious. No reason to be on edge. I was free after all and I was still here. That was what he thought.

And it was true.

But I was not ready for him to turn on me when he found out the truth.

A truth we were getting closer to with every moment.

Every moment we rode on the train and every moment we walked toward Tomasz's family home.

"Now we suspect the wolf used Wolfshadow to mask his scent, but your dad said you could still track him." Tomasz turned the key and entered the house, letting us both through.

Fenrir nodded and moved ahead of us. Saskia ran after him.

"Are you okay?" Tomasz whispered.

No. I was not. I was not okay. Fenrir was about to turn up with nothing and I was about to piss off three people I loved. And a cat.

At least I wouldn't be able to hear Saskia's disappointment.

"Yeah," I lied.

Even if I didn't want to, what was I supposed to say?

No, I'm actually feeling like shit because I fed you lies to get what I want?

I may have liked a little bit of domination with my orgasm, but I wasn't a glutton for punishment.

I stroked his cheek with my thumb and gazed into the wonderful gold specks in his eyes. They seemed brighter.

His gaze, his skin, his entire being sizzled with magic. I helped build that. My cum had given him more confidence, and seeing his family again offered him the last bit of the puzzle he'd been missing to come to his full potential. He wasn't a boy anymore, even though he'd always be one to me. I was so much older than him. And yet I was the blithering idiot.

Me. The thousands-of-years-old god.

He looked back at me with tenderness, and affection. I didn't deserve it. I didn't deserve him.

"Have I told you I adore you?" I asked him.

Because I did. Of course I did.

From the first moment I'd set eyes on him I'd thought he'd looked divine, even if I'd tried to kill him.

And his beauty had only grown the more time I'd spent with him, the more I got to know him and the more I knocked down those silly ideas he'd convinced himself of.

Ideas that he was worthless, useless and loveless.

"Awww, I adore you too." The thrill in his tone made the weight in my heart heavier.

"No, you don't," I said.

He grimaced. "Yeah, I do."

"Well, you shouldn't. I don't deserve it."

Tomasz shook his head and rose onto his toes, lifted his chin and put his lips to mine.

They tasted bittersweet but I didn't deny them. I didn't have the power to.

"If you don't deserve me than I'm doomed because I don't deserve you," he said.

I put my other hand up to his face and held him

tight and close. "Never say that again," I thundered. "Never."

Tomasz nodded and licked his bottom lip before I caught it with my teeth and sucked on it like a hungry, starved man.

I didn't know how much longer I'd be able to do that. I needed something to remember him by when all this was over.

A meow broke the intense silence between us and Tomasz pulled away.

Saskia stood at the other end of the room, staring.

"What did she say?"

"Finn found something."

He had?

How?

Tomasz rushed after Saskia and I followed them into the kitchen where the atrocity had been committed.

Fenrir was crouched in the middle of the room and turned to us as soon as we entered.

"I've got a scent. Follow me," was all he said before his face stretched, his body contorted, his back bent. Bones cracked, flesh ripped and out of the excruciating pain, an ebony wolf, seven-feet-tall, stood before us.

He snapped his jaws and dashed out of the kitchen, into the hallway, out of the house, running into the night.

"That didn't look fun," Tomasz panted, running next to me.

"Yeah, familiars have it easy."

As gods, we didn't.

Saskia held on to Fenrir's wolf form for dear life as he cut through roads, streets, and people. I worked my magic, but there was only so much it could hide when he caused cars to swerve and people to fly across the pavement.

"You know he could have offered to give us a ride too," Tomasz said.

"I'm surprised he lets Saskia ride him. He's very sensitive about who he lets on his back."

"Don't tell Sass she's special. I won't hear the end of it."

I laughed and nodded in agreement.

We kept running, but after a while, even I ran out of breath.

"Hey, big guy! Think of the little-legged people over here," Tomasz shouted at Fenrir, trying to desperately catch his breath. "What's the obsession with these animals to run across London? Have they never heard of the tube? Or buses? Hell, I'd even get a black cab."

And get a black cab, we did.

Tomasz hailed one and I compelled the driver to follow my manic son through the streets of London because once he went hot on a trail, he wouldn't stop even if the world was ending.

We got all the way to Central London, and we ditched the cab to follow him into the alleys of Soho.

Until he stopped in front of a narrow shopfront

on Bateman Street. A neon sign flickered above the door and graffiti covered most of the glass which made it impossible to see inside.

The sound of Fenrir's bones cracking and repairing themselves echoed across the street as my son returned to his human form and looked up at the tattoo parlor called Bewitchink.

"This is it," he said.

"This is what?" I asked.

"The wolf that killed his family. He's here," Fenrir said.

"He is?"

What was happening? Was Fenrir playing tricks on me? He had learned from the best, but this was not the time.

Had he somehow found out that I lied?

"Are you doubting my skills, Dad?" Fenrir asked me, crossing his arms.

I shook my hand with some hesitation as Tomasz took a deep breath.

"This is it, then," he said.

"After you," Fenrir told him. "We'll be right behind you."

Tomasz pushed the door and walked into the brightly lit tattoo parlor that smelled of patchouli and blood, and a bell rang above us.

There was a glass-topped desk with a computer and several books spread out, a couple of them open to pages with intricate colorful designs. A small couch and an even smaller coffee table with a used coffee mug and a dirty ashtray completed the waiting area.

"In the back," shouted someone from behind the graffitied wall.

Tomasz wasted no time.

I rushed behind him and found a young blond man sitting on a chair with a buzzing tattoo pen in his hand, and his other forearm exposed and slick. The blue outline of a thorned rose turned into a beautiful red rose from where his pen had already touched it.

"Sorry. I tend to draw on myself between appointments. How can I help?" he asked us with a big smile.

A whiff of something strange made me wince, but it was neither the blood nor the patchouli permeating the space.

In fact, I didn't think it was a smell at all. It was something else.

Tomasz's chest rose and fell beside me as his breath got heavier and heavier.

"Did you kill my parents?" he asked, barely audible.

The blond man winced. "What did you say?" He leaned forward, turning his ear toward us. "Sorry, you'll have to speak up. I'm not a great lip-reader and I'm hard of hearing."

I turned to Fenrir who was standing a few feet behind me next to Saskia. "Did you say a wolf killed his family?"

He nodded. "Isn't that what you saw with the echo spell?"

The echo spell.

Maybe I shouldn't have fucked with that spell.

"Are you sure?" I whispered.

Fenrir grimaced. "What are you talking about? There was a wolf scent covered by Wolfshadow in that house. I just followed it like you told me."

There...

There had been a wolf scent?

Then that meant the man in front of us had...

He had killed Tomasz's parents.

"He said, did you kill his family!" I cut across the room and grabbed him by the collar.

An inhumane snarl escaped me as I held the man in my hands and I had to fight the urge to snap his neck right there and then.

I couldn't.

Not until Tomasz got his answers.

"Put me down!" the artist shouted.

He dropped his pen and tightened his hands around mine, his feet dangling in the air.

"Don't worry. I will!" I roared.

"You killed my family. Why? Who are you?" Tomasz appeared beside me and glared at the man.

"Answer his question," I told the guy.

His eyes were a striking turquoise that reminded me of someone, but I couldn't figure out who. But it was definitely someone I'd met before.

"And I said...*spinae*!" he growled.

The ink on his neck, the edges of his face, his arms, glowed. Before I could examine what it was, there was a scratching sound and my hands exploded into a million pieces.

LOKI

I fell back, dropping the man. An excruciating pain overtook my body for a long, hard moment and when I looked at my hands I realized they hadn't exploded. However, I had about a hundred spots blood was dripping from.

It was as if he'd...

Looking up at him confirmed my suspicion.

Millions of thorns protruded from his body in different colors, turning his body spiky.

Spinae. Latin for thorns.

He'd cast a spell.

The strange sense I'd gotten when I'd first walked into the shop suddenly made sense. It wasn't the blood or the patchouli that made my hairs stand on edge. It was energy. Magic. Magic in the ink. Both in the bottles on display around the room, and on his skin.

The little fucker had found a way to turn spells into ink, essentially turning his body into a spellbook.

If I hadn't been so angry and in pain, I'd have been impressed.

"Who are you people?" he asked, taking several steps back until he hit the mirror on the wall.

"You don't know me?" Tomasz shouted. "I'm the guy whose family you killed! You filthy monster!"

"What? I didn't kill your family. I don't even know you."

"Exactly. What did they do to you? Huh? What could they have possibly done to deserve death?"

"Tomasz—" Fenrir made an attempt but Tomasz screamed and punched the man's face.

The blond's head crashed back, cracking the mirror behind him and he yelped.

"You are crazy. What the fuck is wrong with you?" he said, holding a hand to his bloody nose.

It was quite the sight to behold. Witnessing the damage Tomasz had inflicted. The blood, the mirror shattering in the shape of a halo. The tears in the tattoo artist's eyes.

"The next one won't be so gentle." I closed my bloodied fists and stepped closer to the young man. "Now speak. We know you're the wolf who killed the Nowaks."

"The-the wolf? I'm not a fucking wolf!" the man shouted.

"Yeah, right." I pulled my hand back and towered

over him, watching his eyes go big and wide staring at my fist.

"Stop!" Fenrir shouted behind us. "He's telling the truth."

"You said you smelled the wolf here," I growled, not turning away from the blond.

"I did, but he doesn't smell like him. He's not your wolf," Fenrir said, his reflection in the mirror approaching behind me.

"I'm not a wolf, full stop. I'm a witch," the guy said with a trembling voice.

I relaxed my fist and eased off him as I looked into my son's eyes in the cracked mirror.

"If not him, who? Who else is here?"

Fenrir shook his head. "No one."

"Are you sure you're not still catching up with your host? You've never had this problem before," I said.

It was possible he was still weak from waking up in his new body. Technically he'd been in it for three years, but being trapped in the Bifröst he hadn't been able to use it, or meet the host's soul.

"I'm sure. Okay."

Of course the more likely explanation was that it was all my fault.

I'd lied and misled Tomasz and Fenrir had misled us because of it.

"Ma-maybe you're looking for Austin," the guy said.

"Who the fuck is Austin?" Tomasz asked.

"He...he's my ex. He came to pick up his shit today. He's a wolf."

He was?

That was convenient.

"And how do I know you're telling the truth?" I started to wrap my hand around his neck when I remembered the fucking prickles around it, so instead I covered his mouth and nose.

"Stop it, Dad," Fenrir said.

"He's lying," I said. "You might be able to smell wolves, but I can smell a liar a mile away."

It was in my blood.

The man sucked desperately for some air, but all he did was tighten the hold I had over him.

"Dad!"

Tomasz put his hand up to my back with a delicate touch and searched for my gaze.

I didn't deserve his touch. I didn't deserve his gaze. I didn't deserve his anything.

"Let him go. Listen to your son," he said.

"But—"

"If he's lying, we'll find out and deal with him appropriately."

He was right.

But as much as I wanted to listen to him, I couldn't just let go of the guy. I wanted to, but I couldn't. It was hard. Almost impossible.

I had to fight with everything I had to breathe again, let alone let go.

But I did and when I managed it, the man fell to the floor, gasping.

"*Uzdrowić.   Uzdrowić.   Uzdrowić,*"   Tomasz whispered.

The pain dissolved from my hands and my thumping heart eased.

I sat on one of the chairs and watched Tomasz help the blond guy to his feet. His skin had turned normal again, although some of the ink he'd had before was missing.

"I'm sorry about the nose." Tomasz offered him some tissue and the man didn't even flinch when he wiped his nose.

My little whisperer had healed him too, even though he probably didn't deserve it.

"Want to tell me who the hell are you people?"

Tomasz introduced himself and told his story while Saskia sat in his lap for emotional support. I wouldn't have put so much faith in the tattoo artist, but I could always torture him with my illusions if he tried to betray Tomasz's trust.

Too bad I couldn't do the same to myself.

"Does that sound like something your boyfriend would do?" Tomasz held one hand in the other as he watched the artist with way too much hope.

"Ex-boyfriend. And there's a reason I dumped him. A few months ago he was kicked out of his pack.

They took his rank, his job, everything. I don't know why. He wouldn't tell me. 'Pack business,' was his excuse every time I prodded. He became a waste of space. He'd got out and not come back for days on end. And then he wouldn't tell me where he'd been or what he'd done."

"Do you think he could do something so bad?" Tomasz asked.

The man shrugged. "No. Yes. I don't know. He's a wolf, isn't he? They all have it in them. No offense." He turned to Fenrir.

"Oh none taken. I'm not a wolf," Fenrir answered him.

The man frowned but didn't ask any further questions that were as clear on his face as his tattoos.

"Do you know where we can find him?" Tomasz asked.

"I'll track him," Fenrir offered.

"Yeah, that worked out last time," I snapped at him.

"Kindly, Dad, fuck off."

"Wait, they're father and son?" The man asked and Tomasz laughed.

Saskia gave a long meow but as usual my Tomasz didn't care to translate.

"It's a long story."

The guy nodded.

"I don't know where he lives now. He got kicked out of his apartment when the pack sent him packing

and he was living with me until I broke up with him.
But..." He paused. "He did leave his hat behind. Do
you think you can track him with it?" He asked
Fenrir.

My son crossed his arms and pouted instead of
answering.

The tattoo artist got up and walked to the front of
the parlor.

"Don't even try it, princess," I warned him.

He stopped, grimaced and shook his head, disappearing behind the wall and returning with a black
beanie hat.

"You're going to kill him, aren't you?" he asked
me, turning the hat in hands.

"It's up to him." I glanced at Tomasz.

The guy took a deep breath and pursed his lips.

I was already sick of his pleas and he hadn't even
started begging us to spare his ex's life.

"Good. Tell him Sandro sent you. I want him to
know it was me."

"I thought you loved him?" Tomasz asked.

Sandro offered him the hat. "I did. Until he killed
my dog."

Their hands connected and Sandro gasped. Saskia
jumped off Tomasz as if her fur was on fire.

The blond man turned dark in front of us. His hair
and his eyes went black and his skin gray.

I sprung up. Tomasz looked at the ghoulish man in
front of him with wide eyes.

"*You're gonna die! You're gonna die soon!*" Sandro said in a voice as terrifying as his appearance.

I snatched him by the neck and pulled him back, away from Tomasz and pinned him against the wall.

Instantly his hair returned to its bright color and his eyes became blue again. Even his skin became rosy pink again, but despite that he looked horrified.

I didn't know why. But no one threatened my Tomasz. No one.

He was going to find out what real horror was like.

"I told you not to try anything!" I snarled.

"I'm sorry. I'm sorry," Sandro cried.

"Tomasz, are you okay?"

"I didn't hurt him. I swear. It's just my power. I can't control it."

Tomasz appeared by my side and cocked his head.

"Wha-what is your power?"

He put his hand around my wrist and pulled it away from Sandro's neck.

"I...I can sense people's death." Sandro rubbed his neck when I let go. "I know it looks scary, but it's just... how it works. I touch someone, I turn into this stupid zombie and I can sense their death."

"That's unique," Fenrir mumbled behind me.

Who did he remind me of?

I was sure he reminded me of someone. Especially now I'd seen his ghoulish form.

"That's cool," Tomasz said.

Sandro shook his head.

"Believe me. It's not. I sense your death, Tomasz. You're going to die," he said.

"What did you say to him?" I pushed the man back into the wall.

"Loki, stop! What's gotten into you?" Tomasz said. "Did you say I was going to die?"

Sandro nodded and I wanted to push him again, to wrap my hands around his neck and snap it like a twig.

How dare he say that to my Tomasz?

"I'm afraid you're a little too late. I already died and came back. Well, almost."

Sandro frowned.

"Tha-that's not...I've never sensed someone's death after it happened before," he said. "But then again, I've never met someone who died before."

Tomasz smiled at Sandro and whispered him some healing before we left the parlor.

But not before Tomasz told Sandro he'd pick up the bill for the damage we'd caused and they exchanged numbers.

"Can you tell me what's wrong with you? You're acting weird. You've been acting weird all day," he said as soon as we were out of Bewitchink.

"I'm not acting strange."

"Yeah, right," Fenrir huffed as Saskia sauntered to him with a yowl.

"You were so mean to Sandro. Even after he explained everything. And you've been on edge since we left home."

"No I haven't."

Tomasz put his hands on my face and pulled me down to him.

"Yes you have. What is it? You can tell me anything, you know that, right?"

I couldn't. I wanted to, but I couldn't. Not this.

"If I do, I'll lose you," I told him in spite of my best interests.

"I can't ever imagine that happening. Just tell me."

"I can't. You'll hate me."

His grip tightened and he pressed his mouth to mine before he returned to staring up at me. "Tell me. That's an order," he whispered, reminding me of every moment we'd spent in his bed.

In the before times.

In the innocent times.

Oh, how I wish we were back in that bed and that I was still bound to him.

Being free and on the cusp of losing him hurt more than it should.

But I owed it to him.

I owed it to myself. To be honest for once in my life.

"I lied to you."

Tomasz smirked. "Which time?"

I deserved that.

"About...about the echo spell. I regretted casting it as soon as I saw the effect it had on you, but I couldn't stop it."

"Oh Loki, that's okay. It was thanks to that spell we've gotten this far." He nuzzled me. He still didn't get it. He didn't get how I'd betrayed him.

"No, Tomasz. I lied to you. I didn't cast a real echo spell. It was a lie. A fake. It was an illusion spell. I showed you what I wanted you to see."

"I don't understand." Tomasz eased from me and took a step back.

The absence of his body from mine already stung.

"I wanted you to believe a wolf had killed your family so you would think it crucial to find my son and save my children," I said, the words tasting bitter on my tongue.

Tomasz glanced at Fenrir before he turned back to me.

"But...why did he find a wolf? Did you lie too?"

"Fenrir didn't know. It wasn't his fault. That's the confusing part. I was scared to tell you Fenrir wouldn't smell anything, but he did."

"So Austin did kill my parents."

"Definitely," Fenrir said.

"Then, it all worked out," he said.

"Yeah, but...I lied to you." Never in my life had a lie felt so bad and admitting the truth felt so good. I wasn't born for truths.

"I know, Loki. You've lied to me before. Somehow it all worked out anyway. I guess Oliwia wasn't kidding when she said to embrace the chaos of my szept."

"But this one was different."

"How?"

I looked at my son then back to my Tomasz.

He wasn't going to be mine after this.

"Because. My plan was to fool you, find my children, free them and…"

"And?"

"And ask Fenrir to kill you so I could be free."

Tomasz's jaw dropped and the tears rolled down my cheeks.

What else could I say after this? What was there to say after you admitted to the man you love that you were planning his demise all along.

Laughter interrupted my depressing train of thought.

"You actually think I was going to kill your master for you?" Fenrir said.

I turned slowly toward him. He was doubled over laughing his guts out.

"Wouldn't you?" I asked.

"You wouldn't?" Tomasz asked at the same time.

Fenrir composed himself and took a deep breath. "Of course not. You were a better father after Heimdall bound you than you were before that. You were present. Predictable. Reliable."

"But he killed the elves after they tried to hurt you," Tomasz said. "How can you say that?"

"Is that what he told you?" Fenrir rolled his eyes. "He killed the elves because he wanted to. He just used us as an excuse."

"They tried to kill you!" I shouted.

How could he say that? How could he say that I used them as an excuse?

I may not have been an honest man, but I loved my children and that was the simple truth.

"One. One elf tried to kill us. And you killed the entire clan. Face it, Dad. You were deranged before Heimdall. I'm not saying he was a saint. What he did was wrong, but..."

"But what?" I asked. What was it that would justify enslavement to a man?

"You were blinded by rage. If he hadn't stopped you, you would have killed us all."

His words hurt.

I'd never harm my children. Everyone else, I wasn't so sure of, but Hela and Fenrir? I'd never lay a finger on them. They were my greatest achievement. The best parts of me.

"I'm sorry, Dad." Fenrir squeezed my shoulder, then grabbed the hat Tomasz was holding and walked away, sniffing it with Saskia following him like a shadow.

"Are you okay?" Tomasz asked, his hands wrapping around mine.

I flinched.

Why was he asking me that after everything I'd done?

"You must hate me."

Tomasz shook his head and touched my face again. "I don't. Don't say that."

"Well, don't you?"

"No. I don't hate you, Loki. I love you."

No, that wasn't true. That was impossible.

"After everything I just told you, after telling you I was planning on having you killed?"

He pulled back and held his hands wide.

This was it. It was happening. He was finally realizing.

"I'm here aren't I? We freed your son and I'm still here. You could have asked him to kill me. You could have asked Hela to let me die. You could have had either one of them kill me while I was asleep, but you didn't. Why?"

Maybe...

Maybe he had a point.

But I'd still lied. I'd done something wrong. And I was going to do worse things.

"Because I love you," I said.

Tomasz waved at people passing by.

"There it is, ladies and gentlemen. Thank you. Thank you. I know you were waiting a long time to hear it. So have I," he said, looking from one to another.

A few of them laughed, a few turned away and sped past us.

I'd never seen him like this. So open, so comfortable out in public.

"You-you're not mad at me?"

Hands on hips. Smirking. Blushing.

I'd missed those red cheeks.

"Why would I be mad that you love me? I love you too, you big, silly demon."

"You do?"

Tomasz rolled his eyes and grabbed my shirt, pulling me into his arms and his mouth.

His tongue slipped into a dance with mine and where he had tasted so bittersweet before, all I could taste now was him. Sweet, beautiful Tomasz.

He squeezed his hand around my nape and his other held my jaw. He deepened our kiss until its effect went straight to my groin.

He'd never been this dominant before. Maybe with his words but not with his lips.

My entire body came alight from something so simple as an earth-shattering kiss.

Who cared about Austin, and the murders, and anyone else when Tomasz was there open with his mouth and his soul, offering me the sweet dessert of forgiveness with a side of arousal?

I was panting when he pulled away. And I leaned in, chasing his lips as if they were my new master and I was the obedient pet.

"Does that answer your question?" he asked.

I nodded.

"Are you coming? Or do you need a moment in that alley? Maybe you'd prefer a bathroom? I hear they've got gloryholes galore," Fenrir said, snapping me back to reality.

Saskia's distinct meow colored the air as I huffed and glared at my son. Tomasz laughed, took my hand and we followed Fenrir's second attempt to find the wolf named Austin.

This time he didn't shift, but that didn't mean he kept a steady pace running through London.

He only slowed down when the familiar dome of St. Paul's Cathedral came within view.

And that was when Tomasz's phone rang.

He took it out of his pocket, read the screen and rejected the call.

But whoever it was, insisted.

"Agh, my gods! I need to block her. She's so annoying!" he groaned before he slid his finger across the screen and answered his aunt's call. "What is it, Ciocia?"

I watched him as his face sank.

"Are you okay? Ciocia, what happened? Where are you?"

He lowered his phone and looked ahead.

"What happened? Where is she?"

Tomasz kept blinking but was otherwise frozen still.

"She's at Java Jinx," he said. "She said she needs help. She sounded distressed."

We were just around the corner from Tomasz's work. Was that a coincidence?

Tomasz ran. Fenrir ran after him. When we got to Java Jinx they stopped and my son grimaced.

"I can smell the wolf in there," he said.

"Why would he take your aunt?"

"To finish what he started? Maybe he thinks she's got zawlanie."

I was sure I'd heard that word before, but if I had, it was thousands of years ago. I searched my mind for the memory but it didn't come to me.

"The question is," Tomasz continued. "What are they both doing here? Do you think Caleb or Lorelai are working with him?"

I shook my head even though I didn't know either of them that well. "Do you think they would?"

Tomasz panted. "I don't know why they would, but...I don't know what to think anymore."

"Well, only one way to find out," Fenrir said and pushed the door open.

As soon as he did, a static-blue energy surrounded him, taking his shape and raising him off the floor and dragging him deeper into the dark café.

"Finn!" Tomasz shouted, running after my son before I could stop him. Saskia yowled and did the same.

We didn't know what other kinds of traps were around.

They both crossed the threshold without a hitch. And the darkness of the shop encompassed them.

I had no other option but to follow him. To follow both of them.

Whatever was on the other side of that door, how much worse could it be than a pissed off, invincible Heimdall?

As the darkness encompassed me too, I saw Tomasz's aunt standing in front of a table with a bejeweled silver egg sitting in the middle of it.

A big brown wolf and a young girl with a pink bob stood on either side of her and Lorelai was behind them, strapped into a chair next to my immobilized son.

"Hello Tomasz," she said, and it finally made sense.

The thing that was so wrong about her when I met her for the first time. The thing that was so wrong now.

Other than the fact she was smiling, she didn't spark like other witches did.

Didn't she say she'd had a vision?

How could she have had one when there wasn't a fiber of magic left in her.

"Ciocia, what's going on?"

The aunt straightened her shoulders and breathed deeply. "What's going on is I'm tired of waiting. And would you, for the love of god, just call me Magda?"

TOMASZ

This picture was all wrong.

When my aunt had called me in distress I didn't expect to find her smiling at me and I didn't expect to find her with my family's heirloom in front of her.

What was Ciocia doing with the pisanka? What was she doing with the magical egg my family had been sworn to protect with their lives?

No, I must be missing some important facts. I'd missed some episodes, that was all.

Maybe she'd found the wolf who'd killed my family, or he'd tried to kill her and she'd taken him prisoner.

However, Lorelai being tied up behind her didn't support that theory.

"What do you mean? Tired of waiting for what? What's going on here? Who are these people?"

I felt Loki's big presence behind me and it offered me some comfort but my aunt's face knocked that right out of me.

Saskia stood between my legs. She was terribly quiet. I couldn't blame her.

Loki came into my field of vision.

"No! Don't take one more step." Ciocia wagged a finger. "I don't know who or what you are, but if you do anything out of line, they pay the price."

She pointed behind her, at Lorelai and Finn. Finn struggled to free himself from the webs of raw energy keeping him restrained, an entrapment spell if I ever saw one.

"Me? What could I possibly do?" Loki put his hands in the air with a chilled manner to his movements and shrugged. I didn't miss the glow of his golden eye, however.

But instead of finally getting to witness his illusions, the tricks he played on people, for the first time, he hissed, fell back and grabbed his head with both hands.

"What happened? What did you do?"

It was crazy I was asking that question to my aunt, but her smugness was undeniable.

Whatever was going on here was her doing.

"Really, Tomasz, I was hoping we'd be having this conversation with you trapped in the spell, but..." She shrugged and lifted a necklace between her fingers. It was a blue gemstone with an intricate golden design around it. "I knew there was something off when I came to see you. I knew my memories were...messy." She turned to Loki and pouted. "You didn't think I wouldn't come prepared, did you?"

"Ciocia, what's going on? What are you talking about? Prepared for what?"

"For the love of—my name is Magda. You and I both know you hate my guts so why even bother calling me Ciocia?"

I'd never seen this color on her. I had to admit, I didn't like it, but it seemed to suit her.

I was never a fan of my mom's sister, but she was family. You couldn't change your family. That had been ingrained in me since I was a baby. And it didn't matter that I didn't like her. She kept mostly out of our business.

"I don't hate you."

"Drop the pretense, will you? I've seen the way you look at me. The way you talk to me. The way you treat me."

I shook my head. She was wrong. She was beyond wrong. Yeah, I may have turned down her calls about the funerals but...

"What do you want? Why are you doing all this?"

"Is he stupid?" the girl next to my aunt said.

I glared at her.

"Isn't it obvious, Tomasz?"

"It is, but I'd like to believe this isn't what I think it is."

"Tomasz I don't like this," Saskia meowed.

I looked down at the table. The pisanka glimmered even in the dark.

I'd never really spent much time with it. I had no reason to. The magical egg belonged to my father until he passed away, or used it, in which case it would pass on to his first-born, Oliwia.

I had no business with the egg. I couldn't even use it because it didn't belong to me, but of course I knew how to activate it in case it ever became mine.

Being the only surviving szeptun of my family meant it now was.

The green and blue gemstones created beautiful patterns across the surface of the silver egg. It looked expensive, just like any Fabergé egg—the pisanka had been the inspiration for the imperial eggs, after all—but it held so much power.

World-shattering power.

It could grant its wielder one wish, whatever that was. Whether it was to restore someone's youth or change the very fabric of reality.

It was an incredible weapon for any szeptun or szeptucha, but that was exactly why our family burden was heavy and secret.

We'd been warned about its power since we'd been in nappies. Even though we had been tasked with using it and protecting it, we weren't supposed to be tempted by it. We were supposed to use it in conjunction with our whisper—to protect, to heal, not to harm.

"I'm afraid it is exactly what you think it is," Magda said.

I swallowed a knot in my throat. "How do you even know about it?" I asked.

"Does it matter, Tomasz? She took it," Saskia said.

I needed to know. I needed to be sure. Maybe I was stupid for not having connected the dots already, but I refused to believe she'd do this.

"I've always suspected." She cast a fleeting glance at my domowik between my feet. "I know the urban myths and Krystyna couldn't even look me in the eye whenever I broached the subject. She told me eventually."

I shook my head and struggled to breathe.

She was talking so casually, so nonchalant about it all, as if she wasn't even talking about her family.

"You killed them?" My voice trembled. My entire body trembled. I blinked away the tears, but it didn't work. "You killed them for a *fucking* egg?"

"An egg. That's...a pisanka, right?" Loki asked. "Is that the heirloom that was stolen from your parents' home?"

He was blurry when I looked at him. I couldn't clear my vision as much as I wanted to keep it together. I nodded.

He hadn't been the only one to lie. I'd kept that from him. We weren't supposed to tell anyone about it. I hoped he would understand that I'd lied, but it didn't surprise me he knew what it was.

"There are only like, two or three of them in the entire world," he said.

I didn't know how many there were. No one did. All the other szeptun families kept it a secret like they were supposed to. No one knew which families had been chosen to guard them. The pisanka in front of us could be the one and only for all anyone knew.

"We simply don't know. But I knew about this one," Magda said.

"That bitch killed Igor, Krys and Oliwia!" Saskia yowled.

"You killed your own sister, your own niece, for a fucking egg?" I whisper-shouted. I couldn't even raise my voice. I could barely use it the way everything inside me was strained and knotted.

"I didn't want to," she replied. "You think I didn't ask your stupid father to help me? You think I didn't beg? But they refused to help me."

"Bullshit!" Saskia shouted.

"I find it hard to believe Dad wouldn't help anyone, let alone family. There was nothing he wouldn't do for others."

"Other than use the pisanka, of course," she said.

"Of course he wouldn't. Do you know how powerful that thing is? Szeptuchas have gone their entire lives not using it because we're only supposed to use it for good. To bring peace. What could you possibly need that couldn't be achieved with a spell or a whisper?"

My aunt's face tightened. Her brows furrowed and the makings of a snarl appeared on her lips. "'Good'? 'Peace'? Those are all subjective. I don't believe for a second there haven't been whisperers in your line who didn't use it for what they thought was good or peaceful when it was all for personal gain. All I asked was for one thing. It would make no difference to him."

"Can I punch her yet? Please tell me I can punch her," Saskia said.

I felt the same energy coursing through me. "And the best next thing you could think of, was killing them? Why? Why would you kill your only family?"

"I didn't kill them, darling. He did." She pointed to the wolf beside her.

He bared his teeth.

"Austin, I presume," I said. "Does that mean you can sleep at night? Does that fact that someone else did your dirty work absolve you of your crime?"

I couldn't even believe I was chatting to her about killing my family—her family—as if it were gossip.

I should've been shouting, screaming, punching and kicking my way to her. But I was just...

Shocked.

Shocked that anyone would do that.

"You think it was easy? You think I wanted to?"

The shock quickly started to dissolve at the fake

solemnity in her expression, the fake sadness. Someone who regretted committing such an atrocity didn't lure their nephew into a trap.

"What could possibly be so important that you would ever kill your family for it?"

"My power, of course."

"What? What power? What are you talking about?"

"She's not a witch," Loki said beside me.

I glanced at him, confused yet again. "What are you talking about? Of course she is. She can see the future. Her gift is vision."

Loki shrugged.

I turned to my aunt. "What is he talking about? You've got your power."

"No," she said. "I don't. A demon stole it from me. They stole it from a lot of people. Like my dear Rita."

Magda stroked the girl's cheek. She leaned into my aunt's touch.

I'd never seen this Rita girl in my life, I had no idea who she was or what she was to my aunt.

"Like the rest of my coven. Our powers were stolen. Our magic was stolen. We have to rely on potions and proxy spells to do even the simplest things. That's what was so important. Our magic. It was stolen and your father refused to restore it."

"And the next logical step was sororicide?"

"I'm sick and tired of waiting for what's rightfully

mine. Do you know what it's like going three years without power?" she screamed.

I laughed.

I didn't even mean to, but that was what came out.

"Are you okay, sweetie?" Saskia asked.

"Tomasz?" Loki said.

"Three years without power?" I ignored them both. "Try a lifetime. I've spent my entire life unable to use my gift for its purpose. I didn't run around killing everyone. I'm guessing you'll kill me now too?"

Magda's eyes narrowed. "I don't have to. I tried to do this the easy way. That's why I sent Maxwell. He was supposed to get the zawlanie from you and he would have let you go, but your friend went and killed him."

"Oh I'm sorry he protected me from who we thought was responsible for my family's death!"

Magda looked away from me and bit her lip. She clenched the table until her knuckles went white.

"Are you gonna open this thing or what?" Rita crossed her hands and tapped her foot.

"Why? So you can kill me?"

"I don't want to kill you Tomasz," Magda said.

"Funny way of showing it." I glanced at Lorelai, at Finn. Even at Loki who stood beside me. He may not have been trapped or tied up, but if he wasn't jumping into action, that meant the necklace dangling from my aunt's neck was some serious business.

"All I want, is the zawlanie. I don't want any more death."

I bit my tongue at that.

She may not want death, but that didn't mean I didn't.

She'd killed everyone I ever loved. She'd taken the life of her own sister. Whatever bullshit she was spouting, I didn't believe her for a second.

"Of course, if I have to hurt you or everyone else, I will. You have no idea how much this means to me, Tomasz."

"I'm getting the idea."

"Let me kill her. Please let me do it." Saskia started to walk toward my aunt, but Austin growled at her.

"Stop," I told my domowik. I didn't want Austin to eat her. I knew she was invincible, but I wasn't willing to see how she'd come back to life after getting mauled.

And I didn't know what kind of power that necklace held.

She'd mentioned using proxy spells, which meant she must have a witch somewhere activating the spell so Magda could use it. There wasn't much use for proxy spells. They couldn't be used between witches and most humans didn't know about our existence to seek out proxies.

"I'll help you," I said. "I'll open the pisanka."

"What?" Saskia and Loki shouted.

I looked at both of them and shook my head, warning them not to do anything stupid.

I need to get closer. I needed to find out what kind of magic she had protecting her.

But when I attempted to approach her, the wolf snarled.

"That's close enough," Rita said.

I paid them no mind. I focused on my aunt and only my aunt. The woman who had the audacity to stand proudly and pretend she'd had no other choice.

"You know I need to whisper the zawlanie to the pisanka." I watched her study my face before she raised the necklace, nodding.

I put one foot in front of the other. How could I even not lose my balance, I didn't know, but I was grateful for it.

The closer to the table and her I got, the more my breath stilled, the anger and hatred swirling inside.

I stood in front of the magic egg and put my hands in my pockets as I leaned into the pisanka.

"Bullshit. Bullshit. Bullshit." My voice turned from whisper to a scream as I straightened and took the Hofund out of my coat pocket.

It grew to its full length in a flash and I took a swing at her. My aunt. The murderer.

It didn't even touch her. But the necklace caught on the blade and the chain snapped.

Austin snarled and jumped onto the table, towering over me.

Pain shot through my body. His teeth dug into my shoulder and I rose from the floor.

A blur of a man flew across the room and onto the beast whose mouth I was trapped in. Not just any man, it was Loki.

Veiny hands latched onto the matted brown fur. His face contorted, turning red. The growl that came out of him turned louder. A golden glow shone from his eye.

The wolf let go, snarling and snapping at air.

Time slowed to a halt as I floated toward the floor. The noise in the café was excruciating. The aroma of coffee replaced by the stench of danger and blood.

I fell on something soft as Loki threw the wolf across the room. He crashed into the floor-to-ceiling windows, smashing them and exposing us to London's evening chill.

Loki wasn't far behind Austin however. He landed on top of the wolf, ignoring the sputtering rain of glass. I felt the softness pulled from beneath me. I hadn't fallen on something soft. I'd fallen on my aunt. But I was focused on my demon who grabbed the wolf's jaws and split them apart.

The tear splintered over all the noise and a sharp yelp brought the silence back.

A boot stomped on my chest. A world of pain spread through my body. A scalding throb tore at my shoulder, pumping, pounding. Blood soaked my clothes and the floor underneath me.

"One more step..." Magda said, the silver blade of the Hofund ringing as it appeared at my throat.

Loki threw his hands up, panting. Magda held the necklace out in front of him with her other hand.

Great. Now what?

"Oh no you don't, bitch," Saskia yowled, jumping onto the counter as the shadows exploded around her.

"What the—" Magda started.

The shadows rose from the floor and wrapped around my aunt's legs, waist, hands, completely swallowing the necklace in the darkness of Saskia's power.

Loki leapt across the room and yanked the Hofund out of Magda's grasp. It turned into a dagger instantly. He flicked his arm back, throwing it at someone behind me.

I turned as Rita slumped to the floor, the Hofund wedged in the back of her head.

Loki seized Magda by the neck and the shadows around my aunt dissolved, the necklace no longer there, but shattered in pieces on the floor.

"Are you okay?" he asked, ignoring Magda.

His voice activated something in me, as if I'd been holding my breath and he reminded me to breathe.

I looked at my wound and the throbbing intensified.

"Nothing a little whispering won't fix," I told him and got to my feet after healing myself.

Saskia jumped onto my newly healed shoulder and hissed at Magda.

"Just tell me the word and she's dead," Loki told me, but my gut clenched.

This didn't feel right.

"What are you waiting for? Do it!" Saskia said.

My aunt's faint green eyes bore into mine as she thrashed in Loki's grip. She was just a shell of the woman from a few moments ago, the woman who had been so confident and calculated.

The woman before me now was terrified.

"No."

Looking into those almost-innocent eyes made me certain this wasn't right. It wasn't right at all.

"No? What do you mean no? If it wasn't for her, they'd all be alive," Saskia growled.

I shook my head and put my cat on the counter behind me.

"No, Saskia. I don't want Loki to kill her."

"Why?" a trace of a shadow appeared around her.

Saskia had never attacked me before, but I wouldn't have put it past her to do so now, only to hurt the woman who had killed her masters.

I walked away from her, toward the back. Lorelai and Finn watched me quietly. Not that either of them could say anything. One was gagged and the other was trapped in a spell.

It wasn't them I was interested in. Not yet.

I bent down, pulled the Hofund from Rita's head, and spun around to face my aunt.

"I want to do it," I said, the sword growing to its full glory.

Loki grimaced. "Are you sure?" he asked, putting my aunt down and holding her by the arms in front of me.

I watched the color return to her face and the arrogance in her eyes and reduced the distance between us.

"Tomasz? Let's be honest, you can't hurt a fly," she said.

I slashed.

Blood burst from her legs and she screamed.

"You're right. I can't hurt a fly. But I can hurt you, because you're worth less than one." I almost didn't recognize my own voice. It was so low and full of hatred. I'd never felt this way about anyone, but she... she deserved it. She deserved my full wrath.

I may not be able to hurt people with my whisper, but I would hurt her with my hands.

"Tomasz, I'm you aunt. I'm family." She was starting to realize there would be no mercy for her tonight.

"You didn't seem to care when you killed mine."

"I'm sorry," she cried. "I'm sorry. I wasn't thinking —I was being impulsive."

I slashed at her stomach. She screamed.

"You think that's going to save you after what you've done?"

I looked away. Bile poisoned my tongue. She was a monster. Was I going to become one if I did this?

I caught a glimpse of the pisanka. In all the chaos of the last few minutes, it had rolled under a chair on the front of the café. The glimmer of the stones mocked me.

"You know what's funny?" I asked her.

I turned to her again and she shook her head, gasping for air. Loki behind her watched me with a raised eyebrow and a pleased grin.

"It's quite ironic, actually. I wonder if the first szeptuchas knew it would come to bite us in the ass one day."

Magda's whole body convulsed, the blood draining from her faster than she could handle. I could heal her. I could heal her just like that. With a whisper.

But she didn't deserve such kindness.

"The zawlanie, the spellword, the word power, whatever you want to call it. The thing that opens that *stupid*, *fucking* egg...it's rodzina. Family." I looked into Loki's eyes and warmth fluttered in my chest.

Maybe I'd lost everyone, but he could be my rodzina. He could be my family from now on.

I slashed.

"You, Magda Pęk, aren't family anymore. You lost that right when you ordered the death of your sister, Krystyna Pęk. Of your brother-in-law, Igor Nowak. And of your niece, Oliwia Nowak."

I watched the life drain out of her leg, her stomach her neck, her mouth. I watched her crumble to the floor and shake until her eyes were as dead as her soul.

And then it lifted.

The weight that had settled over me the day I'd found everyone dead unraveled and soared, leaving me with nothing but grief and tears.

"You're okay. You're okay. You did well, Tomasz. You did great, my love." Loki's arms were around me before I even realized I'd collapsed to the ground, the Hofund feeling heavier than it had ever felt.

Saskia rubbed herself against my leg, purring, also reassuring me that I'd done the right thing.

I wasn't so sure.

I could take it back. I had the power to do so.

But...

I didn't want to.

She hadn't given them a chance, she hadn't shown them mercy, why should I?

"Put your hands up," someone said and I looked up to find a big, tall man standing outside, in front of the smashed glass and the dead wolf.

Whoever he was, he wasn't alone. There was an entire army of people behind him.

And within a second, they were all pointing their guns at us.

Loki

"We can explain," Tomasz said, his hands shooting straight into the air as the group of men and women in dark blue jumpsuits rushed into the café through the broken window.

The man in the lead took in the scene with a bright blue icy gaze. A dead wolf under a sheet of glass. A woman with pink hair turned bloody red. Another one sliced to pieces, bleeding on our very feet.

It didn't make for a particularly good plea case.

"This is my aunt," Tomasz said.

"And you thought you'd repay her by murdering her?" the man said.

"You don't understand. She killed my parents and sister. She made that wolf over—"

The man put his hand in the air, palm flat out, and lowered his voice. A golden pin of angel wings was visible on his lapel, as opposed to everyone else who had the Angel Guard logo printed on their jumpsuits. A symbol of rank, perhaps?

"Let me stop you right there. I'm not here to punish a dead woman for her alleged crimes. I'm here to investigate this one."

A grumble escaped my lips and gained me the attention of the lead Guardian Angel.

"This isn't a crime. This is retribution." I could barely contain the rage bubbling inside me.

How dare he suggest Tomasz was a criminal? How dare he talk to him like that? Didn't he know who Tomasz was? Didn't he know he was the kindest man in this world?

"Retribution is for judges," the man said.

"Since when do witches care for justice and judges?" I hissed.

The Guardian Angel didn't flinch, but he narrowed his eyes and moved his hand to his side, hovering over the gun strapped onto his utility belt.

"No one is exempt from justice," he said.

"And that's exactly what we got."

He didn't like my response. He grabbed the gun and pointed it at us like the rest of his team was. But he didn't shoot.

"I can get us out of this," I told Tomasz.

All it'd take was a little illusion here and there, a bit of compulsion, maybe a punch and a kick just for the fun of it, but we could be out of here in less than a minute and leave these fools to wonder what had happened at the café.

Tomasz looked up at me with his big, gray eyes and shook his head. "No, Loki. They're the good guys."

"I don't care about good guys. I care about you."

A sad smile crept up his face and he put his hand on my arm. "No, Loki. We can explain. We can tell them."

"Identify yourselves," the guy said.

Tomasz took a deep breath and turned his attention to the Guardian Angel, giving him his name. "I work here. Caleb knows me. He can vouch for me. Lorelai knows—" He pointed behind us, at the back, where the fox shifter and my son were still bound.

"Don't move!" the man shouted as soon as he noticed. "Guards!"

The armada of people wasted no time as they all marched into the café and blocked our exit.

"No, you don't understand. My aunt did this. She kidnapped Lorelai and Finn. We came here to stop her," Tomasz said, stretching his hands in front of him as if he could stop their imminent attack.

"You should have called us. You shouldn't have taken matters into your own hands. There are rules—laws—in place," the lead Guardian said.

"How? I didn't have the time. She was gonna kill us before you'd get—"

"Enough! Arrest them."

A few Guardian Angels lowered their weapons and ran toward us. This crap was getting out of hand.

But if they thought we'd go down without a fight, they were mistaken.

I stepped in front of Tomasz, pinning him to my back and my rage threatened to spill. I no longer wanted to contain it. All I needed was the word.

"Just tell me when," I told him.

"No. Stop it. No, Loki." Tomasz came out from behind me and the black cat on the counter yowled. "No, Saskia. All of you, stop. Let us at least explain."

"You can explain in custody," the man said.

Another man, a hairy little thing, snatched Tomasz's hands and pulled him from me.

"Oh no, you don't," I told the man who dared touch mine.

My fist collided with his face and he stumbled back as I dragged Tomasz back toward me.

There was a shot and I watched as a white crystal hurled toward me. The little gemstone shaped like a bullet crashed into my chest and exploded into white, crystalline dust. Its magic tickled me but if it was supposed to have any other effect, I never felt it.

Looking at the woman who'd fired and the confused expression on her face, that was not the expected result.

"You think your little spells are gonna hurt me?" I asked her.

"Loki, please don't—" Tomasz started when a

crystal bullet crashed onto his head and this time, when the dust erupted from the spell, a sparkling, glowing pair of handcuffs bound his wrists.

He winced and let out a pained hiss.

"What did you do to him?" I snatched the woman closest to me by the jumpsuit and yanked the gun out of her hands.

"Loki!" Tomasz said. "Don't. It's gonna be okay. We'll explain everything. Lorelai and Finn will vouch —" A pair of hands came down on him before he finished and dragged him back toward the broken window.

"No! Put him down!" I snarled.

The female officer flailed in my arms before she grabbed my hands and showed me her fangs.

"Stand down," the lead Guardian Angel shouted at me.

"Ouch!" Tomasz groaned and I lost it.

He fought to free himself from the grip of the Guardian who was pulling him away and he didn't seem to care if he was hurting my Tomasz.

All the rage I'd struggled to contain surged out of me.

I could take a lot of shit, but that, I couldn't.

I wouldn't.

"Make me," I growled and snapped the neck of the vampire in one smooth motion.

As expected everyone fired.

But I was done playing games. It was time for mischief.

The illusions soared through the room, drowning everyone before they even had the chance to figure out what was going on. Guardian Angels grabbed their throats, waved their hands, kicked their legs in desperate attempts to save themselves from drowning. I hopped from one to the other to finish the job and put them out of their misery. Soldiers fell around me like dominos and the more I killed the fuller I felt.

I'd missed this. I'd missed indulging.

Being bound to a master meant I only ever got to go on sprees whenever they felt like it, and it wasn't quite as much fun when it wasn't done by my own accord.

This was divine. This was exactly what I'd been born to do.

"Loki, no," Tomasz shouted.

My illusions wavered and those who were alive dropped to their knees coughing their guts out.

I searched for Tomasz.

He was outside in the cold dark alley. The man who had taken him prisoner stared at the events inside the café with wide eyes.

A silver-haired man appeared at their sides and dropped his jaw as soon as he looked inside.

Caleb. Tomasz's boss.

Was he going to blame him for all of this too? Were they going to pin everything on my little whisperer?

I'd love to see them try.

It had been a long time since I'd killed an empath and I couldn't wait to get my hands around his neck.

But it'd have to wait.

Something flew at my face and I lost my balance.

Bullets rained on me but I wasn't concerned with them. I was concerned with the flying furniture that followed them.

A man flicked his hands from the distance and chairs, tables, vases, they all directed themselves at me.

"I didn't say you could do that." I growled and ducked to avoid the small glass candle holder and glamored into a little girl, hopping from place to place to avoid it and everything that followed.

The bullets stopped and the telekinetic witch suspended the furniture in the air while everyone stared at me as a little innocent girl in a flowing dress.

It was so intoxicating seeing everyone so confused, so taken aback by my trickery. It wouldn't last long, that much I knew, but there was nothing more arresting than an innocent creature appearing from nowhere. Everyone wanted to protect a vulnerable child. No one wanted to harm a kid.

Which made my next move all the more satisfying.

"Where the hell did she come fr—" the telekinetic said when I stopped in front of him.

Before he could finish his sentence, I returned to my original form and slammed him against the wall.

He slithered to the floor, leaving a trail of blood on the hard surface.

The bullets started again.

"Loki, no. Loki!" Tomasz screamed, he shouted but I couldn't quite hear him anymore.

There was a certain energy, a certain taste to the air around me that made it impossible to focus on him and not the army of humans laid out before me, practically gifting me their lives.

With every life squashed, there were less and less magic bullets flying around, until there was only one. One person left inside the café.

The leader.

"How does it feel, leading them all to their deaths?" I asked him.

"Loki, you don't have to do this. Stop. Please stop." He was just background noise.

"You don't scare me," the man before me said.

I felt cold all of a sudden. Cold and alone. Someone whispered in my ear, but when I turned, there was no one there.

A phantom appeared before my eyes and disappeared, muttering incomprehensible words.

Something crawled up my legs. I jumped out of its grasp but it only followed me. Claws barely visible but clinging onto me regardless.

"What's wrong, wankface? Are you scared?"

I snapped my attention back to the man and I

recognized the crackle of magic around him, around the entire room.

He was causing this.

An illusion witch?

No, if it were illusions I wouldn't have fallen for it. This was different. This was something else.

His magic extended to the entire room. It bounced off the walls.

I didn't care much what it was, or how he was doing it. I thrust my own illusions back at him and he fell backwards.

"Winston," someone said from outside.

Another man—tall, dark and handsome—stepped through the window in a jumpsuit and ran toward the leader.

"No, Wade. Don't," Caleb warned him from outside. His eyes were teary but the love in his eyes was undeniable.

Ah, the sweet taste of love.

And I was about to crush it. It didn't get better than this.

"What did you do to him?" Wade said.

I raised an eyebrow and winked. "The same thing I'm gonna do to you."

I sent my illusions to get him. Snakes, bats, rats, whatever I could think of, would appear and attack him.

"Please, Loki." I caught Tomasz's voice.

Was he still begging? Couldn't he see how good this was? Couldn't he feel how great it felt?

It didn't matter if he could see or feel it. I could. And that was all that mattered.

I watched my illusions reach Wade and braced myself for the look of fear in his face. I was already salivating.

But the fear never came.

In fact my illusions never even touched him. They wavered inches away from him.

"Your tricks don't work on me," he said and stepped in front of Winston.

My illusions fell off him too.

"Fine." I huffed.

If illusions wouldn't cut it, punches it'd have to be.

I cut the distance between me and the Guardians and shoved my fist in Wade's stomach. Instead of him succumbing to the force, it was my hand that cracked.

I fell back, the pain shooting through my body like a lightning bolt.

"No. Stop. Please. Everyone, stop. Let me go," Tomasz shouted.

I inspected the damage on my hand and the pain renewed when I attempted to flex my fingers.

How the hell had he broken my fingers. What was he?

I threw the same fist back at him, needing an answer. Needing the suffering.

I couldn't help the groan that escaped my lips at

the impact, but neither could I miss the absolute lack of magic around him.

It was peculiar. There was magic everywhere, but none on him.

He was a nullifier. Magic ceased before it reached him.

"Just how many powers do you have?" Wade asked. "What are you?"

"Your worst enemy," I shouted.

Someone reached behind me. I didn't know how I hadn't heard them, or felt, or seen them before, but the *whoosh* of a weapon being drawn rang crystal-clear. I turned just in time to avoid a female Guardian with a sword in her hands—a curved blade that spat out sparkles when it clung to the floor.

I wrapped my good hand around the hilt and kicked her wrist, cracking it, but gaining command of her weapon, which I used to cut her neck open.

"Stop. Loki. No!"

Oh, when would he shut up?

I raised the sword over my head and struck down at Wade. Winston stepped in front of him and took the hit right in the center of his chest.

"No!" everyone screamed.

"Caleb get back," Wade said looking at the silver-haired empath who stepped through the glass crackling with magic.

My chest tightened and shivers ran down my spine. *This is the end. This is the end. This is the end.*

Everything was pointless. I'd killed so many people. There was remorse. No salvation.

This is the end.

Wait a damn minute.

Since when did I feel remorse?

I didn't. It was the witch. The empath. He was making me afraid. He was making me feel guilty.

Well, those tricks didn't work on me.

I pulled the sword out of the dead Guardian and swung it at Wade, buried under the weight of his dead fellow soldier.

He had no time to run, no time to duck, nowhere to go when the blade cut across his chest and gorgeous, beautiful blood poured out of him.

"You're going to pay for this," Caleb said, his face contorting as he sent more crap into my head, thinking it would do anything but bore me.

I closed my eyes, took a deep breath and cast out the voices telling me how bad I was. How evil I was. What a monster I was. How I deserved to die.

I ran toward him, clearing my head and pulling my hand back. I opened my eyes and drove the sword into...

Into...

Into Tomasz.

That was when the shadows wrapped around me and I fell into the darkness.

LOKI

"Tomasz! Tomasz! Oh god. What's going on? What the hell happened?"

"I-I found her, Caleb. I found her," Tomasz said.

Their voices were clear, but I could see nothing.

"Who? You found who?"

"My aunt. She killed them, Caleb. My aunt killed her own family."

Silence.

"Fuck," Caleb answered.

A meow.

"What's your cat doing here?"

"Let him go, Sass. He'd never hurt me," Tomasz mumbled.

There was a growl but the darkness was replaced by images.

Tomasz lying in Caleb's arms, the sword still in his

chest. Blood coming out of his mouth and wound. Caleb's hands stained with it. Saskia standing between me and them.

But my view was limited. And I realized why. My left eye was still in the shadows, covered by the cat's powers.

"Wait, your cat is doing that?" Caleb asked, staring at the domowik.

"She's not an ordinary...cat." He groaned and touched his ribs under the sword. "C-can you...can you do me a favor, Caleb. I know you probably h-hate me but—"

"What is it, sweetie? Tell me."

"Can you pull the sword out?"

Caleb shook his head.

"You'll bleed to death."

Tomasz tried to laugh, but instead coughed out blood.

"It wouldn't be the first time. Please?"

His boss sighed, but he dragged Tomasz and leaned him against a table leg before he stood in front of him and grabbed the sword's hilt. Tomasz was whispering before the blade was even out of his body and within seconds his wound had healed, to Caleb's bewilderment. He jumped to his feet and stood in front of Saskia. His eyes were bright and big and he was drenched in his own blood.

Yet again, he had ended up almost dying because of me. Because of what I'd done.

What had I done?

I didn't need to try to look around me to know the carnage I'd caused was entirely my doing.

I'd taken lives, so many lives and yet I didn't care about any of them. I cared about the life I almost took because I'd been blinded by my rage and thirst for chaos.

"Let him go, Saskia," he said. His eyes were heavy, his shoulders sagged and his breath measured.

I'd put that weight on him. I'd made him like this. Because of what I'd done.

"No. Don't let go," I said to Saskia.

I would love nothing more than to walk over to him, rub his cheeks, taste his lips, look into his beautiful eyes and get drunk on the golden specks in them, but I couldn't.

I didn't trust myself.

"What? Why not?" he asked.

I bit down a gulp of air and squeezed my eyes, forcing the tears away.

"Don't you see? I can't be trusted. I almost killed you."

Tomasz shook his head and stepped over Saskia, reaching for me.

"But you didn't."

I turned away. I didn't deserve to be doted on. I didn't deserve the kind of affection he was offering with his delicate hands, trying to cup my face.

"I could have. I probably would have. If Saskia hadn't stopped me..."

Who knew what I could have done?

"I couldn't hear you, Tomasz. I couldn't...obey you. I didn't care. You kept telling me to stop, and I...I liked it too much."

I couldn't even hear myself, so I don't know how he heard me, but he did.

"You liked what?"

"This. The taste of murder. It was like a game..."

"Does this look like a game to you?" Caleb shouted but I couldn't see where he was. He was out of my limited field of vision.

Besides, I didn't know if I would want to look at him even if I could.

Because he was right. Murder wasn't a game. Innocent lives weren't a game. And yet that was all they'd been only moments ago.

"Maybe I'm just a monster."

"No, don't say that," Tomasz said, grabbing me with both hands now. "You're not a monster."

His expression appeared genuine but I knew the truth. I knew what he thought of me. And even if he didn't, he should. I sure did.

"Tomasz, look around you. Look what I've done. I wanted to murder them all and I did."

My stomach turned at the memory of how much I'd indulged in it. In causing them anguish before I took the most precious thing they had.

"Maybe Heimdall was right."

Wasn't this thirst for blood inside me that had caused him to bind me?

Maybe his vision was right. Maybe I would have burned the world to the ground if he hadn't stopped me.

"Don't say that," Tomasz insisted.

"My Tomasz, you're so innocent. I don't deserve to be here. Kill me. Kill me now. It's the only way to be safe from me."

"Stop it—"

"I need to pay for my sins."

"What sins?" he asked.

He turned away and whispered something before he looked back at me.

"What sins?" he asked again.

Behind him a woman sat up. Another man patted his body. They should be dead. They were dead. And now they weren't.

"Oh my God, Wade! You're alive," Caleb screamed, still out of my field of vision.

They were back. They were alive again. He'd done it. He'd brought them all back to life.

My ears stung but the weight in my heart grew bigger, not smaller.

"That doesn't erase what I did. All my past sins."

The lead Guardian Angel, Winston walked into my peripheral and glared.

"No, Winston, stop. Leave him." Caleb appeared and pushed him back.

It didn't mean Winston stared any less. They were all staring. I could feel it even if I couldn't see all of it.

"Your past sins are in the past," Tomasz said, bringing my attention to him, to his touch. "And let's be fair. Some of your past sins aren't even your own."

"Perhaps..."

"Let him go, Saskia. And please just listen to us." He addressed the last part to Caleb and the Guardian Angels.

"No, Saskia. Don't," I told her.

"Why?" he asked.

"Because what if it happens again? What if someone says or does something, or tries to hurt you? I've waited all my life to be free and now that I am I don't want it. Not if it means hurting people. Not if it means I can't control myself. Not if it means putting you in harm's way."

Tomasz shook his head and his eyes glistened, even in the relative darkness of the café. "Don't talk that way. It was a bad moment. You'll work on yourself. You're out of practice, that's all. You've forgotten what self-control is like."

"I never had it in the first place. Why do you think Heimdall did what he did? I annihilated an entire clan of elves, Tomasz. I took countless lives because I was blinded by rage."

"That was then. This is now."

"And if you hadn't brought them back to life it would have been the same. They'd have sent more people after me and I would have killed all of them. I would have annihilated everyone."

The more we talked about it, the clearer my thoughts and my head got, the more obvious it was becoming. Maybe I was never meant to be free. Maybe I was always supposed to be bound. Maybe my name wasn't meaningless and I really needed to be locked up, to be tied to someone.

"Will you kill me?" I looked him in the eyes and begged. "I want it to be you."

"No!"

"Please. There's no other option."

"There must be. Don't say this is the only way. I don't believe it. I refuse to believe it."

"You can't let me go, Tomasz. I'll kill again." Someone behind him moved toward us. "It's not a threat. It's a warning. I know myself. I thought it wouldn't matter, but..." Staring into Tomasz's eyes, I couldn't withhold my tears. I might be the same demon I'd been thousands of years ago, but I'd never wanted to be different until I'd met him. "But you. I want it to matter. For you. But I don't think I can do it of my own free will. That's why you have to kill me."

"Loki, look at me." I did. "I'm not killing you. No one is. If anyone is going to pay for their crimes, that's me. I invoked you. I forced you to work for me. This is all my fault."

And yet it had been me who caused carnage. Who killed without thought or hesitation.

"Tomasz," I whispered. "There's no other way. Maybe if there was a way to bind me again, but there isn't—"

"You'd do that?" he asked. "You'd bind yourself to someone after everything you've been through?"

I looked into his eyes and I couldn't believe I was saying that but...

"I would. I'd bind myself to you."

Only him. He'd been the only master who had freed me. The only one who saw the good in me. The only one who loved me.

"Are you sure?" he asked.

"Does it matter?" I looked at all the faces in the room, their expressions, their need for retaliation. If only I could make them forget what I'd put them through. If only I could make them see me not as a murderer but the pathetic excuse of a demon I was.

"It does," Tomasz answered.

I turned back to him and nodded. "I would in an instant."

Tomasz took a deep breath and addressed Winston. "If I bind him to me, he will only do what I say. If I do that, will you agree to pardon his transgression?"

"If by transgression you mean killing us—" one of the Guardian Angels said.

"Doing that will mean he will be your own

weapon of mass destruction. How is that any better?" Winston asked him.

Caleb crossed his arms and sighed. "Come on, Winston. I'm a weapon of mass destruction and I'm not behind bars," he said.

"There's a difference. I trust you and my brother to keep you under control," Winston replied.

So Wade was his brother.

"I've known Tomasz for a year and a half and he hasn't hurt a fly. You can trust him."

Winston huffed.

"Then you can trust me. I vouch for him. I never even heard Tomasz raise his voice until his family was killed. He wouldn't hurt a fly."

I didn't even know what it mattered. Why they were arguing. There was no way to bind myself to Tomasz so what was the point of this debate?

"I'm not happy about this," Winston said after what felt like forever.

I didn't even know why Caleb was helping us, or vouching for us. I'd killed his boyfriend. All his friends. It didn't make sense.

"Thank you." Tomasz dropped to the floor and when he stood back up, he was holding the bejeweled egg.

"What are you doing?"

"Do you really want to be bound to me?" he asked.

Again and again I gave him the same answer. There was nothing I wouldn't do for him. Nothing I wouldn't do if it meant I got to see his beautiful eyes every day of my existence.

"I do. I want this."

"And you won't hate me like you did Heimdall?"

I shook my head. This wasn't the same at all. Heimdall hadn't asked. It'd been his choice.

"It's *my* choice now."

Tomasz pursed his lips into a sad smile and looked down at the pisanka. "*Rodzina. Rodzina. Rodzina,*" he whispered.

A mechanical sound whirred as the pisanka parted into three pieces, opening like a flower, revealing the core. It was a silver bottle with a green liquid floating inside.

Tomasz took the bottle out and leaned into me. He removed the cross-shaped lid and touched the rim to my lips. He paused. "Are you sure?"

"I'm sure," There was no question, nor doubt in my answer. If free meant no Tomasz, then I didn't want to be free ever again. "I want to be your rodzina, my little szeptun. If you want."

Tomasz smiled. He tipped the bottle and the liquid wetted my tongue. It tasted thick, sweet and opulent. And ancient.

"Then make your wish, my Loki, my rodzina."

I did. I wished for Tomasz to be my master and I his willing servant. To be bound to him and only him. No sword this time, nothing between us. Just me and him. My master.

I could still feel his touch when he let go the same way I could still taste the old potion from within the pisanka. There was an explosion of magic inside me reaching from the tips of my toes to the follicles on my head, a coolness settling under my skin, hugging me tightly.

"How do you feel?" Tomasz asked.

The same way I'd felt all my existence. "Bound," I answered.

Only this time I had chosen it.

"You can let him go Saskia," he said and the shadows receded until they disappeared and I had full feeling over my body again. "Kiss me."

The order zinged through me, taking over my limbs, my movements. I grabbed Tomasz by the back of the neck and claimed his mouth like I'd been dying to do all this time. It felt good. It felt sweet. It felt fated. To be in his arms and he in mine. To be under his thrall knowing I could never hurt him. It was liberating, no matter the irony. And in that moment, I knew. I knew with all my being that from the minute I was born, I'd been born for him. To be his.

Something throbbed between us, a bright fire spreading from Tomasz's hands, causing him to step back just as the cat at our feet fell to her side and let out a wail.

"Saskia!" he exclaimed and dropped to his knees with the light-shaped egg still in his hands.

TOMASZ

The pisanka rolled to the floor surrounded by light and fire and magic, but it was Saskia I cared about.

She was crying. She was in pain. And in all the years I'd known her, she'd never even had an itch.

"What's wrong, Sass? What happened?"

She didn't answer me. Instead she yowled. The light from the egg intensified, its energy throbbing like a heartbeat.

"Tomasz—" she started when the pisanka exploded into a million sparkles and Saskia lit up like a Christmas tree.

No, that wasn't bright enough.

She lit up like a sun.

When I reached for her, my fingertips burned and I immediately pulled back.

Just like the pisanka, Saskia's light pulsated and grew until it blinded us all.

I threw my hand up to protect my eyes when the darkness returned. When I opened them again everything was a blur. Glitter rained on something big that became clearer that more I blinked.

A woman with long dark hair and smooth white skin crouched on the floor, hands over her head.

"Saskia!"

The woman glared at me with big black eyes.

They might not have been yellow but I'd have recognized those eyes anywhere.

"Tomasz! What happened?" she asked, in the exact same voice I'd been hearing since I was born.

It was weird. It didn't match the woman standing in front of me.

I looked around, searching for the cat I'd known all my life, the pisanka my line had been tasked with protecting, but none of them were there.

"I think..." I started and took a hesitant step toward the naked woman. "I think your duty is done. Your sentence is served."

Her eyes lit up as I crouched in front of her.

She bobbed her head. "The pisanka's gone. It was supposed to pass on to your heirs, but you don't have any. And if the pisanka's gone, I don't need to protect you."

"Bingo," I told her.

Loki offered the cat-turned-human his hand and

she took it, shadows forming around her bare skin, turning into an ethereal dress made as if of smoke.

"Thank you for saving me." Loki kissed the back of her hand and turned to me. "Both of you."

It was so surreal to be in such close proximity to the woman I'd had so many arguments with, to the woman who'd always kept me and my family company.

"Well, I wasn't going to let you kill my Tomasz, even if you're fucking hot."

It was good to know she was just as mouthy as a human, although I didn't miss the rosiness of her cheeks. Maybe spending centuries only being understood by a select few had its effect.

"Oh my God, Wade. Look at this," Caleb said from behind me and I span around to find him over my aunt's dead body.

"What? Don't tell me she's alive." I was pretty sure I hadn't brought her back to life, or either of her accomplices. But if I had, I was happy to rectify my mistake.

"No. She's Magda Pęk, right?" he asked as his boyfriend approached and looked down too.

"How do you know?"

Caleb and Wade exchanged a glance and I didn't miss the relief that crossed their faces.

"She abducted us a few months ago. It was actually Valentine's day. She wanted to use us to get her powers back," Caleb said. "And that's Rita. She was also there that night. We've been looking for them ever since."

So my family weren't the first people she'd hurt in her pursuit for power. How long had she been like this and how much more heartache could have been avoided if we'd known what a monster she was? If we'd seen the signs?

"Why did she think you could give her her powers?"

"Because I took them in the first place." My jaw must have dropped because Caleb laughed. "It's a long story."

And boy was it quite the story. Which he told us while we helped him clean up the café. Apparently my aunt had been such a monster, she and hundreds of other witches had tried to kill the entire human race. It was still impossible for me to reconcile the annoying, traditional aunt with the deranged psychopath killer.

The Angel Guard stayed well out of our way as they freed Lorelai and found the counter-spell to release Finn too.

Winston wanted to take us out for dinner, to get to know us apparently, but I wasn't fooled for a minute. It was a precaution. His way of making sure I hadn't inherited my aunt's killer instincts and I wasn't planning world domination or something stupid like that.

"I'm sorry about the café," I told Caleb after the Guardian Angels had left with the dead bodies and Caleb had restored the broken glass.

"Don't be. It needed a refurb anyway."

"I'll pay for everything," I said.

Caleb raised his eyebrow and smirked. "Of course you will. Didn't think I'd let my extremely powerful, extremely wealthy employee get away without paying the damage, did ya?"

I tried not to show it but I was sure my giddiness wasn't very well-contained. "You mean I still have a job?"

"Well, duh. No one quite whispers coffee like you. But first, you're helping me pick new wallpapers for the refurb."

I was sure a refurb and a little dinner weren't enough to make up for what had happened here tonight, or for what we'd both done, but I was so happy Caleb didn't want to get rid of me. It was good to know I had people in my corner.

Caleb, who didn't seem too bothered by the fact his boyfriend and his friends had died for a few minutes.

Lorelai, who was as shocked and confused as everyone else, especially after I explained how I'd used her.

"I've done a lot worse, for much worse people. Don't lose any sleep, please. It's fine," she said as if we were talking about cheating at poker.

Finn, who wasn't afraid to tell his father how happy he was that he was bound again.

Saskia, who glued herself to the wolf demon, even after he told her he wasn't quite so inclined.

And Loki, who I'd almost lost.

Loki, who'd given himself to me after eons of craving his freedom.

I hoped he wouldn't come to regret it, because I didn't know if I could ever reverse it. Especially without a pisanka anymore.

They were all my family now. Even Winston and the Guardian Angels I'd brought back to life—who Caleb and his boyfriend had cast a memory spell on to forget this traumatic night—they were all my rodzina, unconventional as it might be.

But then again, it wasn't like my conventional one hadn't proven unconventional too.

"So, my Tomasz..." Loki took my hands and pressed them on his chest when we were all alone again.

Alone and willingly bound for the first time.

"What do you want to do next?"

There were so many things I wanted to do with him. To share with him. But first...

"Something I've been waiting a long time to do."

Tomasz

"For if there's a heaven, they're in it now. For if there's a hell, we who were left behind are living it. For if there's peace, they shall find it now. For if there's love, we shall feel it in our hearts forever after."

Loki squeezed me tighter in his arms as I tried to hold back the tears.

Each word was a reminder that they wouldn't come back to me. That they wouldn't ever pick up the phone again, or eat dinner with me while we talked—argued, really—about our lives. Even with Hela around, it wasn't the same. It wasn't the same as talking or seeing them in person. And after some point, they needed to move on to their afterlives and I needed to live my life.

That was why today was so important. For them to

finally get the peace they deserved. I got them their justice, it was time for them to rest.

"Ashes to ashes, your time has come. Dust to dust, you are home. Whisper to whisper, find peace once more."

There was no point anymore. There was no point holding back. I let it out. I let it all out. And when the priestess closed her book, I nearly climbed down with them, six feet under but I didn't. I couldn't.

I had a family that needed me here, they needed me as much as I needed them. And I'd made a promise to myself. That I would live my life in honor to my family, both dead and living.

I dug my hand into the dirt and threw a fistful in each of their graves.

The first one in Mom's.

"I promise I'll love as hard as you, Mom."

The second one Dad's.

"I promise I'll heal the world like you, Dad."

The third, in Oliwia's.

"I promise I'll always strive to be the best version of myself like you, sis."

I had no idea where I found the strength to even speak, let alone speak clearly and not break apart, but when I finished, Loki was there to help me up. To pick me up, like he had every day since he'd bound himself to me.

He'd come such a long way in such a short time. It was as if the act had triggered something in him, a change so deep and personal it had shaken him to his core.

Maybe it was the realization that his freedom came at a cost.

Maybe it was his love for me.

Or maybe it was the fact that I loved him and made no secret about it.

Whatever it was, Loki—my Loki—was not the same, ruthless, manipulative Loki I'd first met.

Of course, he hadn't had a personality transplant overnight. He was still the god of mischief. Still a trickster through and through.

But he was also kinder.

"Are you okay?" he asked me with tears of his own before pressing me to his chest and suffocating me in his embrace.

Having him around was so surreal. A man at my beck and call. Someone with five hundred thousand times the experience I had but who nonetheless looked after me and more importantly, wanted to do it for as long as he breathed.

Which was a pretty long time as a demon.

And apparently, I got to experience the same privileges now that we were together.

I didn't know if I'd ever wrap my head around the idea of living longer than most witches, but then again Mother Red Cap was rumored to be over three hundred and she wasn't a demon as far as I was aware.

I pulled away from my demon boyfriend—

although considering the circumstances, he was more like my demon husband—and watched as Saskia threw dirt in their graves just like I had.

She was dressed in a modest black dress and wore a black fascinator because apparently she'd always wanted to wear one, matched with lace gloves.

If I hadn't lived a lifetime with her, I'd say she resembled a lady. But she was no ordinary lady.

"Rest in peace Igor. Love you always, Oliwia. Look after them for me, Krys," she said and came to stand beside me as Finn and Hela, hand-in-hand, performed the Eastern European custom and they were followed by Caleb, Wade, and Lorelai.

When it was all over we all went back to the family home for coffee and cookies.

"So you decided to move back in, huh?" Caleb asked me as I went around serving everyone in the garden.

It was such a beautiful day. Too beautiful to be wasted inside.

"Yeah. I don't want to let what happened ruin everything my parents worked for. I can't let one terrible moment destroy their legacy."

Caleb squeezed my hand and nodded. "You're right," he said.

Loki came up behind me with the tray of cookies, a recipe right out of my mom's recipe book and whispered with some extra love.

"He's also done something else." He offered them

to Caleb and Wade and glanced at me, waiting for me to pick up the cue.

I took a deep breath and looked Caleb in the eyes, unsure of how he'd react, or what he'd do. "I approached my sister's old boss and asked if I could take over her job."

Caleb froze with a cookie only inches from his lips. Maybe I should have waited for him to eat first and have some of that whispered love swirling inside him before I spoke up.

"You're leaving the café?"

"No, not if you don't want me to. It would only be part-time. I don't think I'm ready to heal full-time. Can you imagine the suspicions it would rouse? It's just a couple of shifts in intensive care. But it does mean I won't be able to work full-time anymore." I hated doing this to him, especially after what I'd done to his life and his café.

Caleb took my hand and smiled. "Don't feel guilty, sweetie. I think that's great. And honestly if you want to do it full-time, I understand. This is your calling. You shouldn't feel stuck with me."

"Really?"

"Really."

A wave of relief washed over me. "I'll start part-time first and let you know if I want to leave Java Jinx."

"Sounds like a plan." Caleb split the cookie in two and passed one half to his boyfriend.

Saskia appeared from nowhere and snatched the

coffee pot from my hands. "People are thirsty," she said. "Me. I'm people!" She then proceeded to fill up the largest cup in the house and shared it with Finn.

"Make sure she doesn't have any more caffeine."

Loki grumbled but hid his frustration with a smile. "I don't want to be on her bad side again," he mumbled before following my accidental order.

I was still getting used to that. To the idea that he would do anything, even die for me if I asked him.

It was a heavy responsibility to have.

"You're gonna be okay," Caleb said. "You've got this."

When I looked back at him, he simply winked and I grabbed a cookie of my own.

"What are you doing with your old flat?" my boss continued.

"Finn is going to take it. He needs a place to stay and Hela is going to live with us until she's an adult..."

"Or gets fed up of you two fucking like bunnies all the time," Saskia shouted from across the garden. I rolled my eyes.

It wasn't *all* the time.

"So...you're keeping the child's body?" Wade asked the little girl on the other side of the table, drinking her coffee quietly.

"It'd be a waste of human life and Elsa deserves better."

She'd already had that conversation with her father, brother and me and she had made up her mind. If she chose a new host, her current body would die since the only reason she could still talk to Elsa was because she was the goddess of the dead. Elsa had died three years ago when Heimdall had used her body to invoke Hela.

"I think that's brave," Caleb told her.

"Oh my gods, I feel sorry for your classmates though," Lorelai chuckled.

Hela cocked her head. "'Classmates'?"

"Well, yeah. You'll have to go to school." Lorelai grabbed another cookie and shoved it into her mouth.

"Is that true?" Hela asked me. I nodded. "Hm... maybe I'll reconsider."

Everyone laughed, although Hela did look very serious.

As serious as she was, I was certain she didn't mean it though. For a creature of death, she had a unique appreciation for life and had formed a bond with Elsa. There was no way in Hel she was changing her mind.

Finn and Lorelai kept teasing Hela, and Caleb and Wade decided to strike up a conversation with Loki, while Saskia sat in a corner and drank coffee out of the pot like a weirdo. Although, I'd probably do the same in her place.

I watched them all, all the people in my life, all the laughter and passion permeating every part of this place, of this house and my heart eased a bit.

This was what this house was made for. To be lived in.

Which only made my decision to move in with Loki and Hela all the more reaffirming.

I couldn't let my family's legacy die with them. And for the first time in my life, I felt like I could carry that legacy too.

I wasn't useless.

I wasn't powerless.

I wasn't a lesser creature because of who I loved.

I wasn't a hater.

I was a healer. A lover. And that was exactly what I'd be for the rest of my long life.

"Hey." The whisper gave me goosebumps as Loki came up behind me and put his hands around me, resting his head on my shoulder. "What are you doing?"

"Thinking."

"About?"

I took a deep breath and turned around so I could embrace the man, the demon god who was mine and only mine. "Life. Me. You. Them. For the first time in a long time I'm happy."

"I'm happy you're happy," he answered with a big beautiful smile.

"I wish they were here, of course. I wish it hadn't taken their death for me to grow into my power and myself, but..."

Loki dipped his head and hovered his lips inches away from mine. "I know," he said. "And I have no doubt they're so proud of you. I know. I checked with Hela."

I chuckled. I was sure he had. And I was sure they were proud of me. I was proud of me too.

"And so am I," he said. "I love you, my Tomasz. I love you, my master."

My chest filled with warmth and fuzzy feelings and I took his lips in mine.

"I love you too, my Loki."

Tomasz

"You guys should trash this place more often," Wade said.

It was the grand reopening of Java Jinx and everyone was there. Even people I'd never seen before who all acted as if they were regulars.

Caleb had decided to do away with the old and tired, pub-like decor and upgrade the café to a hip, cool place for both witches and coffee-addicts alike.

Exposed brick walls, elaborately painted chalkboards, self-watering plants hanging from the ceiling, cozy armchairs and sofas, and even a brand new, clean logo and T-shirts made this previously stuffy place feel fresh and exciting.

Caleb and Lorelai made coffees for everyone and I whispered them with healing and good fortunes.

I still hadn't taken the leap to being a full-time

healer and after the refurb I didn't want to let go of this place and the people.

After all, if it weren't for Caleb, I'd never have ended up here, with Loki in my arms and everything I could ever dream of.

I knew he wouldn't stop being my friend just because I stopped working here, but as much as I enjoyed working at the hospital, I also enjoyed charming coffees for regular, down-on-their-luck people.

"Yeah, we'll make it an annual event." Caleb rolled his eyes but there was no mistaking his smile.

"So...have you hired anyone new?" I asked Caleb as he passed me a soy latte.

"Oh yes. Definitely. He should be here any...time...now."

As if they'd practiced it or something, Finn came out from the back of house, wearing the new branded cream T-shirt and green apron and waved at his dad and me.

"Are you serious?" I knew Finn was looking for a job to fill his time and his new bank account, but I always assumed he'd get a job as a Guardian Angel, or a bodyguard for hire or something.

"Why? Are you mad? Do you not like me taking your job? I'll find something else if you want me to—"

"Finn, you're rambling again," I stopped him. "Of course I'm not mad. I'm just surprised, that's all."

I turned to Loki who was glaring at his son.

"What?" Finn asked him.

"Nothing." Loki shook his head and grinned. "Just remember that next time you pretend you're this big, bad, scary wolf."

Caleb put his hands on Finn's and I pushed my demon off me.

"Are you trying to say a barista can't be big, bad and scary?" I asked.

Loki looked from me, to Caleb, to his son and huffed.

He was talking to a power empath, a literal wolf demon, and the guy who had brought a bunch of fallen Guardian Angels back to life. Maybe being a dangerous creature came with the job perks.

"I'm gonna lose that one, aren't I?" Everyone nodded. "I'm gonna go talk to someone who can't kill me by staring at me."

"I'd avoid the guy in the green jacket then," Caleb warned him.

Finn laughed. "Are you sure you're okay with me taking your job?"

"You're not taking my job. I'm still gonna work here, silly dog."

It was my stepson's turn to frown.

How I had gone from being a virgin to having what were by all accounts stepchildren was beyond me.

Caleb handed me another drink to whisper before pointing to its owner, a man behind me.

He wrapped his hands around the mug, but I barely moved at the familiar set of sparkly black eyes.

The tall, buff man from Craft Royale who'd stopped time just for me.

"Drew! What are you doing here?"

Drew smiled and turned to Caleb. "I work here. What are you doing here?" he answered me.

"I work here. Wait, what do you mean you work here? Since when?"

The time witch took a sip of his coffee as Loki stepped up beside me, placing his hand on my hip and pressing me firmly to him.

"Since now," Drew said, not missing the gesture.

I had to admit, I liked it when Loki showed people I was his. It gave me a rush of desire and a thirst that could only be quenched with a kiss—or more.

"Drew is an excellent mixologist. I thought I'd try something new, so he agreed to do a residency in the evenings. Moon Jinx. We'll serve canapés and the best cocktails in town."

I turned to Caleb in complete disbelief. I may have worked here for almost two years, but this was the first time I'd seen my boss legitimately excited about his business. "That sounds fun," I said.

"Does it?" Loki grumbled, staring at Drew.

I didn't get a chance to answer, because the door burst open and a blond twink ran in, panting. His hair was stuck to his forehead and his gorgeous blue eyes looked pale. So pale they almost appeared white.

"Tomasz. You're here. Thank fuck," he said.

The tattooed man stopped in front of me to catch his breath and I placed my arm around him.

"What is it, Sandro? What's wrong?"

Loki helped me ease him into an armchair and Caleb started working on his coffee straight ahead, while Drew offered him a glass of water.

"I...it happened, Tomasz. It happened. You need to help me."

"What happened?"

Sandro wiped his face and took a sip of the water before he spoke again. "I sensed...I sensed my death. I'm sick. I'm gonna die. You need to help me. Please heal me."

I dropped to my knees and searched his eyes, while taking his shoulders in my hands. "Of course, I will. Do you know what it is?"

Sandro shook his head. "I've had it all my life. I could always feel it, but no doctor has ever been able to find what it is. I knew it would kill me eventually, but —this is the first time I've ever sensed my own death. It's gonna happen and it's gonna happen soon."

I listened to Sandro explain this inexplicable condition and I felt sorry for him.

"It comes and goes. But I have no energy and life seems to be passing me by like I'm just an observer sometimes. I've been on antidepressants my whole life, but they never did anything. It's not a human disease. I know as much. It's like a piece of my soul dies day by day. I just thought I could live with it, even if my life span was shorter than most, but...I didn't think it would be so soon. I'm only twenty-five, Tomasz. I can't die now. I've got so much I ha—"

"Sandro, calm down. Please. It's okay." I soothed him. "Of course, I'll heal you."

I opened my mouth to whisper him but I realized we had an audience so I guided him to the back, Loki never leaving my side. When we had some privacy, I took Sandro's hand, leaning into his ear and whispered in my mother tongue.

"Heal his poison. Heal his poison. Heal his poison."

The energy crackled around me and my magic carried into him. I watched Sandro breathe in and accept my healing as he fell back on the sofa.

I got back to my feet and turned to hug Loki. "Poor guy," I said.

"He's lucky he's got you," Loki answered. "I'm lucky I have you. Everyone is."

It warmed my heart when he said things like that.

"I'm luck—" I started when a dark voice cut through the air like a sharp glass.

"Death is coming for me. Death is here."

The blond Sandro had turned dark again, looking just as horrifying as he had the first time this had happened. He repeated the same words enough times to chill me to the bone before normal, non-scary Sandro returned. He hugged himself and tears streamed down his cheeks. "It didn't work," he said. "It didn't work. I think it made it worse."

I never had my power backfire on me. I didn't know how that was possible. My szept could only heal. It couldn't harm. It shouldn't have made anything worse.

"What am I going to do? What am I going to do? I can't die. I can't—"

"I know what you need." Hela approached and the gravity of her expression and tone distracted Sandro for a moment.

"Hi, little girl. I'm sorry. I'll be okay. I didn't mean to worry you," he told her.

Hela didn't seem affected by his patronizing tone, however. "There's a poison inside you and it can only be cured if you're reunited," she said.

"What? Reunited with who?"

Hela pouted. "An old friend of mine," she answered. "You need to see a witch under Camden Lock. She will help you."

Loki and I exchanged a glance and I took a deep breath.

What the Hel was Hela talking about?

LOKI

"I feel so sorry for Sandro. I hope Mother Red Cap can help him," Tomasz said when we got back home.

"I'm sure she will and he'll be fine," I reassured him.

"It's just...I don't understand why my whisper didn't work."

This was really bothering him. He hadn't stopped talking about it the whole way home.

"I think..." I took his hand and kissed it. "Whatever illness Sandro's suffering from..." I moved onto his neck. "Is older than your magic. That's all."

"Maybe you're right." He sighed and I felt the heaviness pulsing in the air.

"Even if she can't help him, we'll find a way. There's nothing we can't do. Together."

I moved to the other side of his neck and inhaled the beautiful scent of his body.

"What a weird day. First Drew, then—"

"Do not say that name again." I pressed my hand against his neck and stared him down.

Tomasz smirked. "Jealous much?"

I hated that smirk. I wanted to wipe it off his face with my hands, my mouth, my dick.

"Of him? No. Of what he wants to do to you? Yes!" I rumbled.

Tomasz pushed his body against mine, and I navigated my hands down to his firm arse. "You have nothing to worry about. Just because he wants to do something to me doesn't mean he gets to." He alternated between speaking and kissing my face, raising the heat in my body to a dangerous level.

I squeezed his arse and lifted him, claiming his mouth as if it was my sustenance. The only sustenance I needed.

"And what if he stops time and does all the things to you? You won't even know it happened until it's too late."

If it came to it, he'd never go back to Java Jinx. Or I'd make Caleb fire the little time brat who thought he could flirt with other people's men.

"I'm sure he's not a monster, baby. And don't worry. Even if he is and he tries to do something, I'll send my pet after him."

I caught my breath and stared into my little whisperer's beautiful gray eyes with the golden flecks and a groan built out of me.

His pet.

That was me.

His servant.

"Fuck yeah. I'll rip his throat out," I told him. "What else will you ask your pet to do?"

Tomasz raised an eyebrow and ground against my hardness.

"For starters, he has to put his collar on, doesn't he?" he whispered.

I felt every one of my muscles flex with need. I tried to recapture his lips between my teeth, but he pulled back and narrowed his gaze.

"Put me down."

The order coursed through me, pulsing across every inch of my body, forcing me to do as told and my groin tightened.

"Now follow me!" He walked past the hallway and climbed the stairs to the first floor.

When we were inside our bedroom, he opened a drawer and put a dark green box on the bed, sitting next to it.

"What is that?"

"Kneel."

Only when I obeyed him did he run a hand over the box and speak. "I got you a little something. A little gift."

I took his hand, barely able to restrain myself from

putting my whole body on him and taking him right there and then.

No one had ever gotten me anything. They always got me to do things. But never had anyone thought to get me something.

"You didn't need to get me anything."

Tomasz grabbed me by the chin and leaned down to plant a kiss on my lips, squeezing my mouth possessively.

The goosebumps on the back of my neck erupted over my body, making the strain in my pants all the more intense.

"It's just a little something I had especially ordered."

My curiosity was piqued and I looked at him for what felt like centuries before he gave me permission to open it.

I practically tore the lid off to find a silver collar with spiky green emerald studs and a padlock. A small silver chain extended from the collar and ended in a silver bracelet with a single green gemstone resting over an infinity symbol that turned into decorative knots.

"What is this?"

Tomasz leaned back on the bed and rolled his eyes. "It's a banana. I found it in the market and I thought you'd like to eat it."

"Oh I definitely would like to eat it, but what is this?" I lifted the collar in the tips of my fingers and Tomasz laughed.

"I thought a good boy like you deserved to have the best of collars so he can serve his master properly." It was a long way away from the Tomasz I'd met a few weeks ago who was terrified of his own body's needs and who thought he'd never get to experience the joys of sex. "So I had this specifically made for us. The chain and padlock are unbreakable and the gemstones are...let's just say they're aphrodisiac. "Do you like it?""

An indestructible collar with sex spells attached to it? What was not to like?

"A man after my own heart." I ran the pads of my fingers across the decorative surface of the collar and the spells sizzled to the touch, sending wave after wave of desire through me.

Not that I needed the spells for that. I had Tomasz.

"Want to put it on?"

I nodded.

Tomasz took a gorgeous decorative key from his pocket and unlocked the padlock. He then proceeded to snap the thing open, place it around my neck and secure it on me.

The coolness of the metal and the heat of the spells brought me a new flush of sensations that seemed almost alien.

But they paled in comparison to what followed next. Tomasz picked up the bracelet at the end of the chain and clasped it around his wrist.

A series of intoxicating jabs shot straight to my head and my groin. I struggled to keep my eyes open or not fall apart, and looked at my lover. "What did you do?"

Tomasz smirked and sat up in bed. "Tell me to do something," he said.

"Huh?" I cocked my head and studied his face but he gave nothing else away.

"Order me around," he said.

The magic was so hot around my neck it choked me, but that only made me hornier and hungrier for my whisperer. I looked at him from top to bottom. He was so much more comfortable wearing tank tops now and they were positively sinful on him. But even so...

He's still quite dressed. We both are.

"Take your clothes off," I told him.

Tomasz arched his back and his eyes rolled back ,but when he exhaled he laughed. He laughed and grabbed the waistband of his jeans, undoing the buttons.

"Oh this feels good." He slid the fabric down his legs until it was off and then proceeded to do the same with his underwear.

"What does?" I asked.

"This." He raised his bound wrist in the air and the chain linking us dangled. "You like it? It's been magicked for domination. Only I requested ours reversed. So while you wear the collar and I wear the bracelet, I will do whatever you ask of me."

I hung onto his every word as if it was my sustenance but when he finished, I couldn't help the knot that formed in my throat.

"You...you did what?" I asked.

I ignored the pants that dropped to the floor and focused on my gorgeous lover's face.

"I wanted to find a way to give you back some control over your life. A way for you to not feel stuck with me." As he spoke he grabbed the hem of his crop top and lifted it over his head and the garment ended up trapped in his bound hand.

With delicate fingers, Tomasz grabbed the clasp that connected the chain to the bracelet and disconnected the two and threw the top on the floor in the pile of his clothes.

Yet despite being detached from him, there was no disconnect between us. I still felt the magic constricting my neck as strong as before.

"You're lying, right?"

This had to be a joke. He hadn't really found a way to reverse the magic of our relationship. He was pulling my leg.

"Try me," he said and fell back on the bed completely naked.

That was when I realized. I should have felt the *zing* of his order through me. Not just with his last sentence, but with the ones before it. And yet, I hadn't.

"Close your eyes," I told him.

He did.

"Roll over."

He did.

"Touch yourself."

It wasn't as though I was making it hard on him. I would have done all those things in his position, and I'd have done them happily, bound or not.

He smoothed his hands over every part of his body before he got to his long, leaking cock.

I smirked. "Open your eyes. Run your finger over your slit."

Tomasz obeyed without batting an eyelid.

"Taste it."

Tomasz grinned and brought his finger to his mouth. His tongue lashed out at the slickness on his pad and a moan rasped out of him.

He really was under my control, and even if I still had my doubts, I tested him with every order, every move, every minute.

He took off my clothes and kissed me from head to toe before he went down on his knees and worshipped my cock with a fire I hadn't seen in him before.

"Do you like it, baby?" he asked when I told him to push me down on the bed and climb up after me.

"You have no idea." It took all my self-control to refrain from coming just by looking at him.

Not that I let that deter me. The magic of the collar was enough to make me hard again straight away.

I'd never had this. I'd never had those moments

with him while I was free, and of course I never had any moment like this any of the centuries before. There had never been a time when I felt so powerful and not only because I'd been ordered to.

This was truly the best gift he could have given me. I didn't know how I could ever repay him.

But I knew where to start.

"Put lube on your fingers."

Tomasz reached for the open drawer he'd taken the collar from and retrieved a bottle already on its last dregs. That didn't stop him from rubbing the slick between his fingers.

But as he started to put his hand between his legs, I stopped him.

"Use it on me," I said. "I want you to take me. I want you to feel how it feels to be inside someone. I want to share this with you."

Tomasz leaned over me and hovered over my lips taking slow, measured breaths. "Are you sure?" he asked.

I didn't want to waste another moment.

"Fuck me. Fuck me, my little whisperer."

The bliss in Tomasz's face was unparalleled as he finger my tight unused hole and it continued as he eased himself inside me.

Soon we were both hot, sweaty messes stuck to each other for better or for worse, but I wouldn't give up this feeling for anything on Midgard or any of the other realms.

Having him inside me, under my mercy and control, knowing I was his first was more intoxicating than a million orgasms. And if I had anything to do with it, I'd also be his last.

"Come for me, Tomasz." I didn't care if I sounded needy or weak. I didn't care if I wasn't the most powerful, or the most conniving. I was sick and tired of tricks and mischief. At least when it concerned who I shared my bed, my body and my heart with.

I wrapped my legs around his lithe body and pressed him deeper as he thrust and groaned.

The magic mixed with pent-up desire inside me. I was on the brink but I wasn't going to let go until he did. I wanted to feel him come undone inside me, to feel the weight of his body collapsing over me.

He bit my bottom lip, gasping into my mouth and I held his face in my hand for dear life. With my other hand I brought myself over the edge until we were both fighting for breath.

Pleasure and relief rushed through me, through us both and Tomasz collapsed on top of me.

We breathed in tempo, and even our hearts beat in the same tempo.

"You know, I can whisper us the exhaustion away and we can go all night," he said next to my ear and my cock went hard again.

I lifted his face and watched him. Watched how he looked at me. As though I wasn't a criminal. Like I wasn't a loose cannon. Like I wasn't a beast.

And more importantly, like I'd never been any of those things.

He truly had given me so much. And if I had anything to do with it, I'd find a way to repay him for the rest of my long, demonic life.

A life he would share with me now that I was bound to him.

"I love you. I love you, my little whisperer."

And it was true. I did. I *did* love him. He was probably my first and only true love.

"I love you too, my Loki."

I believed him. I had spent millennia waiting to hear those words and, finally, they were real.

"Now do it." I cupped his face with both hands and looked into the eyes of my lover. My master. "Whisper me something good."

Bonus Chapter
Chapter 1: Sandro

Here's a sneak peek of the next book in the series, "Hades and his Witch"

"I'm dying. I know I am. I sensed it."

The older woman in the red robe watched me with bright green eyes that made me uneasy, but she didn't say anything.

The fire blazed in the pit between us and a heavy rumbling bounced through the walls—the sound of the tube picking up speed after stopping at the Camden underground station.

"I don't have long to live."

She didn't believe me.

I didn't know what I was expecting. I'd spent my entire life trying to find a cure for my disease but there was none.

Even my friend, who could bring the recently

deceased back to life with a whisper wasn't able to cure me.

What could an old, strange witch with a flair for stereotypes do for me.

And yet, here I was. In an underground cave waiting for a cure that didn't exist.

Maybe I should just stay here. Spare everyone the trouble of burying me.

"That's dark," the witch said.

I stopped my internal monologue long enough to stare at her. What did she mean? Could she read my thoughts?

"I do believe you, young man."

The fire reflected in her eyes, adding a certain gravity to her words.

But as good as it may be that she believed me, the question was...

"And yes, I can help you."

Yeah, she could definitely read my thoughts. Maybe I should be more careful.

"How? I'm sorry to be rude, but no one's been able to help me. No one can even explain what it is I've got. Not even my parents."

The witch revealed her hands, a small dagger resting in her palm.

"Your disease is old, young man. It's so old its secrets have been long forgotten and hidden by a magic as old as time itself."

I had no idea what that even meant.

"It means that which ails you is shrouded by mystery on purpose. To protect you."

Nothing coming out of her mouth made any sense.

"Protect me? Protect me from who?"

"From those who wish to hurt him," she answered but she might as well have spoken in tongues.

"Hurt who?"

The witch didn't reply. She got to her feet and walked over to me with the dagger she held looking sharper and sharper the closer she got.

Was I in danger? Had my friends led me into a trap? Was this Mother Red Cap witch going to hurt me?

"Your mind might have forgotten his name, but your soul clings on to him. It calls to him. It needs him. That's why you're sick." She sat beside me.

I held my breath, afraid of what might happen if I moved an inch. "I don't understand what you're talking about. And how can you know what's wrong with me if everyone else has forgotten?"

She smirked. "Because I've got...special abilities. I can see things other creatures can't."

Whatever that was supposed to mean.

"Are you ready to meet him?" She held the knife up in front of me and goosebumps pricked my skin.

"Meet who?"

Mother Red Cap puckered her lips and a small grin appeared on her face.

"Your disease...it's rare."

Yeah, no *fucking* kidding.

"Your soul, it's reacting to his absence. It needs him to survive. And if you're not reunited with him, you will die."

There it was again.

Him.

Who was *him*?

Why did she have to speak in riddles? Why couldn't she just tell me who the hell she was talking about?

"I swear to god, if you don't start explaining, I'll walk out of here." I didn't know if that was even a threat, considering it would be me who would lose if I did that.

"Your soulmate," she said. "Your soul is missing its mate. We need to reunite them."

My throat went dry and I paused. "'Soulmate'?"

What did my soulmate have to do with my sickness?

Most witches never found their soulmate, their familiar, their fated lover and none of them died for it.

"That's not the kind of soulmate reserved for you," the witch said. "You're not fated to a familiar."

This whole mind-reading thing was getting really irritating. Hadn't anyone told this woman it was rude to do that without permission.

"If he's not a familiar, then what is he?"

Mother Red Cap smirked again, taking my hand in hers and holding the tip of the knife against my finger.

"Do you really want to know?"

I nodded.

"Your mate is a...god. And you need your godmate to survive," she said and pierced my skin, drawing blood.

———

Want more?
Join my Patreon to read the chapters as I write them!
Or Join my newsletter so you don't miss it when the book comes out.

Huge thanks to my Patrons
for their support.
Anka, Laora, Donna and Sandra
you're the best.

A Letter from Rhys

I had so much fun with this book and I hope you did too.

If you enjoyed Tomasz, Loki and their mischief, make sure you leave a review or rating on Amazon! And share the book with your friends! The more people know about it, the better.

The inspiration for Loki and his Master came from an illustration, believe it or not. An illustration of two men bound together by chains, one of them seemingly in control.

I've also been wanting to do a Loki story for a while and as I was researching Loki's mythology things started to fall into place. From the ambiguous meanings of his name, to his enemies and lovers the more I worked on the story, the more it made sense for Loki to be bound to a human and a great way for me to use the inspiration from the illustration in a story.

What may surprise you however (or not, depending on how many authors you follow) was the fact Loki was supposed to be a standalone novel. It was supposed to serve a function of bridging two different series together but the more I worked on the world of this book the more gods came to the front needing their attention and stories told.

So of course it turned into a series.

And I'm so looking forward to sharing the next one. I think you're gonna love Sandro and Hades together.

Until then, make sure to join my newsletter so you don't miss the next release in the series and in general, and if you're so inclined, you can join my Facebook group, **Rhys Everly After**, where I announce everything about new projects, share snippets of my work-in-progress, and more.

If this is your first book of mine and you're curious about Caleb and Wade's story, then you want to go and grab Killer Heart and dive into the first book of the Cursed Hearts universe!

Rhys Lawless, March 2023

Audiobooks

My books are coming in audio. For an up-to-date list visit my website at rhyswritesromance.com/audio

Rhys Lawless

Killer romance. One spell at a time.

Cursed Hearts Series:

Narrated by John York

Killer Heart, Book 1

Roman & Jude Series:

Narrated by John York

Elven Duty, Book 1

Elven Game, Book 2

Elven Heir, Book 3

––––––

Rhys Everly

Sexy romance with all the feels

A Proper Education Series

Narrated by John York

Teach for Treat

Beau Pair

Me Three

Your Only Fan

Missing Linc

CEDARWOOD BEACH SERIES

NARRATED BY NICK HUDSON

Fresh Start, Book 1

ABOUT THE AUTHOR

Rhys Everly-Lawless is a hopeless romantic who loves happily-ever-afters.

Which would explain why he loves writing them.

When he's not passionately typing out his next book, you can find him cuddling his dog, feeding his husband, or taking long walks letting those plot bunnies breed ferociously in his head.

He writes contemporary gay romances as Rhys Everly and LGBTQ+ urban fantasy and paranormal romances as Rhys Lawless.

You can find out more about him and his works-in-progress by joining his Facebook group or visiting his website rhyswritesromance.com

Printed in Great Britain
by Amazon

24851168R00225